I0627929

Diary
Of
Murder

Diary
of
Murder

A Logan & Cafferty
Mystery/Suspense Novel

Jean Henry Mead

Copyright © 2011 by Jean Henry Mead

All rights reserved. No part of this book may be reproduced or transmitted in any form or by any means, electronic or mechanical, including photocopying, recording, or by any information storage and retrieval system, without written permission from the author, except for the inclusion of brief quotations in a review.

Printed in the United States of America

ISBN: 978-1-931415-19-4
Cover design by Bill Mead
First edition, 2011
Second edition 2011

Dedication

In loving memory of my daughter Lisa

Diary of Murder Reviews

Mead does a masterful job in taking her readers down dark treacherous paths of betrayal, deceit and greed. Many people are involved in this mystery-suspense thriller--there's much more to the story than the death of Dana's sister. Many characters take part in the story, yet Mead keeps them sorted out, making Diary of Murder a riveting, satisfying read.

~Mary Trimble, award-winning author

Fans of Dana Logan & Sarah Cafferty are sure to love this second novel in the Logan & Cafferty mystery/suspense series. Non-stop action with an ever-growing cast of suspects keeps this Wyoming mystery moving as fast as its gale-force winds. The murder victim, Dana Logan's sister, Georgi, is said to have taken her own life but Dana and her friend Sarah Cafferty set out to prove that it was murder. Dana and Sarah are believable protagonists, and this story is a fun read.

~Mark W. Danielson, mystery author and international airline pilot

Chapter One

"There's nothing worse than a Rocky Mountain blizzard," Dana complained. "Not even our San Joaquin Valley fog."

Her friend whimpered like a frightened puppy when the motorhome swerved on the ice. A massive storm had assaulted them without warning, spattering the windshield with flakes the size of sand dollars. They had already decided that March was *not* the month to travel Colorado.

"We should have listened to the weather report."

"That wouldn't have stopped me, Sarah. I have to know why Georgi died."

"But they said it was suicide." Sarah's grip on the safety handle was turning her fingers blue.

"My sister would never have taken her own life, and I'm going to prove it."

"If we don't get off this highway soon, we're going to kill *ourselves*."

Dana lifted her foot from the accelerator. "If I pull off now, we could wind up in a ditch. Or hit by an eighteen wheeler." Activating emergency lights, she squinted to locate the center line, which had already disappeared under a thickening layer of snow.

Snowfall increased, forcing Dana to adjust the wipers. At their highest speed, they clattered like a band of castanets. The motorhome swayed, causing something to crash to the floor behind them.

"My laptop," Sarah wailed. "I forgot to put it away."

Snow was swamping the wipers. Their only hope was to prevent the coach from leaving the northbound, two-lane highway. Wind had picked up, driving snow in hypnotic swirls. Nauseated, Dana blinked repeatedly, feeling trapped inside a kaleidoscope. Snow was falling so heavily that it seemed they were standing still.

"We'll never get out of this," Sarah shouted over the wiper's clattering noise.

"Sure we will," she shouted back, doubting her own words. "Watch for exit signs and delineator posts."

"I can't see until we're on them, Dana." Her voice bordered on hysteria.

The lonely stretch of interstate between Denver and the Wyoming border had already drifted in, with visibility reduced to less than twenty feet. If they managed to survive, Dana vowed to never leave an RV Park again, without a weather report. A brief glance at the temperature gauge told her it was twelve degrees. So why did she feel that she had just stepped out of the shower?

Hours seemed to pass before visibility increased. Then intermittent lights appeared in the midst of a blinding whiteout.

"Snowplow," Sarah said. "Stay a ways behind him."

"Or her."

"Women don't drive snowplows, Dana. At least not while I lived in Nebraska."

"That was before the snowplow was invented, Sarah."

Their laughter helped to relieve the stress, but Dana's fingers would have to be pried from the wheel when they reached their destination. *If* they reached it.

"Steer into a skid," her friend advised. "At least I remember that much."

"Maybe you'd like to drive."

"No, no, you're doing fine." Peering through the side window, Sarah said, "An off ramp should be coming up soon. I can't wait to wade through all that white stuff in my tennis shoes."

"And I can't wait to reach Wyoming." Dana swallowed a lump in her throat when she thought of her sister Georgi.

Snow had tapered off by the time they reached Cheyenne, where an early lunch at a truck stop revived them. Sarah replaced her shoes with boots while Dana fueled the motorhome. Impatient to resume their trip, she hurriedly removed ice from the wipers and swiped at the windshield. Road grime coated the front of her parka and their new RV appeared to have developed Progeria, rapid aging disease. Dana sighed, feeling a similar fate.

Snowflakes disappeared a few miles north of Wheatland, and she relaxed enough to loosen her grip on the wheel. Checking the map, Sarah said they had less than two hours remaining. Reaching across the console to pat Dana's arm, she said, "Illnesses often cause people to react in strange ways."

"Georgi would have told me if she were sick."

"Tell me again what her husband said."

"Rob was nearly incoherent when he called. He found her in bed when he arrived home at noon. Georgi was still in her nightgown and had a hand to her throat as though she were choking."

"What kind of sickness would cause that?"

"I wish I knew, Sarah. That's something we need to find out. We also need to talk to her doctor and insist on an autopsy."

"What if her husband objects?"

"I assume he'll agree, but I really don't know him that well."

They rode the rest of the way in silence. Before they reached the outskirts of town, Dana called her sister's number. Her brother-in-law answered and gave her directions to a rural subdivision. Before they reached the circular drive, they stopped to stare in awe at the elaborately built house with its towers, wings and gables.

"Dana, this place looks like Queen Elizabeth's castle."

"It's actually a Queen Anne colonial. Breathtaking, isn't it?"

A shiny black sports car, with its engine running, was parked in the three-stall garage.

"Nice car," Sarah said. "Looks like somebody's leaving."

Georgi had mentioned the sports car, a birthday gift from her husband. Why was it running now when Rob was expecting them? Dana climbed down from the motorhome and opened the passenger door. "Take a deep breath." she said, "We've got some investigating to do."

A tall, tanned, well-built man opened the entry door. For a moment she didn't recognize him. He seemed older and more haggard than Dana remembered. Rob Turnsby gasped when he noticed her standing on the expansive wood porch.

"I thought you were expecting us, Rob."

"I'm sorry, I forgot how much you look like Georgi."

"I'm a year older but some thought we looked like twins." We were once as close as twins, she thought as she stepped across the threshold.

She wasn't sure why Rob made her uneasy. Maybe it was his standoffishness, as though he didn't want anyone invading his space. He led them into the living room and motioned them into two matching arm chairs. After introducing Sarah, she glanced about the well-appointed room with its mahogany mantle, large landscape paintings, and Oriental rug. The oak floor gleamed as though recently polished. Rob had done well for himself since marrying her sister.

"Can I get you something to drink?"

"Thank you, Rob. I'll have some herbal tea." She glanced at Sarah, who nodded her agreement.

"I was thinking of something a bit more relaxing, after your long trip," he said.

"Tea's fine, if you have it."

"I'm sure there's some in the cupboard." His eyelids appeared to twitch.

Glancing again at Sarah, she noticed her questioning expression.

Rob started from the room but turned back to say, "If you don't mind, I'll have a drink."

"Of course not. You look as though you need one."

His face seemed to have lost its previous tan. "What are you implying, Dana?"

"Nothing, you just seem on edge."

His sigh was drawn-out and heavy. "It's been a nightmare since Georgi's death."

"Please sit down. The drinks can wait."

"No, I insist." He turned and left the room.

Sarah leaned toward her, whispering, "What's going on?"

"I don't know but we're going to find out." She left her chair and moved to a large, elaborately draped window. From the corner of her eye she noticed a young woman carrying a packing box into the garage. She turned to watch as a shapely redhead slid into the car and backed it from its stall. *Who can that be? Isn't that Georgi's new car?*

Dana resumed her seat. "Keep your eyes and ears open," she whispered.

Patting her short blond curls into place, Sarah nodded and glanced about the room. "What did you say Rob does for a living?"

"He owns a construction company."

"He built this gorgeous house?"

"I believe he did."

"Very expensive house and furnishings. He must be quite successful."

"I've noticed."

"And young."

"Yes, ten years younger than Georgi."

"Sounds like a novel plot."

Dana shifted uneasily in her chair. "Strange that you should say that. Are you aware that Georgi was a writer?"

"Yes, you mentioned it."

"Did I tell you she's been writing mystery novels?"

"No, is that why you had so many in your library?"

"Partly. Her books piqued my interest in the genre. She was a very gifted writer." Dana quickly wiped the dampness from her eyes. She then nodded in the direction Rob had taken. Raising a finger to her lips, she settled back in her chair, resting her head against the leather back. Within seconds Rob returned with a tray.

"I hope you don't mind that I microwaved your tea," he said. "The kettle takes forever."

Sarah smiled. "As long as you don't microwave dinner."

"My friend's been reading alternative medicine books," she said, reaching to squeeze Sarah's arm. "We need to discuss Georgi's death certificate as well as the funeral arrangements."

"Already taken care of." He set the china tea service on a marble-topped coffee table. "I wasn't sure you would arrive in time, so I took care of the arrangements, myself."

"But Georgi's only been gone two days."

Rob excused himself and made his way to the bar in an alcove adjoining the living room. He returned with a cocktail. "I knew you would be exhausted from your long trip and I didn't want to burden you with it."

"What are the arrangements?"

"Cremation tomorrow morning."

"Cremation? But Georgi wouldn't–"

6

"She said that's what she wanted, Dana. I'm surprised you didn't know."

"She had a living will?"

"No, but there's an estate will. I thought that would interest you."

"Why?"

"She left you some money as well as her books. You're her only blood relative, other than your daughter, Kerrie, so naturally she would leave you something."

"I see."

"By the way, where is Kerrie?"

"Working as an editorial assistant for a news magazine in California. I haven't called her yet."

Rob seated himself in a burgundy leather recliner. "Georgi didn't leave you much because the majority of our assets are tied up in the construction business."

Dana felt her scalp prickle. "I didn't expect—"

"The housekeeper's packing her books so you can take them with you."

"We'll have to put them in storage for the time being."

"In that case, you're welcome to leave them here until you've finished traveling." He smiled benevolently.

"Thank you, Rob. That's very accommodating. By the way, was that the housekeeper I noticed leaving in Georgi's sports car?" She watched him wipe his shiny upper lip.

"Uh-yes, I'm allowing her use of the car until her pickup is repaired. She's been very helpful about packing Georgi's things."

"What are you planning to do with them?"

"Give them to charities."

"Would you mind if I go through them and keep a few mementos for Kerrie and myself?"

He shrugged. "By all means. I know that sisters have a special bond. I'm sure you'd like some of her things."

"You're most generous." Dana rose and offered Sarah her hand.

"You can do that tomorrow after the memorial service," he said, sitting upright.

"Would you mind if we look through them before the housekeeper finishes packing?"

"Not at all. I'll show you to her room." He glanced at his watch. "I have a business meeting in half an hour. I should be back in time for dinner."

"You're not taking time off to grieve Georgi's death?"

"We all handle grief in our own way," he said. "I have a business to run and I need to stay busy."

Dana shivered as he guided them up the oak stairs to his wife's room, which was filled with packing boxes. He left before she could ask about the official cause of death. Mentally tabling the question for his return, she opened the closet door.

Shocked, she turned to Sarah. "It's empty. My sister has only been gone two days and he's already getting rid of her clothes."

"I wouldn't be surprised if the housekeeper's making off with them, Dana."

"From the looks of her, she's already taken Georgi's place, including Rob and the sports car."

"We need evidence to go to the police."

"I have to stop the cremation so cause of death can be determined."

"How?"

"I'll think of something. Let's go through these packing boxes to see what we can find."

The first carton contained leisure clothing, the second high-heeled shoes. Five additional boxes were filled with formal wear wrapped haphazardly as though dirty laundry. Dana cringed when she noticed the expensive labels. Her sister must have worn them while married to her former husband, a San Francisco lawyer.

While sorting through a box of designer jeans, Sarah said, "Look at this. A locked, black velvet box. "

"It must be Georgi's jewelry. I'm surprised it's still here."

"It's heavy, Dana. Do you think we should open it?"

"How? Pry it open? I don't feel right about that."

"The key must be here somewhere." Sarah opened dresser drawers to feel beneath them. Disappointed, she turned to the white Victorian desk that matched the four-poster bed. Opening the drawer, she extracted a carved wooden pill bottle, which rattled when she shook it. Removing the lid, she discovered a key.

"This has to be the one."

Dana was surprised when the box opened. Carefully lifting the lid, she discovered a matching book, its black velvet cover etched in gold with the name Georgiana Turnsby. Hands trembling, she opened the cover and discovered a diary. The beginning entry was dated June 21st, which she quietly read aloud:

I had serious misgivings about moving to Wyoming, but it's beautiful here. I miss San Francisco Bay, but the air is so clear that you can see the mountains forever. I'm glad I allowed Rob to talk me into moving to his home state.

"Sounds like she was happy, Dana."

She scanned the next few pages and stopped. "Listen to this:"

I can't tell anyone that I've made a terrible mistake. I should have listened to my friend, Angela. Now, I'm too embarrassed and ashamed to tell anyone. How could I have been so blind that I allowed myself to be fooled and rushed into this. What am I going to do?

"Oh, my." Sarah dropped a black sequined dress back into a packing box. "What do you think she's referring to?"

"If my instincts are right, she's referring to her marriage, but the entry was written nearly two years ago. Why didn't she confide in me?"

"She said she was embarrassed, Dana."

Turning the page, she noticed the next entry was dated four days later.

I've decided to make the best of it. I've secretly transferred half my divorce settlement to an offshore account. The rest has been loaned to my husband for the business. He promised to build me the most beautiful house in the state, and seems so eager to please me. How can I turn him down?

"Sounds as though she changed her mind." Sarah picked up another box and set it on the bed.

"Georgi was a generous person. I'm sure she was willing to help Rob establish himself in business."

"Then why would he kill the proverbial goose?"

"The housekeeper, maybe. Georgi may have discovered they were having an affair and threatened to divorce him."

"Wasn't there a prenuptial agreement?"

"I would hope she was smart enough to have one, but Rob's a former salesman and a very charming guy. He could have talked her into nearly anything." Dana had turned another page when she heard a door slam somewhere in the house. Thrusting the diary into its box, she hid them under a pile of clothing.

Chapter Two

The bedroom door burst open and the same redhead she had seen earlier appeared. Her reaction was similar to Rob's when she noticed Dana, who rose from her chair, towering over the young woman.

"I'm Mrs. Turnsby's sister. My brother-in-law gave us permission to go through her things."

The redhead held a hand to her chest. "I thought you was–"

"Georgiana?"

"I didn't know there was two of you."

"We did look very much alike."

"Rob–Mr. Turnsby–didn't tell me about you."

Impatient, Dana said, "Are these all her things or have you disposed of some of them?"

"All but a few boxes of clothes."

"Where did you take them?" Dana noticed she was wearing a wedding ring.

The housekeeper hesitated. "The thrift shop."

"We're going to need them back."

The woman's expression changed. "Oh, so you're one of them relatives who rushes in and takes everything before the others get here. I know your kind."

"Really? I noticed you're driving my sister's new sports car."

"Rob said I could use it till my truck gets fixed."

I'll bet that never happens.

Sarah stepped between them. "Ladies," she said, holding her hands in a peaceful manner, "there's no reason to argue. We're here to see that Georgi is put to rest and her things disposed of in the best way possible."

Dana sighed. "You're right. We need to work together, and we need those clothes back, if only temporarily, Mrs.—?"

"Beardsly," the woman said grudgingly.

"First name?"

"Tonya."

"Please drive back to the thrift shop and retrieve the clothing. Tell them you'll bring them back tomorrow."

The housekeeper glared a moment before turning to leave the room. They could hear her stomping down the stairs before the front door slammed. It wasn't long before Georgi's sports car roared down the drive and onto the road.

"I doubt Rob's seriously involved with her," Sarah said as she picked up another box. "She's too—"

"Unrefined?"

"Yes, and married."

"Marriage doesn't stop some people. Especially if the lover has a nice home and even nicer bank account."

Sarah made a face. "So I've heard."

"Why don't you continue going through the boxes while I read the diary."

"Better hurry before someone else gets here."

"Rob probably won't be back for hours and the housekeeper will take her time."

"I'll bet she's going home, instead of the thrift shop."

"My thoughts exactly." Dana turned another page in the diary and read an entry dated September 3rd:

The foundation has been poured and it's exciting to see our house plans beginning to take shape. Rob really loves me or he wouldn't go to all this trouble to please me. I'm so happy.

Dana sighed and turned the page. Dated September 30th, Georgi had written:

Nothing seems to be getting done and Rob's excuses are getting tiresome. He comes in late and claims to be exhausted. He goes straight to his computer to play solitaire. He didn't even notice my new hair style. No matter what I do, I can't seem to please him.

"Sounds like the honeymoon was over." Sarah said, carefully repacking a box of dresses.

The next few cartons, containing lingerie, were placed against the wall. Dana put the diary aside to help Sarah sort through the remaining boxes. Half an hour later they heard the sound of brakes as the sports car came to a stop below the bedroom window. A car door slammed, as did the entry door a moment later.

"Sounds like Tonya wears combat boots," Dana said, as the housekeeper stomped up the stairs.

The bedroom door flew open and the housekeeper dropped a box to the floor. "There's another one in the car." Before they could answer, she left the room, the door banging closed behind her.

"No combat boots but she's definitely wearing heavy wedgies, with a temper to match." Dana shook her head and reached for the box, which had obviously been hurriedly packed. A dark green velvet sleeve hung from beneath the lid, along with a silk ruffle. Opening the lid and sorting through the clothing, she gasped.

"Look at this." She carefully pulled a blue silk scarf from the box and examined the fringed border.

"That looks like dried blood."

"It sure does."

"Do you think it was Georgi's?"

"Who else could it belong to?"

"Maybe he strangled your sister with it. That would explain her hand on her throat."

"I think the examining doctor would have known if she were strangled."

"Unless the two of them are in cahoots."

"That's pretty far-fetched, don't you think, Sarah?"

"You're right. Rob would have gotten rid of the evidence instead of tossing it in a box. And if the housekeeper's involved, I don't think she'd return it."

"Maybe she forgot about it being there."

"She's no genius but I doubt she's that stupid."

They heard the entry door close and the sound of carefully placed shoes on the oak stairs. They waited for the door to open and realized she was listening on the other side.

Dana held a finger to her lips and nodded toward the door. Projecting her voice, she said, "I don't think it will take long to go through the rest of these boxes, do you, Sarah?"

"There's nothing here of real value, unless you're planning a yard sale."

"I think the housekeeper can take them back to the thrift shop later this afternoon. I haven't found anything that I want to keep."

The door opened and the redhead stood on the threshold, holding another box.

"This's the last of 'em," she said.

Dana forced a smile. "Thank you, Mrs. Beardsly. Just put it down anywhere. We'll be finished soon. You can return later this afternoon for all of them."

The woman stood uncertainly for a moment, then placed her box near the door. "I'd be glad to help."

"That's not necessary. I don't want to keep you from your family. Thanks again."

"No problem."

14

They said nothing more until they heard the sports car's engine.

"She's definitely got a heavy foot." Sarah glanced through the window. "I hope there are no kids playing in the road. I wonder if she has some of her own."

"She may have and I doubt she's more than Rob's temporary plaything. He must already be looking to replace Georgi with another wealthy woman." Dana's hand moved to her midsection. "This entire affair is literally making me sick. Georgi didn't deserve to be betrayed by her own husband."

"The husband is always the prime suspect, Dana."

"I know, but I still can't believe that he would–"

"Kill her in her own bed? It's not that uncommon."

"Her own bed. Why did they have separate rooms?"

"Maybe Rob snores."

"Knowing Georgi, she would have found a way to help him overcome a snoring problem. I find it hard to believe that she would solve the problem by sleeping in another room. They haven't been married that long."

"None of us are spring chickens, Dana."

"I don't think that was the problem. Rob may be ten years younger, but Georgi was heavily into exercise, health food, and youthful procedures. She could have kept up with him."

"I have a feeling we'll find the answers in your sister's diary."

Chapter Three

The following entries chronicled the building project with little, if any, references to Georgi's relationship with her husband. Frustrated, Dana put the diary aside to help Sarah sort through the remaining boxes. Before they finished, they heard a car pull into the driveway. Sarah peered through the lace curtains and quietly announced that Rob had returned. Hiding the diary under Georgi's bed, Dana stood to straighten her sweater and jeans. They would finish looking through the few remaining cartons after dinner.

Rob seemed agitated when they found him in the living room. Dana wondered whether the housekeeper had called him to complain. She decided to wait for Rob to bring up the subject.

"How was your day?" she asked, taking a nearby chair.

He grumbled something inaudible.

"Things not going well at the office?"

"No, everything's fine."

"Georgi's death has taken a toll on both of us, Rob. We need time to recover."

He waved his hand dismissively, avoiding her gaze.

"I'm worried about you. Something's obviously wrong."

"Nothing I can't handle," he said gruffly, rising from his chair. Walking rapidly to the alcove, he poured himself a drink.

"Can I get you ladies something?" he called over his shoulder.

They both declined.

"Going through Georgi's things must have been tiring," he said when he returned with his drink. "Did you find what you were looking for?"

"Looking for?"

Rob sat on the edge of his chair. "I had a call from Tonya, the housekeeper. She was upset that you were rummaging through the boxes, as though you were searching for something."

"I'm searching for answers, Rob. I can't believe my sister took her own life."

He repositioned himself in the chair, nearly spilling his drink. Sighing, he said, "Georgi's been depressed. I urged her to get professional help, but she wouldn't listen. She thought she could handle whatever was bothering her. "

"Depressed? About what?"

He briskly rubbed his chin. "I've been so busy with the construction business that I haven't spent much time with her lately."

"I see." Dana leaned to touch his arm "Forgive me for asking, but is that why you had separate rooms?"

"That wasn't my idea. I sometimes talk in my sleep."

Dana leaned back in her chair. "Were you having marital problems?"

"I don't think that's any of your business."

"I'm simply trying to understand what happened."

"That's immaterial now, isn't it? She's gone and nothing will bring her back."

Her reply was interrupted by the housekeeper, who announced that dinner was ready. Tonya Beardsly was working overtime. Dana wondered whether she also served as a bed warmer.

Rob rose from his chair and offered them each an arm. He seemed relieved that the conversation had ended. Once they reached the formal dining room, he pulled a chair for them both, then placed himself at the head of the mahogany table. The housekeeper appeared as though on cue, carrying a platter of roast pork. Dana didn't miss the brief, intimate smile exchanged between them.

Groaning inwardly she glanced across the table at Sarah, who seemed more interested in the platter of food than what was happening at the table. Rob filled his plate before he brought up the subject of Georgi's cremation. Dana thought it was an inappropriate subject to discuss during the meal. Even Sarah stopped eating long enough to gape at him.

"We'll be holding a brief memorial service at two tomorrow afternoon, following cremation," he said, pushing his potatoes around on his plate.

"It's too soon." Dana gripped the edge of the table, her voice rising.

"Why?"

"We haven't determined the cause of death."

"The attending physician signed the death certificate. Georgi swallowed a bottle of sleeping pills."

"I know my sister. Suicide was never an option, no matter how depressed she might be." Dana rose from the table, flinging the napkin to her plate.

Ever the gentleman, Rob rose to his feet, seemingly stunned. "I can't drag this thing out," he said. "There's no reason to prolong it any longer."

"I'm going to call the authorities to have cremation delayed long enough to conduct an autopsy."

"I can't allow them to slice up Georgi's beautiful body."

"You're planning to incinerate her body. That's much worse."

"Fine, I'll get you the number. The sheriff's my brother, Will."

"I suppose the coroner is your Uncle Larry."

"Actually, he's a cousin on my mother's side."

"This is no time for jokes."

"I'm quite serious."

"Then why aren't you interested in getting to the truth?"

"I told you, Dana. The matter is settled."

"Not as far as I'm concerned."

"It's too late," he said, resuming his seat.

Dana swallowed hard and lowered her voice. "We still have a few boxes to go through. Do you mind if Sarah and I spend the night in Georgi's room?"

Rob hesitated. "As long as you leave after the memorial service."

"Agreed. By the way, what time is the cremation?"

Rob clenched his jaw. "First thing tomorrow morning."

Or sooner, if you can arrange it. She motioned her friend to accompany her upstairs, but Sarah hung back, finishing the food on her plate. Once the door closed behind them, she complained that she had missed dessert.

Irritated, Dana said, "I'd be worried about the food. I'm glad I didn't eat dinner."

"Aren't you being paranoid?"

"Not at all. Rob doesn't want us raising questions about my sister's death. There's too much money at stake."

"I wondered why he didn't show you her will. Aren't you interested in how much money she left you?"

"You heard him. The amount is insignificant. What matters is how and why Georgi died."

Sarah rushed to lock the bedroom door. In a near whisper, she said, "I'd be more comfortable sleeping in the motorhome. We could be murdered in Georgi's bed."

"Or the motorhome could be tampered with."

Sarah's blue eyes widened and she appeared panic-stricken. "Let's get out of here. I won't sleep a wink."

"Not before we go through the rest of these boxes."

In the last carton Dana found her sister's address book. Slipping it into her purse, she knelt on the plush carpet to retrieve the diary from under the bed. Quietly opening the door, they crept down the stairs and stopped to listen. Muffled voices could be heard from the dining room, and Dana was undecided whether to move close enough to listen. A moment later she handed her friend the diary and motioned her to stay in place. She then tiptoed to the dining room door. The voices were audible and she held her breath to listen.

Rob's voice was angry. "If you interfere again, I'll fire you on the spot."

"But I'm leaving Johnny to move in with you."

"How would that look?"

"Lotsa housekeepers live in."

"You're not bringing your brats here to live."

"They're good kids. They won't cause—"

"Go home to your family, Tonya."

"I told Johnny I'd be late. I thought we'd–"

"Not tonight with my nosy sister-in-law in the house."

"Is she leaving tomorrow?"

"She'll leave, all right."

When a moment passed in silence, Dana put her ear to the door. She heard dishes rattle before the door was jerked open.

Chapter Four

"Hear something interesting?"

"Excuse me, Rob. I came downstairs to ask where the service is being held." Dana's crossed fingers hid behind her back. "I was afraid we might miss you when you leave in the morning."

"I see." He straightened to his full height, several inches taller than his guest. "Is that the only reason?" His voice took on an arrogant tone, one she had never heard before.

"Of course. I apologize for my behavior at dinner. You must realize how upset I am."

"No more than I am. I loved your sister more than–"

Her money? "Georgi told me how good you were to her, building this beautiful home."

"I'm glad you changed your mind," he said, drawing her into a hug. "We need to mourn her death together."

She resisted the urge to pull away. "You're right, Rob. I'm sorry I upset you."

Releasing her, he gripped her chin, turning her face upward. "Seeing you is both hurtful and exhilarating. It's like having my Georgi back." He lowered his head and began to cry.

Stunned, she reached to pat his back. "Get some rest," she said. "We'll talk in the morning."

Nodding, he made his way to the foyer. Remembering that she left Sarah at the entry door, she hurried after him, but her friend was nowhere in sight. Maybe she had retreated to Georgi's room when she heard their voices in the hall. When Rob's bedroom door closed, she quietly ascended the stairs, but Sarah wasn't there. She must have gone to the motorhome. Relieved that she had taken the diary, Dana retraced her steps.

The motorhome door was locked and no interior lights were visible. Tapping lightly she waited for the door to open. When it did, a night light illuminated someone perched on the landing, holding a weapon in striking position.

"It's Dana," she whispered. "Put the bat down." She heard a sigh of relief.

"Georgi's car is still in the garage. Is the housekeeper spending the night?"

"Rob told her to go home but she's clearing away the dishes."

"Maybe we were wrong about your brother-in-law."

"I hope you're right, but I'm not convinced."

"Come inside. It's colder than a frozen pizza."

"Don't you ever take your mind off food?"

"Not when I'm nervous." She closed and locked the door. "What did you find out?"

"There's definitely something going on between Rob and Tonya. And Rob seems anxious to break it off."

"You think the housekeeper's blackmailing him?"

"That's a possibility."

"What do you plan to do?"

"Set the alarm for six o'clock. I'll call the coroner's office first thing in the morning. If that doesn't work, I'll call the state attorney general's office to stop the cremation and force an autopsy."

"What can I do to help?"

"Just being here for moral support means a lot. Keep your eyes open and jot down anything you think might be relevant."

"By the way, Dana, it's getting hard to swallow. You think the housekeeper put something in my food?"

"I'm sorry I was paranoid about dinner. You probably have a strep throat." Dana opened the refrigerator. "All that snow and wind would make anyone sick." Pulling a carton of cottage cheese and leftover pineapple from a shelf, she placed them on the table. When she looked up, her friend had a hand to her throat. Within seconds she was gasping for air.

She slapped Sarah's back repeatedly but it didn't seem to help. Wild-eyed, she was choking as though something were caught in her throat.

Frantic, Dana reached for her phone. Punching in 911, she hurriedly told the dispatcher what had happened and gave her the address. She then tried pulling Sarah from the small dining booth. She seemed to be losing consciousness and was wedged in so tightly that Dana was unable to start CPR.

By the time the ambulance arrived, Rob and Tonya were banging on the motorhome door. Dana yelled at them to make room for the EMTs, realizing she had lost control and possibly her best friend. Bursting into tears, she found it difficult to communicate with the ambulance crew.

An hour later in the hospital, her recollections were a blur. Rob had driven her to the emergency room, following the ambulance, asking what had caused Sarah's collapse. She couldn't remember whether she had accused him of poisoning her friend or if she had imagined it. She glanced at him from the corner of her eye. Seated next to the ICU, his head cradled in his hands, he appeared to be shaking. He was probably crying again. She didn't know and at this point didn't care. All that concerned her now was Sarah's survival. Something in the food must have caused her throat to swell and she had nearly asphyxiated. Is that how Georgi had died and was *she*, not Sarah, the intended victim?

The door opened and the attending physician appeared, looking older than his apparent years. *He's exhausted*, she thought, *or has bad news.*

"How is she, doctor?"

"Time will tell," he said. "She's going to have a restless night. We treated her with Epinephrine but she came very close to needing a tracheostomy, a tube inserted in her throat."

Dana's lip quivered. *It's my fault. I shouldn't have dragged her into this.* "Do you know what caused it?"

"The lab's very busy tonight but we should know by morning."

Dana thanked him and noticed Rob standing nearby. He had obviously heard what the doctor said, and apologized again for Sarah's plight.

"We ate the same food and nothing happened to me."

"I'm aware of that."

"Does she have any food allergies?"

"None that I'm aware of. She eats too much of everything." Dana got to her feet and began to pace the lobby.

"You're welcome to stay at the house until your friend's out of the hospital."

"Thank you, Rob, but I need to find an RV Park."

"No need for that. You can stay in Georgi's room."

Dana shuddered. "I don't think–"

"Not afraid of ghosts, are you?"

"Of course not, but what happens in the next twenty four hours will determine what I do."

He hesitated. "I understand. Your friend's condition is most important right now."

"Yes, it is." *That's what you want me to concentrate on, isn't it, Rob?"*

He reached into his pocket and withdrew a set of keys. Selecting one from the ring, he handed it her. "This will open the front door. Use it whenever."

"That's very generous."

"We're still family as far as I'm concerned."

"Really?"

"Yes." A slight smile curled the edges of his ample lips. "In that case I think you should fire your housekeeper–"

"I've already taken care of it."

"You gave her notice or a temporary vacation?"

"She won't be coming back and I don't intend to furnish a reference."

"Is there a possibility that she was responsible for Georgi's death?"

The expression on his face was one of shock. "Of course not. She had no reason to harm Georgi."

"Are you sure? We've both heard of women murdering their rivals, or attempting to get rid of them."

Rob sighed and hung his head.

"This is not the place to discuss your indiscretions, Rob. Let's wait until we're back at the house."

He nodded and they took the elevator down to the lobby. Dana glanced at her watch, which said nearly midnight. She didn't know how she was going to get through the following day. And by the looks of Rob, he was in no better shape. Physical strength aside, she thought, men are the weaker sex.

Chapter Five

When Rob drove her back to the house, she insisted she would be more comfortable in the motorhome. She needed privacy when she called the state attorney general's office to postpone the cremation. No matter how nice Rob was attempting to be, she didn't trust him. She told him they needed to talk, but he put her off, saying that later that morning would be a better time. They were both too tired to be coherent at that late hour.

When she couldn't fall asleep, she searched for the diary. Sarah had hidden it in a cabinet above her bed. Flipping through the pages, she found the last entry she had read. On the following page, Georgi had written:

Whenever I decide to leave him, Rob turns on the charm and convinces me that he will change, and he does for a short while. But he's so self-absorbed that it takes real effort on his part to concentrate on the needs of others, especially mine. Whenever I'm not feeling well, he takes it as a personal affront, as though I'm deliberately trying to inconvenience him. I wonder how many women put up with this kind of mistreatment.

A tear hesitated on Dana's cheek as she experienced Georgi's grief, along with her own feelings of hatred for Rob. How dare he betray her sister and make her life so miserable. Setting the alarm for six, she wrapped the diary in a pillow case and placed it back in the cabinet. She had to prove Rob's involvement in Georgi's death and she wasn't going to get much sleep until she did. Exhausted, she lay back on her pillow and promptly nodded off, but the dreams that came to her during the night left her even more tired when she awoke next morning.

Groping for a pad and pen, she wrote down actions that needed to be taken that day. After she showered and made herself presentable, she would enter the house to prepare Rob's breakfast. They would then have their talk.

At 6:35 she inserted his key in the lock and discovered the house was empty. Where had he gone and in whose bed had he slept? Dana wanted to scream and rid herself of the anger and hatred she felt for him. She had to act fast to stop the cremation. Locating a telephone book, she wrote down the numbers for the sheriff and coroner's offices. She then called information for the attorney general's office.

Promptly at seven she called the coroner. Hearing a recording, she hung up and called the sheriff. A dispatcher said the sheriff was investigating a crime in another part of the county. Frustrated, she hung up and called the hospital to ask about Sarah. She was told that only relatives would be given that information.

Relatives? I've got to get in touch with Sarah's children.

Before she replaced the receiver, she thought to ask about her sister. "Was she brought to the hospital the day she died?"

"I believe she was," a southern voice said.

"Who was the attending physician?"

A moment later she was told, "Doctor Whilton."

"Where was her body taken?"

"Kirby," the nurse said. "Weren't you notified?"

"I just arrived from California."

"I believe her husband ordered cremation first thing this morning."

"Do you know what time?"

"I think it starts at 9 o'clock. By that time they've heated up the furnace–"

Dana hung up on the insensitive woman and flipped through the yellow pages. Kirby's Funeral Home and Crematorium was located on South Main Street. She called the number and heard a recorded message. She left one of her own, telling them to postpone the cremation. She would be there as soon as possible. She next called the state attorney general's office. A receptionist answered and asked for Dana's phone number. Someone would return her call. She glanced at her watch. It was 8:05 and she still needed to call Sarah's family.

Eyes closed, she practiced deep breathing for several minutes before she hurried to the motorhome. She would call the funeral home on the way and ask for directions. In the meantime she prayed that a live person would answer the phone.

Dana maneuvered the motorhome into the parking lot at 8:35, and hurried to the massive office door. She found it locked. Pounding with her fist, her voice grew louder with each stroke. Swearing, she rubbed her aching hand.

The door finally opened and a smiling, elderly woman apologized for neglecting to unlock the door.

"You've got to stop my sister's cremation," Dana said, nearly out of breath.

"I have no authority—"

"Then take me to the director *now.*"

"Calm down, dear, and have a seat. I'll see if he's available."

"He's going to have a lawsuit on his hands if he's not."

"I don't think you can stop–"

"If blood relatives object to the cremation, it can't be carried out. And my daughter and I are her only living relatives." She hoped she was right and that the woman was no expert on funeral law.

"I see," she said anxiously. "Wait here and I'll find him."

Dana sank into the nearest chair, breathing shallowly. Peering at her watch, she knew the furnace had been fired by now and that only seventeen minutes remained until Georgi's body was cremated.

If the funeral director isn't here in sixty seconds I'm going to find him myself. She watched the second hand crawl around the dial and was ready to spring into action when a short, paunchy man with graying hair appeared in the doorway.

"What's all the fuss about," he said as though speaking to a wayward child.

"I'm Georgiana Turnby's sister and I object to her cremation. There's strong evidence that she was murdered and you're about to destroy it."

"Her husband has durable power of attorney–"

Dana was on her feet. Glaring down at him, she said, "Stop the cremation now or I'll sue you for every penny you have, and then some."

Plucking a cell phone from his pocket, he punched in a number and turned his back. A long moment passed before she heard him say, "Russ, the Turnsby cremation is on hold. You haven't started–?"

She held her breath.

He turned, grim faced, and said, "I'm afraid it's too late."

Dana's knees nearly buckled. Dropping into the nearest chair, she struggled to hold back the tears. "It's only 8:47. It can't be too late."

"I'm going over there right now. Come along, if you wish."

She nearly leaped from the chair to follow him.

The long, narrow hallway opened into a small, barren courtyard. Beyond was a neutral colored building, rectangular in shape with a round, thickly constructed chimney. Smoke curled upward and a strange smell caused Dana to wince.

The funeral director turned back and frowned when he noticed her distress. "I don't think you should have come," he said.

"That's my *sister* you're cremating."

"Very well."

"What is that awful smell?"

"Crematory emissions. Mercury, nitrogen oxides, carbon monoxide and–"

"You're burning my sister *and* polluting the atmosphere?"

He pushed open the door and hurried to another room. "That's the cremator," he said, as though a tour guide. "The coffin is placed into the retort as quickly as possible so that heat won't be lost. . ." Taking a breath, he continued: "The retort is lined with refractory bricks to hold the heat–"

"Enough," she said, covering her ears." I don't want to hear any more."

A balding man stooped before the box-like apparatus and pushed a button to lift the furnace door. When it rose a few inches, he inspected the progress inside. Shaking his head, he turned a dial.

Dana was near hysterics. *It's too late. Georgi's gone.*

The door opened behind her and she was surprised by the sound of a familiar voice. "Dana, what are you doing here?"

"Why are *you* here, Rob? To keep me from stopping the cremation?"

"I wanted to say goodbye to my Georgi, but it seems I'm too late."

"Really, or are you trying to insure the evidence is destroyed along with my sister?"

"Don't make this more difficult."

The door opened again and another body was wheeled into the room. Dana noticed brightly painted toenails peeking from the white shroud of the cardboard coffin.

The attendant pulled back a section of material covering the body and began to inspect it.

The funeral director edged closer. "He's checking the body for jewelry."

"Oh, my God." Dana moved closer to the coffin. Something about the exposed arm and toes were familiar.

Rob followed her. "What's wrong?"

Dana jerked the shroud from the corpse's head and gasped. "It's Georgi."

"No," the attendant said. "This is Gladys Connelly."

"You have your bodies mixed up, sir. That's my sister and you're *not* cremating her. Not now or *ever*."

"Call my brother, Will," Rob said. "He'll take care of this."

Dana's cell phone rang. Turning her back, she answered.

"Dana Logan?" the caller asked. "John Mason from the attorney general's office returning your call. I understand you were calling about a possible homicide."

"Yes, and they're trying to destroy the evidence by cremating my sister. Please do something before it's too late. I'm here in the crematory with the funeral director and my sister's body. And my friend is critically ill in the hospital because of something she ate at my sister's home last night."

"Put Mr. Kirby on the phone."

Sighing with relief, she handed him her cell phone. A moment later he told an attendant to remove the body. He apologized to Rob and glared at Dana. "This is only a temporary postponement," he said. "A special agent will be arriving after lunch to check out your story." He turned and left the room.

"Satisfied, Dana?"

"Humor me, Rob. After the autopsy, you can cremate Georgi's body."

"You won't interfere?"

"You have my word."

"Good," he said, his tone sarcastic. "You'd better go to the hospital to visit your friend."

Dana tucked her cell phone into her purse. "I'll be back at the house by one o'clock to meet with the agent."

"I'll be there as well. We've got to put these suspicions of yours to rest."

Chapter Six

Sarah was in good spirits despite her harrowing experience. She had injured her back when Dana tried to pull her from the dining booth, so she would be spending a few days in the hospital. She had been advised not to use her voice for the rest of the day, so she scribbled a message to Dana, asking that she wait to notify her children in California.

I don't want to worry them, the note said. I'll send postcards as soon as I leave the hospital to tell them we're still traveling.

Dana understood and was hesitant to call her own daughter Kerrie. She would be devastated when she learned of her favorite aunt's death.

When she told Sarah of her plan to meet with an agent from the attorney general's office, Sarah wagged her head and began to write. Be careful, she warned. I don't trust Georgi's husband. He tops my suspects' list. Along with that Tonya person.

Dana assured her that she wouldn't be alone with Rob again, and that she planned to find an RV Park near the hospital. Checking her watch, she decided it was time to drive to Georgi's house. She might spot an RV park along the way.

* * *

It was time for lunch but she wasn't hungry. Maybe after Georgi's autopsy, she would think about food. The gas gauge was registering empty. She had already passed the last service station before the turnoff to the rural subdivision. Turning back might make her late for her appointment with the agent. If she continued on, there wouldn't be enough fuel to return to town following the meeting. Sighing, she pulled off the road and waited for traffic to clear. Checking her rearview mirror, she saw a black sports car pull off the road a few hundred yards behind her. *Is that Georgi's car? If so, who's driving?*

Traffic cleared and Dana made a hazardous U-turn, narrowly missing a sign on the opposite side of the road. When she was even with the sports car, she noticed that a newspaper blocked the driver from view. Shivering, she watched as the car spun around to follow her. It wasn't far to the service station and she pulled in at the outside pump to watch the street. She sighed with relief when the sports car slowly drove past. I'm getting paranoid, she thought. It's probably just a coincidence.

She slid a credit card down the front of the pump and hurriedly filled the tank. Within minutes she was back on the road. Watching her mirrors for the sports car, she was relieved it wasn't following. When she pulled into the circle drive, an official looking car was parked near the entry door. Rob's red pickup truck was parked close behind.

Dana sat at the wheel for a full minute, eyes closed, and breathing deeply. It's all going to work out, she told herself. This nightmare's going to end. When she opened her eyes, she noticed that the door had opened and two tall, dark-haired men were shaking hands on the porch. *The agent's leaving. What did Rob tell him?*

She opened her door and nearly fell from the motorhome steps. Rushing to the porch, she apologized for her tardiness. The agent smiled. "It's all right, Ms. Logan. Mr. Turnsby filled me in with all the pertinent details."

"I'll bet he has, but I'd like to speak with you privately." She motioned him to follow her into the motorhome.

The pleasant looking agent hesitated but decided to follow. When they were seated in the dining booth, she told him what she suspected and that Georgi had left a diary.

"That's evidence I'll have to take back to Cheyenne," he said.

"When I've finished reading it."

"I'm afraid that's not possible. I can't order an autopsy without evidence."

"Are you a relative of Rob Turnsby?"

"No, I just met the man today."

"I–uh–left the diary with a friend who won't be home until tomorrow morning." She crossed her fingers under the table. "I was afraid that whoever killed my sister would try to steal it."

"Then there's nothing I can do. I have to get back to the office."

Something told her she'd never see the diary again. "I'll have to call the governor's office and explain what happened to one of this country's leading writers. I'm sure the governor is a fan of Georgiana Turnsby."

"The mystery writer?"

"News of her death has been reported in the national media."

The agent grimaced. "Well, that does change things. I'll call and get an authorization to spend the night in town."

"Fine. I'll meet you here at eight tomorrow morning."

When he left, she followed him at a distance back to town, leaving Rob standing on his porch. When she made sure no one was following, she would find a photocopy store and print the contents of Georgi's diary. But first she would park the motorhome and rent an inconspicuous car. She worried that whoever was driving the sports car would forcibly take the diary from her.

After the RV was hooked up to campground utilities, she called the rent-a-car agency that advertised pick-up service. The only vehicle available was a dark blue compact sedan that required a shoe horn for tall drivers. Although cramped, Dana felt anonymous. She hoped no one would tell Rob they had seen her at the rental agency.

With the diary hidden in a large purse, she drove the main street of town, looking for a copy shop. She also watched for familiar cars in her rearview mirrors. Suddenly hungry, she pulled into a fast food drive-through to order a milk shake. She then backed the car into a corner of the lot, where she watched the traffic drive past. Ten minutes later she decided it was safe to find a copy shop.

The diary contained at least 300 pages and she didn't trust the woman at the counter. She could be Rob's sister. Fortunately, there were machines located away from the windows and she finished in a little more than two hours. Overheated and exhausted, she paid the clerk and stuffed the diary and copies into her travel purse. Few people were in the parking lot and she hurried to unlock the car. Dana banged her head on the frame but managed to close the door before the real pain began. Damn this little sardine can, she thought. Why couldn't I have rented a real car.

"Dear Lord, please help me get back to the motorhome to read the diary," she said, a hand clamped to the top of her head. "I'm too tired to fight off a killer, even with Sarah's bat."

The pain finally subsided and she left the parking lot. When she reached the RV Park, she drove through several times to make sure she had not been followed. It would be easy for a stalker to spot the small car parked beside the RV although it was nearing twilight.

Gathering the heavy purse under her arm, she eased herself from the car, which seemed the size of a roller skate after driving the motorhome. The keys were in her hand when she noticed someone standing near the door. *What can I use for a weapon? My purse?* She then remembered the pepper spray cylinder on her key chain. Could she adjust the lid and aim before she was attacked?

A man stepped forward from the shadows. "Good evening, Miz Logan. I came by to see if you were able to hookup your hoses?"

She gasped when she recognized the park manager. "You don't know how close you came to getting sprayed," she said, dropping her arm.

"I guess I oughta be more careful. I came by earlier but you weren't here." When she didn't respond, he said, "I know how hard it is for a single lady to connect to the utilities."

Sighing heavily, she tried a key in the motorhome door. "I'm not alone. My best friend is spending a few days in the hospital. We'll be leaving as soon as she's discharged."

"Sorry to hear that. If there's anything I can do to help–"

She turned back to thank him. "As a matter of fact, I've been followed. If you notice a black sports car or red pickup truck circling the park, please call the police."

"I'd be happy to do that, ma'am. I'll keep a close eye on your space."

She resisted the urge to kiss him. Before long she was propped with pillows in bed, reading Georgi's diary. A cup of hot coffee sat on the nightstand between the two bunks, which she hoped would prevent her from dozing off. Thumbing through the pages, she read about the construction progress and how the neighbors ignored her sister. One such entry jarred her fully awake:

Californians are not liked here. Some of the antagonism must stem from people who sell their expensive homes on the West Coast and inflate prices by paying top dollar for retirement property here. I can't blame the locals for disliking people who want to change the status quo, but I'm really too sensitive to take their antagonism. Sometimes I think someone is going to throw a rock through my front window, or shoot at the house with a shotgun. It makes me very nervous, but Rob just laughs and calls me a wimp.

So Rob was unsympathetic to her sister's fears. She wasn't surprised. Poor Georgi was alone in a strange place with no real friends to talk to:

The rural mailboxes are lined up together a mile down the road. No one speaks when they stop on the way home from town. I thought it was because I'm a stranger that no one talks to me, but as I sat in my car going through the mail, I noticed that everyone ignores one another. How strange. I thought that only happened in big cities. Of course, when Rob accompanies me, the young women who stop at the mailboxes flirt with him because he gives them all a wink and big smile. Doesn't he know how that makes me feel? He acts the same way when we go shopping, as though he's single and on the prowl.

"Damn you, Rob," Dana said aloud. "Why did you humiliate Georgi in public? And why didn't you introduce her to other people? You king-sized ass." *I wonder why Georgi stayed with him.* Several pages later, she thought she may have found the answer.

Rob has been complaining about the phone bill. I told him that I'm lonely and miss my friends back home. I asked him why he doesn't invite people over for a visit. He said that I'm too beautiful and that he's afraid that one of his friends or business associates will steal me away. I didn't realize that he's so insecure.

Dana thought she heard a clicking sound at the door. Laying the diary aside, she turned off the reading lamp and reached for Sarah's bat. Tiptoeing forward, she placed her ear against the door to listen. She heard the sound again. Someone was trying to insert a key in the lock.

"Who's there?" She struggled to keep the fear from her voice.

"Jus' me, sweet cheeks. My key don't work."

"You've got the wrong RV," she shouted.

"No, I don't. I live here." His words were slurred.

"Go away or I'll call the police."

"If dat's the way you feel, I'll go sleep with Mary."

"Do that right now before I pick up the phone."

"I'm gone," the male voice said, fading into the distance.

Dana imagined him staggering off into the darkness in search of another woman. She briefly felt guilty about the man's wife or girlfriend who must be waiting for him. She then returned to the bedroom. Noticing that her bookmark was only halfway through the diary, she decided to read in her recliner chair near the front of the coach. She had to prevent herself from falling asleep. She returned to the page she had been reading:

I didn't realize he's so insecure. That must be why he flirts so outrageously with any woman in sight, no matter her age. People look at me with pity in their eyes, wondering, I'm sure, why I'm still married to such a womanizer. I'm beginning to wonder, myself. Am I really that desperate? I've blamed myself for his behavior and I've turned myself inside out, trying to please him. Nothing works. He just seems to get worse. He's so unbelievably immature.

"Oh, Georgi, why didn't you tell me? Why didn't you just leave that moron?"

Her cell phone rang, startling her. The voice on the other end sounded familiar but she couldn't place him.

"Ms. Logan, this is Agent Brown. I'm having a drink at the Oasis and thought you might join me."

"How did you get my cell number?"

"From your brother-in-law."

"Former brother-in-law."

"I hope you don't mind."

"I do mind, actually. I'm in my pajamas and really very tired."

"There are a few details about your sister's death that I would like to discuss with you. If you don't want to come here, why don't I stop by–"

"I don't want to seem rude but I really need some sleep. Can't we talk this over in the morning?"

"I have a case in Cheyenne that needs attending to tomorrow morning."

"I see."

"I thought perhaps you could call your friend who has the diary and get it from her tonight."

She sighed. The agent was persistent and she needed his help to have Georgi autopsied.

"All right. I'll call and see if she can drop it by. Call me back in ten mintues."

"I'll do that," he said and hung up.

Grumbling, she pulled off her night clothes and dressed in a sweat shirt and jeans. She then placed bookmarks in the diary for pages that she considered crucial to the case. Stuffing the photocopied diary in an overhead cabinet, she returned to her chair. Flipping through the pages, she made sure that Georgi had not hidden any notes or objects in the back of the diary. She then resumed reading until her phone rang again.

"My friend will be here in five minutes. How long before you get here?"

"I can be there in ten, if that's convenient."

She checked her watch. It was 9:47. "That's fine. I'm looking forward to seeing you."

He chuckled and Dana imagined him thinking: I'll just bet you are.

Someone knocked at precisely 9:57 and she asked who was there.

"It's me," a man said.

"Don't play games with me. You're not the first man to knock on my door tonight."

"Sorry, Ms. Logan. It's Agent Brown."

"Agent is a strange first name," she said when he was seated opposite her in the motorhome. "What's your real name?"

"Matherson."

"That's original."

"Not really. It was my grandfather's name."

"So you're Matherson the second."

"Actually, I'm the fourth, but you can call me Matt."

She was unnerved by his change in attitude. Was this his after-hours *modus operandi*?

She decided to play along.

"In that case, you can call me Dana."

"Mrs. Turnsby's only sister?"

"I am and I'm convinced that her husband is responsible for her untimely death."

"What makes you think he killed her?"

"Georgi was a kind, loving, carefree person who would *never* take her own life."

"How can you be sure?"

"We were very close and I knew her better than anyone. She was a successful, talented writer."

"I'm aware of that."

"I overheard Rob and his housekeeper talking about their affair–"

"Mr. Turnsby told me about that."

Dana frowned. "He did?"

"It seems the housekeeper made several sexually explicit advances to him and that's why he fired her."

She laughed. "He lied to you, Agent Brown."

"Matt."

"Did he tell you that he gave her the use of my sister's new sports car? Does that sound like a one-sided affair?"

Matt Brown retrieved a small notepad from his suit pocket and began to take notes. "What about the diary?" he said.

"I have it here and it's very dear to me, so I need your promise to return it."

"Yes, of course, I'll give you a receipt."

Wary, she handed it to him. "I've bookmarked certain pages that I feel are most important to the case, but I haven't had time to read the entire diary. Please read the marked pages tonight and order an autopsy in the morning."

"It's not that simple but I'll see what I can do."

"I'm depending on you . . . Matt."

As he wrote an official receipt, she told him that her friend had been poisoned the previous evening at dinner.

Apparently surprised, he wondered aloud why Rob hadn't told him.

"I'm sure he wants to keep the matter quiet," she said. "You might want to accompany me in the morning when I visit my friend Sarah. I hope, by then, that her doctor will know what type of poison nearly killed her."

"I'll do that before I return to Cheyenne."

"And after you order the autopsy?"

He briefly chewed his lip. "We'll see. It depends on the diary and what the doctor has to say."

"I guess I'll have to settle for that." She extended her hand, saying, "Thank you, Matt. You're a God send."

The agent nodded and prepared to leave. "Eight o'clock tomorrow? I'll pick you up."

"I'll be waiting."

After he left, she retrieved the photocopy and resumed her reading. Checking her watch, she realized that she would have to skim the remaining pages if she wanted to get some sleep. She prayed the diary would convince him to order the autopsy.

She was nodding off around midnight when a passage jumped out at her:

My blood pressure has increased dramatically and I can't imagine why. My doctor put me on beta blockers, which helped but I've always had low pressure. Maybe it's the stress that I'm under. Callers that hang up when I answer the phone, sometimes ten times a day. Is Rob having an affair or is someone trying to drive me crazy? His work keeps him on the job later and later and I rarely see him at all . . .

"Of course he was having an affair, Georgi. Probably multiple affairs."

The phone rang and she dropped the pages into her lap.

"It's Matt Brown. I hope I didn't wake you. I've been reading the diary and all I've found is evidence of a cheating husband."

"But surely you must see that he had motive to kill her."

"If your sister was as rich as it seems, why kill–"

"The golden goose?"

"Yes, why kill off his main source of income?"

"I don't know how much money is involved and I haven't seen the will, but he must have talked her into leaving everything to *him*. Everything but the books he said she left to me."

"Looks like I'll have to hang around tomorrow morning after all. This case is getting more interesting by the minute."

"I know you haven't had time to read the entire diary. Don't you think you should?"

She heard him sigh.

"Looks like it's going to be an all-nighter."

"It doesn't have to be, Matt. Can't you extend your stay long enough to thoroughly investigate?"

"I suppose I can."

"Thank you. I owe you a steak dinner."

"Make that home cooked and you've got a deal."

"If you don't mind cramped quarters . . ."

"Not at all. I'm not much of a cook myself and I'm tired of eating out."

She smiled to herself and said goodnight. Finally, some progress.

Chapter Seven

He knocked on the motorhome door at precisely eight o'clock, freshly shaven and smelling of Old Spice. She hadn't noticed before the intenseness of his hazel eyes or the way his gray-tinged hair curled around his ears. He was apparently in his mid-fifties and had a pleasant smile.

"I thought we might stop for breakfast before we drive to the hospital," he said.

"I've already had breakfast, but I can fix you something before we leave."

"A cup of coffee will do."

"I just happen to have some." Dana stepped aside as he climbed the steps. She didn't mind pouring him a cup of coffee but wondered whether they were becoming too friendly.

"Good coffee," he said after a sip. "I hope you realize there are procedures I have to follow."

"I'm well aware of that. I have a sheriff friend in California. We solved a multiple murder case together." She filled him in on the case while he finished his coffee.

"Well, well, an amateur sleuth. Did your sister write about the case?"

"I believe she was planning to . . ."

He placed a sympathetic hand on her shoulder when her lips trembled. "Let's get going," he said as he set his empty cup on the counter. "I'm seventy-five percent convinced that I should order an autopsy."

"What's it going to take to convince you a hundred percent?"

"An interview with your friend should do it."

"Then let's go."

They arrived at the hospital within fifteen minutes and boarded the elevator to the third floor. Sarah was having breakfast and managed a smile.

"I'm ready to leave," she said, but they won't discharge me until the lab decides what caused the problem."

Dana introduced Matt Brown, who proceeded to interrogate her friend. At least he was nicer to Sarah than he had originally been with her. He was obviously accustomed to dealing with criminals. She wondered which mode he had been in when he questioned her former brother-in-law. And what was his impression of Rob now that he had read the diary?

Sarah's doctor arrived with the lab results. "Are you allergic to turmeric?" he asked.

She lifted her shoulders, apparently confused.

"Turmeric was in the contents of your stomach. The lab didn't find anything else that could have caused your throat to swell."

"I can't remember what it is." she said.

"It's a south Asian spice, an ingredient in East Indian curry. Turmeric has been used as a dye as well as a medicinal herb, to which you, unfortunately, seem to be allergic. By the way, did you take a pain killer such as ibupropen last night?"

"Yes, I had some arthritis pain."

So Sarah had taken a pain killer while alone in the motorhome. But why did it cause her throat to swell?

The doctor said, "The pain medication combined with Turmeric could have caused a drug interaction which triggered an allergy. You're lucky you made it to the hospital in time."

Matt frowned. "So she wasn't poisoned?"

"Apparently not."

His mouth twisted into an expression that Dana read as undecided.

"You're still going to order the autopsy, aren't you, Matt?"

"I'm not sure."

"My friend loves to eat and she must have had turmeric before, with no adverse reaction."

Sarah obligingly wagged her head up and down.

"Turnsby couldn't have known about your friend's reaction to the herb–"

"You haven't read the entire diary, have you?"

He admitted that he had fallen asleep sometime after 4:00 a.m.

"Then let's find a quiet place where you can finish reading."

"All right, Ms. Logan," he said. "Lead the way."

So now it's Ms. Logan. He's back in professional mode.

They rode the elevator down to the first floor after she had hugged and kissed her friend. She was relieved that Sarah would be discharged the following morning.

"I noticed a park a few blocks from here," she said. "The kids are in school so it should be quiet for a few hours."

He smiled and started the engine. "You should have been a professional detective, Dana. You seem to have a knack for ferreting out things."

"I read a lot of mystery novels. That's one legacy my sister left me."

He turned his head to stare at her. "I'll let you know what I've decided as soon as I read the rest of her diary. You won't be too upset if I turn you down?"

"Upset? Of course not, Matt. I'll simply call your supervisor."

"You probably would. You're one determined woman."

"And don't you forget it." Dana smiled but meant every word.

When they reached the park, they sat in the car, reading aloud. While she was reading, he reached for the diary to make sure she wasn't ad-libbing. Satisfied, he reclined his seat and closed his eyes. They had been reading for several hours when she noticed he had fallen asleep. She decided to let him sleep while she hurried across the street to the fast food restaurant. There she ordered cheeseburgers and coffee to go. He was snoring when she returned.

"Come on, Matt," she said. "We've got work to do."

Startled, he bolted upright and reached for his shoulder holster.

Dana ducked and stifled a laugh. "It's lunchtime, my friend. Let's eat and resume reading."

"You left me here asleep while you–"

"I walked across to the Lucky Inn."

Matt patted his back pocket, apparently to make sure his wallet was still there. "What if some pickpocket came along–?"

"Sorry, I didn't think of that. I couldn't let you sleep the afternoon away. I thought that food would wake you up."

"Food makes me sleepy, but I'll do my best."

"Why don't we walk around the park while reading? That should keep us both awake."

"Okay, you read, I'll steer. Then we'll switch."

After they had eaten, Dana wrapped a wool scarf around her head and re-buttoned her coat against the freezing wind. She read for half an hour while Matt held her arm. She stumbled twice and nearly fell, but was determined to finish the job. When his turn came, he had been reading several minutes when he stopped.

"What's wrong?" she asked.

He merely snorted and continued reading:

Rob has been acting peculiarly the last few days. He's been talking incoherently in his sleep and tossing and turning so much that I can't rest. This morning he suggested that we sleep in separate rooms. I, of course, objected, but he said that we both need our sleep, that it was just a temporary arrangement. So I agreed.

Dana said, "He told me that separate bedrooms was Georgi's idea."

"If he was having an affair, it would make it easier for him to sneak out at night. But that doesn't make him a killer."

Dana cursed beneath her breath.

The agent turned to the following page and read:

I couldn't sleep so I went into Rob's room at 3:15 this morning. His bed hadn't been slept in. I should have known that was the reason for separate rooms. When he returned home this evening, I told him I was going to divorce him. He pleaded with me to stay. He said that he couldn't sleep, so he took a drive into the country. He doesn't want a divorce and was so upset that he cried. Could I be wrong about him?

"Of course she wasn't wrong," Dana said heatedly.

"How can you be sure?"

"Keep reading, Matt."

The following pages were filled with descriptions of the presents and flowers he gave her, including tickets for a second honeymoon trip to the French Riviera.

I was so wrong about Rob. He's been simply wonderful to me and has insisted that I move back into our room. His work load has robbed him of his sleep and I'm worried about his health. The second honeymoon trip is scheduled for the 24th of next month. I can't wait... It will do us both wonders.

"Move back into his room? But Georgi had her own room when she died."

"Such is married life."

"That sounds cynical. You must be divorced."

"Right you are."

"I think your failed marriage is clouding your judgment, Agent Brown."

"Matt."

"All marriages are not battlegrounds or chess games."

"How do you know?" One eyebrow raised and a smirk slid into place.

"My own marriage and my parents had–oh, never mind," she said. "Let's get back to the diary."

"Okay, on September 12ᵗʰ she wrote:

I'm finally getting some work done. I've been too depressed to write for some time, but now that I know Rob really loves me, I'm back at the computer at least six hours a day. My latest mystery novel is going quite well and it certainly takes my mind off our past differences. If only he would show an interest in my work, as I do in his.

"Typical marriage," he said. "Husband works hard to provide his wife with everything she needs and wants, and all she does is complain."

"You can't be serious."

"I'm not convinced that your sister was murdered."

"Keep reading. I know the reason for her death is in the diary."

"Pushy woman," he said grinning. Turning the page he read:

My deadline is fast approaching to submit my latest manuscript but I'm suffering from writer's block. I've only finished seven chapters. Why is this happening? My new prescription was supposed to lift my spirits but instead it nauseates me. I have no appetite and can't sleep. I'm so restless that Rob asked me again to sleep in the other room.

"Stop right there," Dana said. "Rob was switching Georgi's medications so he'd have an excuse for her to switch bedrooms. *Again.*"

The expression on his face said, *Oh, come on.*

"You're not being objective, Matt. Just because your own marriage went sour–"

"Let's leave my marriage out of this."

Dana clasped her hands as though in prayer. "Please order the autopsy. If you don't, you'll always wonder whether you let a killer go free."

"All right," he said, exasperated. "You've worn me down. I'll call to arrange an autopsy for tomorrow morning."

Dana kissed his cheek and thanked him. She then said, "I hope you'll finish reading the diary. I have a feeling that Georgi named her killer."

Chapter Eight

Matt dropped her off at the RV Park, promising to order an autopsy before he returned to Cheyenne. Dana impulsively planted another kiss on his right cheek before leaving the car. Smiling, he said, "I'll be in touch."

Exhausted, she dropped onto the motorhome's couch and immediately fell asleep. It was twilight when she awoke, hungry and ready to resume reading the rest of the photocopied diary. She first called the third floor nursing station. The nurse in charge said that Sarah wouldn't be going home the following day because she had developed an infection. She was sedated and would probably sleep through the night.

Torn between rushing to the hospital and finishing the diary, Dana decided to do both. No longer hungry, she retrieved the photocopy from the overhead cabinet and rummaged through her purse for the rental car keys.

* * *

When she arrived at the hospital, she questioned a nurse at the station near Sarah's room. The young woman had just come on duty and wasn't aware of her condition. She promised to let her know before her shift was over. Dana found Sarah snoring softly. Kissing her forehead, she stroked her arm and said a short prayer for her recovery. She then took a seat next to the bed and switched on an overhead reading lamp. Opening the manila envelope, she found the page where Matt had stopped reading. Georgi had written:

I've lost six pounds this week and I'm so nervous that I can't hold a fork long enough to eat. What's wrong with me? Rob promised to take me to the doctor this morning but he was so late getting home that I missed my appointment. He picked up a refill at the pharmacy and told me to take two capsules instead of one. I don't think I will.

What kind of pills had Georgi been taking? Matt needed to pay her doctor a visit. Gritting her teeth, she hoped that he read the same passage and already ordered Rob's arrest. Turning the page, she noticed that the next entry was dated three days later:

I'm feeling much better since I stopped taking the pills. My hands have stopped shaking and I'm ravenously hungry. Rob was angry when I told him that I must be allergic to the last prescription. He said the doctor told him that I had to take the medicine to get better. So I've been flushing one of them down the toilet every morning.

"My poor Georgi," she said aloud. She heard Sarah groan and placed a hand across her own lips. *What a nightmare.* Leaning back in the chair, she dropped the pages into her lap. She hadn't practiced transcendental meditation since they started the trip. Now seemed a good time. Closing her eyes, she repeated her mantra several times before thoughts began to swirl through her mind, her body gradually relaxing. Her hands and feet soon grew numb and a peacefulness settled over her, which was suddenly shattered by a nearby voice.

"What's that in your lap?" he said.

Dana gasped as though she'd been assaulted.

"Looks like Georgi's writing." He lifted a page and started reading. "Where did you get this?"

Dana grabbed for the page but it was jerked out of reach.

"Why are you here, Rob?"

"I came to see how your friend's doing. I heard she had a relapse."

"God help you if you had something to do with it."

"Are you out of your mind?"

"No, but I'm sure you are. How did you hear about Sarah?"

"I have several pharmacy friends, including one who works here."

"I see. You mean like your housekeeper friend?"

"I told you I fired her."

Dana stood and reached for the page, but he refused to return it. Turning his back he said, "This looks like a diary entry. How did you get it?"

"Georgi left me all her books, including the diary. Remember?"

"A diary's different. You have no right to it," he said, turning to grab the rest of the sheets. A tug of war was in progress when a night nurse entered the room.

"I'll have to ask you both to leave. You're going to disturb my patient."

Momentarily distracted, Dana loosened her grip and Rob tore the pages from her hands. He immediately turned and left the room. Hurrying after him, she reached the elevator as the door was closing, and suppressed an urge to scream. After a moment of indecision, she returned to the room to retrieve her purse. The nurse was checking Sarah's vital signs with her back turned, so Dana blew her sleeping friend a kiss and hurried back to the elevator. In the lobby she sat in an overstuffed chair to review her cell phone calls. Matt Brown was listed first and she punched in the number.

A groggy voice answered during the fifth ring.

"Matt, this is Dana. Rob Turnsby stole my copy of Georgi's diary."

"Copy? You didn't tell me there was a copy." His voice took on a more alert tone.

"I guess I forgot to tell you."

"Where did it happen?"

Dana briefly told him all that had transpired since he dropped her off at the motorhome.

"You should know that withholding evidence is a crime."

"Georgi left me all her books, Matt, including the diary. Rob obviously didn't know about it."

"So you didn't trust me enough to work the case on my own. You had to play amateur detective."

"What if the victim were your sister, Matt?"

She could hear him grumbling on the other end. "I'll see you in the morning. Where will you be? The hospital?"

"I'll be in Sarah's room."

"See you by ten."

Before she could ask what he intended to do about Rob, she heard a click and Matt was gone.

She returned to Sarah's room, which seemed smaller each time she visited. Fortunately, the nurse had gone. Placing a palm on her friend's brow, she noticed that it was warm, much warmer than it should have been. Panicking, she hurried to the nurse's station. The young nurse she had talked to earlier was missing and she rang the bell on her desk. An older woman came down the hall, an aggravated expression on her face.

"Visiting hours are over," she said. "What do you need?"

"Sarah Cafferty in room 387 has a high fever. What kind of infection does she have?"

"I can only release that information to her family."

"But we're traveling together—"

"As I said—"

"All right. I'll get in touch with her children. In the meantime, would you please check on my friend?"

Satisfied that she would, Dana started down the hall toward the elevator. Once she reached the lobby, she would call information for Sarah's daughter's number. Checking her watch, she hoped she was still awake.

Jennifer Cafferty sounded on the verge of tears. She said she would call the hospital about her mother's condition. She'd also get in touch with her brother Charley, and book a flight out of Long Beach for the following morning. Dana paced the lobby for twenty minutes before she again called Jennifer's number. It rang a number of times with no answer. How was she going to learn what had caused Sarah's relapse? She would have to keep calling. She decided to return to the nurse's station. Maybe the young nurse was back on duty. The moment she left the elevator, she noticed that the station was still unoccupied, and knew the older nurse would have her evicted.

Tiptoeing down the hall, she heard a commotion coming from room 387. Dana peered around the door in time to watch a doctor apply a heart starting apparatus to Sarah's chest. When she gasped, a nurse turned and immediately blocked her entry.

"Wait in the lobby," she said, closing the door.

Dana steadied herself against the wall. All she could do now was pray. "Dear Lord," she began but anger seemed to throttle her. Rob was responsible for not only Georgi's death but Sarah's, *if* she failed to survive.

Chapter Nine

Jennifer arrived at the Natrona County airport the following morning with her younger brother Charley. They both looked as though they hadn't slept. Dana noticed their striking resemblance to their mother and immediately hugged them both. As soon as they collected their luggage, she drove them to the hospital.

She had stayed at the hospital the previous night until she knew Sarah was out of danger, but asked Jennifer again what the doctor said about her mother's condition.

"The infection's under control and mom's sleeping soundly."

When they reached Sarah's room, she briefly looked in on her friend before returning to the hall to allow them privacy. She found a chair and began a few moments of meditation. She had dozed off when someone touched her shoulder, saying, "Dana, I need to talk to you."

Her chin snapped back from her chest and she blinked to clear her vision. Standing before her was a slightly disheveled Agent Brown.

"What's wrong, Matt?"

"We've got another body on our hands."

"Who?"

"The housekeeper, Tonya Beardsly."

"What happened?"

"She was found not far from here. A couple of stray dogs dug her out of a snow bank along the railroad tracks."

Dana shuddered. Had Tonya's husband found out about her affair with Rob? Or had Rob killed her to prevent her from testifying about Georgi's murder?

"How was she killed, Matt?"

"Hard to tell after the dogs…"

She held up her hand to stop him from telling the rest. "What about Georgi's autopsy results?"

"Won't know for several days."

She closed her eyes and slumped in her chair.

"You need some rest," he said. "I'm going to take you back to the motorhome."

She told him Sarah's children were in their mother's room, and had nowhere to stay. Would he help them find a hotel?

"I'll do what I can," he said, taking her arm. "But let's attend to you first." They stopped briefly in Sarah's room, then rode the elevator down to the main floor. As soon as they were seated in his car, she asked if he had questioned Rob about the housekeeper's death.

"Not yet. My first concern was you and your friend."

"Sarah needs a guard. The hospital orderlies can't watch her every second."

"I'll see that she gets one, Dana, but I'm more concerned about you. You shouldn't be running around investigating on your own. I don't want you to wind up like the housekeeper."

"I can take care of myself, Matt."

"I'm not so sure of that. Why not ride along with me as my unofficial partner. At least until your friend is out of the hospital?"

"What will your superiors say?"

"I'm in charge of the investigation and I don't want my witnesses disappearing."

"All right, what time will you pick me up in the morning?"

"How about seven, partner?"

"I'll be waiting."

"Lock yourself in and don't answer the door tonight for anyone. Hear me, Dana?"

She nodded and left the car. Matt waited until she was safely inside and had turned on a light. She noticed that he was still sitting there five minutes later.

* * *

Coffee and a crescent roll were waiting when he arrived at 6: 45 the following morning. He was cleanly shaven and smelled again of Old Spice. Shaking her head, she reminded herself that this was strictly business. Her new partner was going to help solve her sister's murder.

"What's first on the agenda?" she asked when he had wolfed down the roll and drained his coffee.

"Interviews."

"With whom?"

"First, your brother-in-law."

"Former brother-in-law."

"Right. I went by his house last night and no one was there. I checked again about midnight, so I assume that he's not a cautious man. Maybe even careless."

"Cautious is not a word I would assign to Rob."

"He's either sleeping elsewhere or left town."

"What about the diary, Matt? Have you finished reading it?"

"I'm afraid not."

"I'm worried that the reason he left was my sister's diary."

"That's a possibility."

"Would you mind if I read the original while you conduct your interviews?"

"I'm afraid I can't do that, Dana. It's state's evidence."

"But I gave it to you."

"I know," he said, smiling. Reaching into the back seat, he retrieved his briefcase. Unlocking it, he withdrew the diary and handed it to her. "I'm trusting you not to lose or damage it in any way," he said. "It could cost me my job."

"I'll guard it with my life."

"That's what worries me."

"I'll read while you drive. You can have it back when you drop me off at the RV Park."

"That's a deal, partner."

She flipped pages until she came to the last entry she had read about flushing the prescriptions. Three days later, Georgi wrote:

Rob hasn't spoken to me since he learned that I wasn't taking the pills. He won't even look at me and didn't come home last night. I think he's trying to wear me down and I don't know what to do. I'm so tired from not sleeping that I can't think straight, but I'm not going to take any more prescriptions.

"Why didn't you leave him?" Dana said aloud and continued reading.

The next entry was written a week later. It read:

Rob came home smiling and acting as though nothing has happened between us. He's been the perfect husband and I'm beginning to doubt my own sanity. Have I been imagining his abuse or simply dreaming about it? He keeps me completely off balance. Whenever I convince myself that I should pack up and leave, he charms me back into line. Please, God, help me.

"I'm going to strangle that S.O.B. when we find him," Dana said.

"Why, what does the diary say?"

She read him the passage and watched his jaw tighten. "I just might help you do it, Dana." He turned onto the gravel road and they were soon in the circle drive. Matt told her to stay put while he went to the door. After knocking and

66

waiting several minutes, he opened the garage and looked inside.

"You didn't see me do that," he warned when he was back behind the wheel.

"See what, Matt? Was his car in the garage?"

"No cars in the garage."

"Not even Georgi's sports car?"

"No."

"I wonder who's driving it *now*?"

Matt shrugged his shoulders. "I think I'll talk to one of the neighbors."

"Good idea, partner. Where shall we start?"

"How about the house across the road?"

"Makes sense to me."

She stayed in the car reading while he interviewed Rob's neighbor. When he returned he was scowling. "Seems that Turnsby hasn't been home for two days. The neighbor saw a blond woman driving away in the sports car, with Turnsby following in his pickup. He hasn't been seen here since."

"What now?"

"Put out an APB."

"He could be anywhere by now."

"Don't worry, we'll find him."

"If you don't mind, Matt, I'd like to stop by the hospital to check on Sarah."

"You betcha. We also need to stop by the hotel to pick up her kids."

"They're great people, Matt, just like their mother." Dana turned to stare at his profile. "By the way, have I told you what a great guy *you* are?"

"Just doin' my job, partner." He immediately reached for his phone to call in Rob's description and the make and model of his pickup truck.

Her gaze lingered on his profile much longer than she had intended.

Chapter Ten

Sarah appeared exhausted, which brought tears to her daughter's eyes. Her doctor, a gaunt man in his early sixties, assured them Sarah would recover following another round of antibiotics. When asked about the infection, he shook his head, saying, "Some patients' immune systems are stronger than others and they react differently to medications."

"No better place to get an infection than a hospital," Dana muttered when the doctor left the room.

"We'll stay with Mom while you help the detective," Jennifer said. Sarah nodded from her hospital bed and motioned Dana to leave.

After hugging her friend and giving Jennifer her cell number, she followed Matt to the elevator. Noticing her troubled expression, he said softly, "It's a lot for one person to bear."

She forced a smile. "I'm fine. Let's get this investigation into high gear before the price of gas goes any higher."

"Yes, ma'am. The tank's full and the state's paying for it."

The elevator door opened and they rode down three floors in silence. Dana's mind was filled with questions. Where had Rob escaped to? Who was the blonde driving Georgi's car? Was she another one of Rob's girlfriends? How were they going to prove that Georgi had been murdered and who had killed the housekeeper? At least some of the answers had to be found in the diary. She was determined to read nonstop until she found Rob's motive for murder.

Matt opened the car door and helped her inside. "I'm not a rickety old lady, "she protested.

He looked amused. "How old *are* you, by the way?"

"A young sixty."

"Could have fooled me. I would have guessed maybe fifty. And by the way, has anyone told you that you look like my favorite actress, Gina Davis?"

"Yes, but she's much better looking."

"Oh, I don't know. I do know that I was pissed when they took her TV show off the air. I'd vote for that lady as many times as the machines would allow."

Curious, she said, "And you, Agent Brown? How many years have you been on this planet?"

"I'm 56, and have always been attracted to older women."

"Let's stay focused on the murder, shall we?"

"I'll do my best."

"Who's next on your interview list?" She reached for the diary.

"The coroner's office to check on your sister's autopsy as well as Tonya Beardsly's."

"I'll read Georgi's diary while you sift through the coroner's reports."

"I don't blame you. The morgue isn't exactly Macy's perfume counter."

"I've been in morgues, Agent Brown. That wouldn't deter me in the least."

"Then don't let me keep you from your research."

Before they reached the morgue, she remembered Rob telling her that the coroner was his cousin. When she told him, Matt shook his head. "Well, if that's true, it could certainly alter the lab results. I'll keep that in mind."

Once they reached the morgue, she read for nearly half an hour without finding a clue. An entry then surprised her:

An alternative medicine sales woman came to the house today with a case of samples and a catalog of hundreds of products. I've always been interested in natural cures so I invited her in, amazed that there are still door-to-door salespeople, especially out here in the boondocks. She's a young blonde with a bubbly personality, so I enjoyed her visit. She sold me some bilberry for my eyes, melatonin for insomnia, and vitamin B 12 for energy. She promised that I would be feeling better soon.

The following entry said:

I don't know whether it's the alternative medicine or mind over matter, but I do feel better. I can't wait for Laura to return so that I can sample more of her products . . .

Laura who? Dana flipped ahead to find her last name, but Georgi didn't mention it.

. . . I haven't told Rob about the supplements I'm taking but I'm sure he's noticed my improvement. He stopped insisting that I take the prescriptions about the same time that Laura appeared. I wonder . . .

I wonder too, Dana thought as she returned to the first page describing Laura's appearance. Could Laura be the same blonde who drove Georgi's car away?

Matt startled her by opening the driver's door. He didn't look pleased with his own research.

"No luck?" she asked.

"Nothing yet, but I'm gonna keep hounding them till I get some answers."

"Did you talk to the coroner?"

"He's out of town."

"Maybe he has a large area to cover."

"Probably."

"Couldn't anyone else give you the results?"

"They won't release their findings without the coroner's approval."

Dana sighed and closed the diary. "Now what?"

"We check with the sheriff to see if he's come up with any leads on Turnsby and his latest girlfriend."

"I hate to tell you this, Matt, but the sheriff is Rob's brother."

"You've got to be kidding."

"I wish I were."

"I should have known," he said, starting the car. "Everyone in these small towns seem to be related."

"I guess it's natural to intermarry, unless they still have mail order brides."

He grinned. "There are catalogs if you have the money and don't mind brides that speak broken English."

Matt tried unsuccessfully to reach the sheriff by phone, so they drove to his office just off the highway. Dana continued to read while Matt conducted another interview. When he returned to the car, he said, "The word must be out *not* to talk to me. Everybody decided to leave town at once."

"What about the APB, Matt?"

"I checked with the office while I was in there and an APB *has* been issued. So far no results on that either."

"I wonder if there's a mountain cabin where the entire family has congregated."

"I wouldn't be surprised."

Dana asked about Tonya Beardsly. "Shouldn't you interview her family, especially her husband?"

"He's next on my list. When we're finished with him, we'll take a drive over to Turnsby Construction to see if anybody knows where the boss has gone."

Good luck, Matt, she thought. The employees are probably Turnsby cousins.

Chapter Eleven

Johnny Beardsly was evasive when questioned about his wife's activities. "We were talkin' divorce," he finally said, when Matt pressed him.

"So you decided to get rid of her and save yourself some alimony."

"Hell, no, I wouldn't kill my kids' mother." Beardsly's complexion darkened and Dana noticed his clenched fists. "I still love the woman, no matter what she done."

"You wouldn't be the first–"

"Tonya was messin' around with her boss."

"And you killed her in a jealous rage."

Beardsly shook his head. "Her boss musta killed her to keep her quiet about his own wife's murder."

"Why do you think my sister was murdered?" Dana asked. She then noticed Matt scowling at her. He had allowed her to accompany him to the interview, which he must now regret.

"I overheard Tonya talkin' to Turnsby on the phone a few days back. She was tellin' him not to worry. That nobody would ever find out."

"How do you know it was her boss?" Matt asked.

"She called him Rob Baby." Beardsly's lips twisted in disgust.

"What else did she say?"

"Nothin,' I guess she saw me standin' in the hall. She hung up."

When they left the Beardsly home, she asked his impressions of the housekeeper's widower.

"He didn't kill his wife, Dana."

"What makes you think–?"

"His eyes. I've interviewed a lot of suspects and more than a few guilty ones."

"His eyes told you he's innocent?"

Matt nodded.

"What about his body language?"

"That too. The guy's grieving and probably scared to death of raising his own kids."

"Well, he's not bad looking and will probably remarry soon."

"If he can find a mail order bride, you mean?"

She managed a smile as Matt started the engine and headed for Turnsby Construction on the other side of town. When they arrived they found the doors locked and a prominent closed sign hanging diagonally across the front window.

"Looks like Turnsby has relocated to another area."

Disappointed, she sighed. "I hope he hasn't absconded with the rest of Georgi's money."

"We'll find him. From what you've told me, he's not the smartest rock in the box."

"He's not exactly the dumbest, Matt. I think he had this whole thing planned for some time."

"Even the smartest criminals make stupid mistakes. We'll just keep digging for answers."

Dana picked up the diary and began to read. "Listen to this:"

I've been going through the bank statements when Rob's not home. He's been spending a lot of money on travel vouchers lately. Maybe he's planning to surprise me with another exotic vacation like our second honeymoon. He's been a lot nicer and I think he still loves me.

"When did she write that, Dana?"

"Six months ago."

Matt whistled. "You're right. He's been planning this for a while."

"The bastard," she said beneath her breath.

"Keeping reading," he said, "while I check in with Cheyenne."

Dana's anger deepened as she read glowing accounts of her sister receiving flowers on a daily basis. There was also jewelry and other gifts. Her husband had obviously decided to keep Georgi off guard. She wondered how much of her money he was spending on his girlfriends.

"Matt, I think we should check the company's books to see how much money Rob embezzled."

He raised an index finger to indicate that he was still receiving information from Cheyenne, so she returned to the diary.

Laura came by today with a new batch of samples. She insisted that I try some new vitamins for mature women. She said that I may feel light-headed or a little dizzy at first, but that they would make me feel twenty years younger. Now, that I look forward to, and I'm sure Rob will as well.

Light-headed? Vitamins weren't supposed to make you dizzy. Georgi was an intelligent woman. How could she have been taken in by a door-to-door saleswoman? Matt was still talking to the head office so she read Georgi's next entry:

Laura was right about the dizziness but it's getting better. And I am feeling years younger. I've gone back to work on my mystery novel. My protagonist is an older woman married to a younger man, who is cheating on her. I'm not sure whether he's going to kill her or whether the housekeeper will do the dirty deed. I've awakened several nights in a row thinking about the murder and how it should be executed, but it seems that I've suddenly developed writer's block. I think I'll spend a few days reading some of my favorite mysteries. Maybe that will get me started again.

"Good grief, Georgi. You were writing about you own murder."

Matt hung up the phone. His questioning look said, *Did I hear you right?*

Dana read him the passage and they both shook their heads. "You don't suppose she read some of her book to Rob, which gave him the idea to kill her?"

"I guess if he followed the plot, the housekeeper killed your sister and Rob killed the housekeeper. End of story."

"Not quite, Matt. What about the blonde who drove Georgi's car away?"

"Rob Turnsby is quite a ladies' man, isn't he?"

"I wonder how many other women he's been involved with."

"I'm sure they'll resurface when the newspapers get hold of the story."

"Unless they've already been cremated."

"That's pretty ghoulish, partner. You've been reading a lot of mystery novels, haven't you?"

"You have no idea how many."

The investigator chuckled to himself as he stared through the windshield.

Deciding to change the subject, she said, "What about your call to Cheyenne? Was there any information about Rob?"

"Not yet."

"You were on quite a while for no information."

His flirtatious mood ended and he was now all business. "I have other cases pending."

"And you want to wrap this one up as soon as possible."

He nodded grimly.

Dana reread him Georgi's earlier entry about the amount of money Rob was spending on gifts. He agreed that they should check the construction company's bank records. She also told him about the vitamins that made her sister dizzy.

"Anything else in there that I should know?"

"I'll keep you informed." She continued to read while Matt stopped at one of the local banks. He returned a few minutes later saying, "Not the right one."

"Maybe some of the records are at the house. I happen to have a key."

Matt eyed her curiously. "A key to the house?"

"Rob gave it to me when I first arrived. I forgot to return it."

"That should save some time." He smiled at her appreciatively.

"At least we'll know which bank held their money."

"So you think your former brother-in-law wiped out all the bank accounts before he left?"

"Wouldn't you, if you were running for your life?"

Matt laughed. "If I'd killed my ex-wife, there wouldn't be a place on earth where I could hide. Her relatives are all in the travel and tour business."

"They could certainly help us find Rob," Dana said, returning to the diary:

I finally broke my writer's block today and the words are literally flowing onto the computer screen. This is definitely a muse. It was going so well that I wrote right through the dinner hour (I'm not sure why Tonya didn't tell me she wasn't going to prepare dinner before she left), and I wasn't aware that Rob was late until he opened my office door at 8:30. He said that he was surprised to find me smiling. I guess I haven't done much of that lately, but I'm only truly happy when the words are coming so fast that I can't type fast enough to keep up with them. I can see the characters in my mind and hear their words as I type, but I sometimes lose part of their conversations. They're not telling me who killed my protagonist. I'll have to listen more closely.

It sounds as though she had a film strip running through her head, Dana thought as she turned the page. The thought that her sister might have been losing her mind gave her cold chills.

Chapter Twelve

"This is deja vu, Matt."

"Why's that?"

"Not long ago I was riding around the San Joaquin Valley with Sheriff Grayson, helping him solve the murders of our friends."

"Did you catch the perp?"

She smiled. "You bet we did. And we're going to catch Georgi's killer too."

"What have I been saying all along?" His grin resembled a smirk.

Matt stopped midway in the Turnsby's circle drive. Before he had time to walk around to open her door, she was on the porch, her key at the ready.

"Try not to disturb any evidence," he said as she opened the door into the foyer. Everything seemed in place, with no sign of a hurried departure. Dana led the way to Rob's home office, which they found locked.

"No problem," he said, taking a small leather case from his pocket. "You didn't watch me do this, either, Dana." He removed a long thin blade from the case and inserted it into the lock. Within seconds the door creaked open.

Although the rest of the house was undisturbed, Rob's office resembled the aftermath of a tornado. The floor was covered with papers, his desk haphazardly piled with what appeared to be work orders.

"We're in luck," Matt said, retrieving a bank statement from the floor. "This is two years old but at least we know the name of the bank. Let's get over there."

"But what about all of this?" she said, her arms wide.

"First things first." His foot turned over a stack of documents.

Dana asked if he had notified the sheriff of the possible murder.

"We don't want the suspect's relatives disposing of evidence, now do we?"

She said nothing, disliking his arrogant tone. *Men. Why do they think they have all the answers?* "Why don't I stay here," she said, "and go through all these papers while you're gone?"

He looked at her as though she were insane. "Because the killer might decide he left some incriminating evidence." When she made a sour face, he said, "We'll pick up some take-out after we leave the bank. Then come back for a thorough search."

At Matt's suggestion, she stayed in the car while he interviewed a vice president about the Turnsby accounts. She was three-quarters of the way through the diary and had to finish soon. Resisting the urge to flip ahead to the end, she forced herself to methodically plod through the rest of the text. She didn't want to miss a single clue.

Before she resumed reading, she retrieved her cell phone from her purse. Sarah should be well enough by now to talk. Her daughter answered the bedside phone and sounded optimistic about her mother's recovery. Sarah's voice was scratchy but she was obviously glad to hear from her friend.

"How's the investigation going?" she asked.

"Frustrating, but at least the investigator from Cheyenne thinks that Georgi was murdered. I'm not sure that he believes that Rob killed her."

"What do *you* believe?"

"I'm sure Rob killed my sister. He left town not long after he discovered me reading her diary."

"That's awfully suspicious. Did the housekeeper go with him?"

Dana hesitated. She wasn't sure whether she should tell her that Tonya Beardsly had been murdered. Not while she was confined to a hospital bed.

"What aren't you telling me, Dana?"

"I don't want to worry you but–well–Tonya Beardsly's body was found yesterday."

"My gosh, Dana. That means *you're* in danger."

"Not really. I've partnered with Matt Brown, the investigator. He insists that I ride along with him while he conducts his interviews, so he can protect me at the same time."

"Another lawman? What is it about you that attracts them like foxes to a hen house."

"It's not like that, Sarah. It's strictly business. We need Matt to help find Georgi's killer."

"You're already on a first name basis, I see."

"Would you rather that I looked for clues on my own?"

"Not at all."

"Let's talk about *you*. When will you be ready to leave the hospital?"

Sarah coughed and her voice sounded weaker. "Not nearly soon enough. The doctor says maybe the end of the week. But I'll have to take it easy for a while."

"I'll see that you do. By then we should have this case wrapped up and the killer awaiting trial."

"I hope so, my friend. I'm so sorry about your sister's death."

Dana gulped back a lump in her throat and said goodbye. She decided to visit her friend the following morning. Meanwhile, finishing Georgi's dairy was her first priority. Backtracking a few pages, she read forward to:

I've never had quite so much fun as I'm having writing this novel. I know that novelists write about events from their own lives, and I'm amazed how much this book parallels my own, with the exception of my death, of course. Rob has been so sweet and kind that he would never consider killing me, especially the way my antagonist murdered his wife.

At long last, Dana thought, turning the page. She's going to reveal how she was killed. But Georgi continued to write platitudes about her wonderful husband. Nauseated, Dana decided to find her sister's manuscript to discover how the woman in her novel was killed. Unless Georgi had already mailed the completed script to her New York agent. She had to get back to the house.

It was nearly an hour before Matt returned to the car. Dana was not only agitated with the diary, but furious with Matt for insisting she come along. "We need to go back to the house as soon as possible," she said.

"What's the hurry? I'm hungry. What'll it be? Pizza or a burger?"

"Whatever."

"What's got a hornet in your bonnet, partner? Something you read?"

"Among other things."

"Such as?" His eyes narrowed as he fastened his seat belt.

Dana rested her head against the seat and slowly exhaled. "Make mine a cheeseburger."

He smiled. "The lady's hungry after all."

"This lady is more concerned with finding evidence to convict Rob Turnsby. Let's get back to the house."

"Oh, so that's it. You're upset because I didn't leave you there alone."

"I'm capable of taking care of myself."

"I'm sure Tonya Beardsly felt the same way."

She knew he was right but wouldn't admit it. The man was infuriating. "What did you discover at the bank?"

"You were right. The accounts have all been closed."

"So I was right about something." She fumed in silence while Matt drove to the fast food restaurant and placed their orders. They ate while he drove and she didn't speak to him again until they reached the house.

"I'm going to Georgi's office to find her latest manuscript," she said, "while you sort through the papers in Rob's office."

He nodded and left her at the foot of the stairs. "Don't keep any evidence from me," he said over his shoulder. "This isn't a case for amateur detectives."

She stomped up the stairs and slammed the door to Georgi's office. "Amateur detectives we may be, but we're quite capable of solving murders." When Sarah left the hospital, they would team up and sift carefully through all the evidence. Matt couldn't keep them out of her own sister's house. Or could he?

Chapter Thirteen

Georgi's office had not been rifled, which made her job easier. There had to be a copy of her sister's latest manuscript somewhere, probably in the file cabinet. She found it locked. Frustrated, she searched the desk, finding nothing resembling a key. Maybe Georgi had hidden a copy in her bedroom. Dana rushed down the hall and began opening dresser drawers. All of them were empty. *Good work, Tonya,* she thought, remembering the housekeeper's systematic removal of her sister's possessions. Maybe Georgi's things were still at the Beardsly house, but why hadn't Tonya removed everything from the office? Writing equipment and books probably didn't interest the housekeeper.

She returned downstairs and crossed the living room, which adjoined Rob's office. She found Matt on his hands and knees sifting through a pile of papers. When he looked up he was frowning.

"Nothing here but a bunch of old work orders," he grumbled.

"We need to go back to the Beardsly house," she said, after explaining their need to retrieve Georgi's manuscript.

"Let's open that file cabinet first. It might save us a trip." Once upstairs he used his blade to open the cabinet, which was jammed with manuscripts.

"What's the name of the novel?" he asked, sorting through the top drawer.

She hesitated. "I'm not sure."

"Then I suggest you finish the diary." He turned and left the room.

Embarrassed, she began reading the titles of each folder. Pulling out the bottom drawer she noticed that it was filled with research notes. It could take a month to read through all of them. Maybe Matt was right. She needed to finish the diary.

Dana froze when the phone rang on Georgi's desk. Would Matt pick it up downstairs or allow the answering machine to record a message. She hesitated. The phone rang four times and beeped. A woman's voice then came on the line:

"Georgi? This is Angela. I'm leaving tomorrow morning and I'm worried because I haven't heard from you. Are you still planning to meet me at the airport?"

Dana reached for the phone but stopped when she heard Matt's voice calling from downstairs. "Don't pick up," he demanded.

"Why? It's Georgi's best friend in San Francisco."

"Don't pick up," he repeated.

"All right," she said to herself, "but you'd better have a good reason."

"Please call me." Angela's voice sounded on the verge of tears. "I'll never forgive myself for not coming sooner if something's happened to you."

Disregarding Matt's order, Dana picked up the phone in time to hear the disconnect.

"Damn it, Matt, you should have let me talk to her." She angrily slammed down the receiver and turned to see him standing in the doorway.

"I'll return her call and officially record the conversation."

"Angela's not a suspect."

"She may have vital information from previous phone conversations with your sister. We also need to access Mrs. Turnsby's computer for email messages."

"We don't know her password, Matt."

"There are ways–"

"I see." *Governmental spying*, she thought as she slipped past him in the doorway and made her way back to the car to retrieve the diary. She would read the rest of it in Georgi's room and report back to him on what she had learned. She didn't care to talk to him until then.

Settling herself on Georgi's bed, she began to read. Skimming past the delusional compliments, she at last found something she considered valuable information:

Rob didn't come home until eleven o'clock last night. He didn't call and said he had lost his cell phone. No wonder I couldn't reach him. When I asked him where he had been, he said that his pickup had stalled on a gravel road when he drove out to make a construction estimate. A farmer gave him a lift into town. Poor dear. He was exhausted and went straight to bed.

"Lost his cell phone, my Aunt Fanny. I'm surprised that he didn't say he ran over it."

Further proof that Rob had completely fooled his wife was on the following page:

Rob came home early today with a bunch of red roses. I was thrilled that he brought them for no particular reason, except to say "I love you." How lucky I am to have such a sweet husband.

Dana groaned. Lucky, Georgi? As in lucky to have still been alive? Clenching her teeth she continued reading: *I talked to Angela today and convinced her that she needed to come for a visit. She asked if she needed to wear western boots and a ten gallon hat. I told her that jeans and T-shirts would suffice. I can hardly wait to see her.*

Dana checked the date. It was exactly four months ago to the day. What had taken Angela so long to plan the trip?

A sharp knock at the bedroom door startled her. Matt stepped inside, saying, "I don't know about you, but I'm pooped. Why don't I take you back to the motorhome? I'll pick you up at eight in the morning."

She rolled off the bed and checked her watch. It was 8:35. Where had the time gone?

"I need to visit Sarah in the morning. Could you drop me off? My rental car's still in the parking lot."

He puffed his cheeks as though deep in thought. "I guess I could do that. How long you do you plan to stay?"

"Several hours. We've got a lot of catching up to do."

"Call me and I'll pick you up."

"No need, Matt. I can drive the rental car over here for lunch."

He shook his head and she noticed a dark shadow covering his chin. He looked as though he hadn't slept in days. "I don't know whether it's safe for you to be driving around alone."

"It's only a couple of miles from here. I'll pick up a pizza on the way for lunch."

"All right, but no stopovers anywhere else."

"I promise," she said, crossing fingers behind her back. She grabbed the diary and followed him downstairs. He dropped her off at the RV Park, exacting a promise that she lock herself in for the night.

"No worries," she said, remembering her previous unscheduled visitors several nights before. "I have no plans to venture out into the darkness with my trusty magnifying glass."

Matt's mouth set in a grim line. "I've dealt with stubborn women like you before, Dana Logan. In fact, I married one."

"Learned your lesson, didn't you?"

His sharp laugh sounded angry and she left the car without another word. Tomorrow she would learn as much as she could on her own, whether he liked it or not. She hoped he hadn't noticed the diary under her arm instead of in his briefcase. There was still a lot of reading to do.

Chapter Fourteen

Seated in the recliner, she elevated her feet and checked her watch. It was too late to call Sarah at the hospital. Maybe her kids were back at the hotel by now. She retrieved Jennifer's cell phone number from her purse and punched it in. A sleepy voice answered.

"How's your mother doing, dear?"

"Much better, Dana. She's pestering the doctor to discharge her."

"That's my Sarah. I can't wait to see her in the morning."

"She's anxious to discuss the murder case with you."

"I'm sure she is. I'll see the three of you tomorrow."

She made herself a cup of chai tea and settled back for a long evening of reading. She could hopefully finish the diary that night. Skimming through the glowing reports about Rob, she stopped short to read an entry dated over a month earlier:

Something's wrong. I woke in the middle of the night with a killer headache and pains in my chest. I thought I was having a heart attack. When I woke Rob to tell him, he just laughed and went back to sleep. I was devastated. I even thought of calling an ambulance, but the pain finally subsided.

He laughed and went back to sleep? The diary dropped into her lap and she clenched her fists. *If he comes back to town, he's a dead man.*

Later that day, Georgi wrote:

I asked Rob how he could be so insensitive and he said he thought he was having a nightmare, and why didn't I call an ambulance? He seems to think I'm a hypochondriac. I wasn't imagining the pain. Did he really think he was having a dream?

"Oh, Georgi, why didn't you tell me? I would have flown out here to take you away from that monster." Dana closed her eyes and tried to prevent the tears. The lump in her throat was ready to throttle her. Reading the diary was too painful. How was she going to get through to the end? She took another sip of tea and forced herself to read.

I called my doctor this morning for an appointment and was told that he's out of town. They told me to go to the emergency room at the hospital if the pains persist. The housekeeper is on vacation this week so I'm on my own. I've got to keep my cell phone handy.

Her doctor must be another of Rob's relatives. It was too much of a coincidence that the housekeeper was gone at the same time. If the plan was to leave Georgi stranded, why wasn't she killed that week? Dana shivered. The entire episode was beyond her comprehension. Unless it was a dress rehearsal to determine how Georgi would react.

Her eyes burned from lack of sleep. She closed them and reclined in the chair. A few minutes of meditation would refresh her before she returned to reading. When she opened her eyes, dim light filtered through the window beside her chair. Her watch said 6:45. She had slept for hours and it was nearly time for Matt to pick her up. Pulling herself upright, her body felt as though she had taken part in a wrestling match. Sharp pains stabbed at her neck as she carefully undressed and stepped into the small shower. Dressed in faded jeans and her favorite sweatshirt, she was combing her hair when she heard him knock. He was scowling and she nearly closed the door in his face. She was in no mood to deal with a cranky man.

"Which side of the couch did you roll out on?" she asked, backing up to allow him access to the motorhome.

"Probably the same side you did, from the looks of you." He sat on the couch. "What did you do, read all night?"

"Not quite."

"I don't remember saying you could take the diary with you."

"How do you expect me to finish it, Agent Brown? ESP?"

"I was planning to read it myself last night, Ms. Logan."

She was undecided whether to give him the diary or leave it under her pillow. She then recalled one of Sarah's favorite sayings: honey draws more flies than vinegar. She mentally bit her lip and decided to charm him. Flashing him her best smile, she said, "Let's work together on this, Matt. Time's running out and Rob's getting away."

"Oh, all right," he grumbled. "What does the diary say?"

She told him about the *nightmare* incident and Georgi's apparent heart problem.

He shook his head. "When men work hard, they sleep hard. You can't base a murder indictment on something like that."

Here we go again. "You're right, of course. I'll keep reading."

"I think I'll have a go at it while you're at the hospital," he said, rising from the couch. "We'd better get over there now."

Reluctantly, she retrieved the diary and handed it to him. "You'll give it back when you're finished, won't you, Matt?"

He sighed. "We'll see."

"Why don't we make another copy so we can both read."

"Not a good idea. Someone else might get their hands on it."

"I'll guard it with my life."

"You may have to. The killer's still running loose."

Well, at least he believes Georgi was murdered. That's a start. She retrieved her coat and followed him to the car. He stopped by a coffee kiosk on the way to the hospital and bought them coffee and breakfast rolls. When they arrived at the emergency room parking lot, she spotted her rental car.

"I'll see you back at the house," she said, handing him the key.

"I'm allowing you this against my better judgment. Come straight to the house when you leave the hospital."

She nodded and hurried to the hospital entrance. When she reached the door, she turned to see if Matt had left. Was he planning to read the diary there? Maybe his car was visible from Sarah's room.

* * *

Sarah was smiling and in good spirits. She was still connected to an IV but the oxygen tube was missing. Jennifer and Charley had not yet arrived, so they had a few catch-up moments. After Sarah filled her in on her condition, she asked about the murder investigation.

"I'm afraid it's not going well. We've got another Sheriff Grayson on our hands."

"That incompetent, Dana?"

"Not quite as bad but just as stubborn and arrogant."

"It's a man thing. They don't think women know a hoot about criminal investigation. Did you tell him we solved the murders of our friends in California?"

"He doesn't care about that, Sarah. He thinks his way is the only way to solve crimes."

"Just wait till I get out of here. We'll show him a thing or two."

"He's got a tight leash on me at the moment, but I'm going to slip the knot and do some investigating on my own."

"Be careful, Logan. I think you should wait until I'm out of here."

"You're in no shape to chase clues, Cafferty. Your job is to get well and provide moral support."

"At least we can do some brainstorming."

"Yes, I look forward to it. . . By the way, can you see the parking lot from your window."

"I saw you arrive a few minutes ago."

Dana moved around the bed to peer through the large panes. "He's still out there, and making sure I don't leave without him."

"I'm glad he's protecting you. I've been worried about the man who showed up at the motorhome. He could have been the killer or someone in cahoots."

Dana made a face. "I doubt it."

"Nothing surprises me, Dana. Especially after the housekeeper was killed."

"Yes, you're right. I'll be careful."

Chapter Fifteen

Matt Brown's car was where she had left it. Head down, he was apparently engrossed in what he was reading. She might be able to reach the rental car without him noticing her. She hesitated in the glassed entry until three men walked through on their way to the parking lot. Fortunately, they were tall. Keeping them between herself and Matt, she made her way to the car.

Quickly unlocking the door, she started the engine, praying he wouldn't hear. As she slowly backed into a lane some hundred feet behind him, she watched the back of his head. When she reached the street, she resisted the urge to floorboard the sardine can. She reached the nearest corner and checked her rearview mirror. No sign of him. She then made another right turn and drove down the main street.

The Beardsly home was somewhere south of Main Street. She hoped she could find it again. If need be, she'd call information and ask the operator to look up the address. It was then she noticed a red light flashing in her mirrors. When she pulled over, his angry face was at her window before she could switch off the engine.

"Where do you think you're going?"

"To the pizza parlor. Remember I said I'd bring some back for lunch?" She held her crossed fingers below the seat.

"It's on the other side of town."

She took a deep breath before she said, "I have no sense of direction, Matt. I'll turn around and follow *you*."

"See that you do."

"You have no right to order me around."

"You're a material witness and I could have you locked up in protective custody."

"You wouldn't."

"I would. Have you forgotten about the sheriff, the coroner, and God knows how many other public officials are related to your former brother-in-law?"

"Why would they harm *me*?"

"You're Georgiana Turnsby's closest relative and heir. Her husband probably promised them all a slice of her fortune, *if* they cooperated."

"But Rob said all she left me were her books and a small amount of money."

"Have you seen the will?"

"Not yet."

"I rest my case."

Dana closed her eyes and rested her head against the steering wheel. Maybe she *was* in danger.

"I'm also worried about your friend in the hospital."

"You think someone would try again to kill her?"

"I don't know, but I have a strong feeling that you were the intended victim, not your friend. Whoever made Ms. Cafferty sick was probably using the scattergun method. I think they were actually after you. Without you, the cremation would go ahead as scheduled."

When he noticed her trembling hands, he offered to drive her back to her sister's house. She refused, saying, "I'll be fine. And I promise to behave myself if you agree to listen to my ideas about solving the murders."

"All right, let's go. I'll follow you."

Skipping the pizza parlor, she drove straight to the house. There had to be something edible in the cupboards. She would dazzle him with her culinary skills.

Nothing in the house seemed to have been disturbed. Instead of climbing stairs to her sister's office, she headed for the kitchen. She found some questionable bread and a can of tuna in the cupboard. Maybe there were frozen entrees in the freezer. While pulling packages from the lower section, she spotted a plastic bag in the ice cube compartment. Wrapped in a large freezer bag were several stacks of money. Another bag, beneath a carton of broccoli, contained expensive looking jewelry.

Dana sat down heavily in the nearest chair. Had Georgi hidden her valuables there, or had Rob stashed them and forgotten to take them with him. Maybe the housekeeper stole them and hid them there from Rob. Undecided whether she could trust Matt, she quietly carried them upstairs and hid them under Georgi's bed. She then returned to the kitchen.

He startled her with, "What's for lunch?"

"I found some au-graten potatoes in the freezer."

When he made a face, she said, "How about pasta and chicken?"

"Sounds good to me."

"Find anything interesting?"

He shook his head. "You?"

"Not a thing, Matt. I was trying to decide how to impress you with a gourmet lunch."

"A cheeseburger and beer would be fine."

Why am I not surprised?

"I heard you going upstairs. Find anything I should know about?"

"Bathroom break. I prefer the one in Georgi's bedroom."

"You're looking guilty about something. I think you'd better tell me now."

"More threats, Agent Brown?"

"Listen to me, Ms. Logan. I have very few clues to go on. If you've found something, it will certainly help me crack this case before we find another body. Hopefully not yours or your friend's. And need I remind you that withholding evidence is punishable under the law."

"All right, but I want them inventoried before I turn them over to you."

"Whatever." His eyes rolled toward the ceiling.

Dana returned upstairs and carried the thawing evidence back to the kitchen.

Matt looked as though he had won the lottery. Pulling a pair of latex gloves from his pocket, he began the inventory. When finished, he said, "Twenty thousand in hundred dollar bills. I'm not a jeweler but all this bling looks like a hundred thousand in gold, diamonds and rubies."

"I'd like a receipt, if you don't mind."

"I didn't figure you for a gold digger, Dana."

"You figured right. I don't want any more of Georgi's things disappearing, especially in some crime lab."

"You don't trust anyone, do you?"

"Very few."

She prepared lunch while he wrote descriptions of the jewelry. They ate in silence, each somewhat wary of the other. When he pushed back his plate, she said, "What are you going to do with them?"

"Pack them in a carton and ship them by special courier to Cheyenne."

"In an armored Brink's truck, I hope."

"Anything to satisfy *you*, Ms. Logan."

Dana closed her eyes and leaned her head against her palms, elbows on the table.

"You're not going to cry, are you?" he asked, sounding a bit nervous.

"And if I do?"

"I'd have to arrest you for intimidating an officer."

She stifled a laugh as they both rose from the table.

"We've got to work together, Dana. Don't hold anything back from me. I want to solve the murders almost as much as you do."

"I believe you. Let's get back to work."

She helped him wrap the jewelry in paper towels and place them in plastic bags. Recounting the money, they stacked the bills and bound them with rubber bands before storing them in plastic freezer bags. When he had sealed the carton, he placed a call to the Brinks global service number.

"You're in luck," he said, replacing his cell phone in his pocket. "They're in town today and can pick up the carton in about two hours. We'll meet them at the bank to save them a trip out here."

Dana nodded, noticing that the cuffs of his jacket were frayed and his shirt was more than a little wrinkled. You need someone to take care of you, she thought, but it certainly won't be me.

"What about my sister's friend, Angela?"

"I called her and broke the news. She took it pretty hard, but said she would fly out for the memorial service. Has that been arranged?"

"No, Matt. I've been waiting for the autopsy report."

He handed her Angela's number and asked that she call when the arrangements had been made.

"By the way, did anything in the diary convince you that Rob's the murderer?"

The expression on his face said no. "That husband of hers is a class A jerk, if nothing else. I don't understand why she stayed with him so long."

"Some women are like a dog with a well-chewed bone, Matt. They can't let go, no matter how rotten the object of their affection is."

"Yeah, I recall a few wives who were shot by the husband's girlfriend, but they stayed with the morons. Or maybe the wives were morons–"

"Are you calling my sister a moron?"

"No, but I'd sure like to know what kept her here."

"She was sick because he was poisoning her with prescriptions."

"We only have her suspicions, Dana."

"Then we should search the house for prescription bottles and get a printout from the pharmacy where they originated."

He smiled. "Good idea. Why didn't I think of that?"

Dana bit her tongue. Now was not the time for sarcasm.

"You take the upstairs bedrooms and baths and I'll search down here," he said. "Let's get it done."

She searched Georgi's medicine cabinet as well as under the sink. Everything had been removed. Even the trash cans had been emptied. There had to be at least one overlooked prescription bottle, but where?

She moved on to Rob's bedroom, which had apparently been abandoned in a hurry. Several pairs of slacks were crumpled on the floor along with discarded underwear. A few shirts still hung in the closet. Beneath them were a couple of pairs of shoes. The bathroom door was closed and she hesitated before entering. She had seen too many horror films with killers lurking in the shower.

His shower stall was empty as was his medicine cabinet. She checked the trash can and found an empty bottle of Percadon. Had Georgi been given capsules from the bottle? She took the container downstairs to Matt, who had found several prescriptions in a cabinet in Rob's office. "Look at these," he said, "Oxycodone, Methadone and Coumadin. They're in his name but the pharmacy's name and the doctor's have been blacked out with a felt tip pen."

"He may have been giving them to Georgi."

"You're probably right. We'll have to contact the issuing doctor to find out."

"If he's not another relative of Rob's."

"This is a dangerous collection of drugs, especially if taken together. Oxycodone is derived from codeine and can cause dizziness, nausea, and emotional disorders. Taken with Percadon, you've got a double whammy pain killer."

"So that's how he made Georgi sick."

"Methodone withdrawal alone could have caused your sister's problems. Anxiety, depression, exhaustion, flu-like symptoms. It's been called a living hell by users in methodone clinics, and is responsible for more than a few deaths."

"How do you know so much about prescription drugs, Matt?"

"It's my job to know. I also served as a corpsman in the Marine Corps."

"You did?"

When he nodded, she turned the prescription bottle around in her hand to read the label. "What about this one, Coumadin?"

"It's an anticoagulant, a blood thinner, originally marketed as a rat killer."

"Damn that bastard–" Dana threw the prescription bottle with such force that it ricocheted off the desk, striking Matt's arm.

He winced in pain. "Listen, partner, if you're going to take your anger out on me, I think it's time for either protective armor or protective custody. Your choice."

Dana apologized before asking, "What else did he give her, Matt, besides rat poison and nightmares?"

Chapter Sixteen

Dana insisted they search the Beardsly home after the Brinks truck picked up the evidence carton.

"What do you have in mind?"

"The housekeeper might not have returned all the boxes she took home with her, including some prescription bottles."

"That might prove theft but we can't prosecute a murder victim."

"Tonya Beardsly may have hidden evidence of Georgi's murder."

"It'll take time to get a warrant, *but* you could ask Tonya's husband if he'll allow you to look through the boxes because you're the victim's sister. It's worth a try."

When they located the house, Johnny Beardsly answered the door. Red-eyed and unshaven, he had lost his job and was searching the help wanted ads. Beer cans stacked around his chair confirmed Dana's suspicion that he had a hangover.

"Got the kids off to school, but the place's a mess."

"We understand," she said. "It's hard for a man to raise children on his own." She looked away when his face crumpled and tears ran down his ruddy cheeks.

Matt cleared his throat. "We hate to bother you but Ms. Logan needs to look in the boxes your wife brought back from the Turnsby house."

He led them to a storage room off the kitchen. "They're all here. I told her she oughta take 'em to the thrift store but she wanted to keep some of 'em. Don't know why. She didn't have no place to wear them fancy duds."

Dana touched his arm and smiled sympathetically. "Women like to have pretty things hanging in their closets, although they may never wear them." *I'll bet Sonya planned to wear them when she and Rob left the country.*

Matt was already pulling dresses from one of the boxes. "Nothing here," he said.

Dana carefully repacked them as he started on another. "If you don't mind," she said to Beardsley, "I'll come back later to get these."

"Take 'em all. I don't wanna look at 'em. They remind me of Tonya."

"You haven't removed her things from the closet, have you?" she asked.

"No, come on in the bedroom and have a look."

Matt nodded and she followed him down a long, narrow hall. The unmade bed was heaped with dirty clothes and the closet door was open. Quickly scanning the closet shelf, she pushed clothing aside and knelt to inspect the floor.

"Do ya know who killed my wife," he said from somewhere behind her.

She turned to look at him. "No, do you have any idea who may have killed her?"

"Prob'ly her boss. I hear he got away."

"We don't know yet, but it certainly looks like he may have killed my sister *and* your wife."

Clinching his fists, he said, "I'll kill the slimy–"

"Think of your children," she said, rising from the floor. "They need you. They've already lost their mother."

When he hung his head, she said, "Is there anyone who can help with the children?"

"Ma's comin' from Abilene. She's a widow lady."

Dana sighed. "Thank goodness."

Matt was in the doorway, waving her out of the room. "I've found something," he said.

She followed him back to the storage room, which was in worse shape than Beardsly's bedroom. Why were men so messy? Thank God Georgi didn't know what had happened to her beautiful clothes. Or did she?

Matt held up a cardboard box filled with prescription bottles. Some rattled while others were empty. When they examined them, they found that most of them contained Rob's name.

"No wonder he was able to give Georgi so many prescriptions, but where did he find a doctor to prescribe them?"

"Look closely, Dana. The doctor's name has been blacked out."

"But how did he convince Georgi to take prescriptions assigned to him?"

"Her name is on a few of them."

"So you think he refilled hers with his own prescriptions?"

"Pretty clever, wouldn't you say?"

"But how did he get the ones with her name on them?"

"You can buy anything on the Internet. All kinds of medications without a prescription."

"Have you looked through all the boxes?"

"I found these in the last one."

"Good, I'll start repacking."

When she finished, she gave Beardsley a brief hug and they returned to the car.

"You're a regular mother hen," he said, chuckling. "I wouldn't have guessed that about you."

"I'm not all needles and tacks, Agent Brown. Just don't think you can take advantage of my soft spot for grieving widowers."

"Never entered my mind."

"Good. What's next on the agenda?"

"More interviews."

"With whom?"

"I thought we'd start with the gardener. The woman across the road said that everyone in the neighborhood has the same lawn service. Some old guy comes out from town."

"So you've been holding out on me."

"Official business, ma'am. I don't have to share all my leads with you."

"Pretty one-sided if you ask me."

Musgrove's Lawn Service was located one block off Main Street in a small quonset hut. Various models of lawn mowers were displayed out front. If Musgrove were a woman, he would have been described as petite. Dana wondered if he could actually reach the pedals of a riding lawn mower.

Not a young man, by any means, he removed his cap and smiled at them with a few missing teeth. "Need the snow pushed off your driveway?" he asked.

"No, but we have some questions for you." Matt flashed his badge and the little man grinned.

"Don't tell me my tractor ran over somebody's yard lights."

"Nothing like that. I'm investigating the death of Georgiana Turnsby."

Musgrove's smile dissolved. "Nice lady," he said, "but always looked so sad. I think she was homesick for California."

"What about her husband?"

"Hardly ever saw him. He wasn't home much."

"Did you ever hear the couple fighting or see him with another woman?"

"No fighting that I could hear. My equipment makes a lot of noise. But everybody knew her husband was chasing skirts. Gossip's the main source of entertainment around here. Not much going on, otherwise."

"Do you know the names of the women he was seeing?"

"Oh, sure, but–" He hesitated and looked away.

"It's important, Mr. Musgrove," Dana said. "My sister and Tonya Beardsly were murdered. The other women Rob's seeing could also be in danger."

"Well, in that case I guess I could remember their names."

She patted his shoulder and thanked him. Matt then wrote down the names of five women.

"Were any of them blondes?" Dana asked.

"Three of them as I recall. But you don't know what color a woman's hair's gonna be from one day to the next."

Matt agreed, thanked him again, and they left.

When they were again seated in his car, she said, "I'm disappointed that none of them are named Laura. I was sure she's involved."

"Laura may have been an alias, Dana. Too bad your sister didn't describe her more accurately."

"She said blonde and bubbly. That's a start."

"Well, let's start with the first blonde on our list, a Sharon Zumwell."

Chapter Seventeen

Sharon was a tiny blonde in her mid-twenties with sparkling sapphire eyes. She lived in a small house behind the grocery store, where she worked, according to Musgrove. She didn't answer her door so they crossed the street to the store. Dana picked up a box of tissues and Matt replenished his supply of sunflower seeds. Only one blonde was working at the checkout counters so they stood in her line.

"Miss Zumwell?" Matt asked when he had paid for his purchase.

She smiled up at him and nodded.

"We need to talk to you about Rob Turnsby."

Her face fell and she said, "Rob who?"

His badge convinced her to close her counter and lead them to the employee's lounge, which was unoccupied. She claimed that she had only dated Rob Turnsby a few times before she broke it off.

"You must have known he was married."

"He said he was getting a divorce."

"And you believed him?"

"At first, but all he wanted to do was–well, you know." Apparently embarrassed, she lowered her head. "I found out that he was seeing other women."

"Do you know their names, and how long ago did you break it off?"

"Amanda Smelton and Linda Johnsbury. I dumped the jerk about six months ago."

Matt checked the names against his list. "Did he say why he was divorcing his wife?"

"He said she was always accusing him of cheating on her."

Matt laughed. "I wonder why."

"I asked if he would rob a bank if she accused him of it."

"Did you ever sell alternative medicine?"

"We sell a few things here."

"How about door-to-door?"

"No way."

They thanked her and left.

They found Amanda Smelton at work at the Lucky Inn, the fast food restaurant across from the park. She was a well-built blonde in her late twenties. One blue eye winked at him when Matt asked to speak with her privately.

"I get off work at six," she said with a broad smile.

"I need to talk to you *now* about Rob Turnsby."

Her reaction was similar to that of Sharon Zumwell. It took longer, however, to convince her to leave her post and submit to questioning. Rob had lied to her as he had to Zumwell, with one exception. He promised to take her to the Bahamas with him in May.

"What happened?"

"I caught him with another woman."

"Who?"

"Linda Johnsbury. I guess she didn't know about me *or* his wife."

"Did Rob ever ask you to sell vitamin supplements door-to-door?"

"Are you serious?"

Later, when they reached the car, Dana said, "I've always felt that anyone who has an affair with a married man deserves what she gets, but Rob can charm magpies out of trees."

"Yeah, a real snake charmer."

"When did he have time to work, and what kind of man preys on unsuspecting women?"

"He's an insecure boy who will never grow up," Matt replied. "All he cares about are his own pleasures."

"But why kill Georgi if he was getting what he wanted and keeping her caged like a helpless bird?"

"Doesn't make sense, does it?"

"Unless one of his girlfriends insisted he leave Georgi to marry *her*."

"We have three more girlfriends on the list. There may be more."

Dana checked her watch. "We've got enough time for at least one more interview before sundown."

"We may have to work overtime."

"Fine with me, Matt. Who's next?"

"Linda Johnsbury, the unsuspecting paramour."

She was getting off work at the convenience store when they pulled into the last parking space. Small and brunette, she had a nice smile and beautiful hazel eyes, like Matt's. She couldn't have been out of her teens.

Linda insisted she didn't have time for an interview. She had a small child at day care that she needed to pick up. "No problem," Matt said, they would follow her home. Seated again behind the wheel, he said, "She's going to try to lose us. Keep your eye on her in traffic in case she turns on a side street."

"How do you know she'll run?"

"Trust me, Dana. I know her type. She's young and she's scared."

Dana shook her head. "I don't understand how a 48-year-old man can attract all these young women? If he's such a svengali, why risk everything by killing his wife?"

"Stupidity, pure and simple."

"Womanizers have serious character flaws," she said. "I wouldn't trust them with an empty piggy bank."

"I've found that to be true of serial killers," he said, watching his mirrors. "Sociopaths have no sympathy for anyone."

Dana leaned to peer through the windshield in the dwindling light. "She's getting away, Matt." The faded green subcompact turned right and picked up speed. Matt immediately went after her. She made another right, then left, and right again, but was no match for Matt, as Dana had earlier experienced. She wondered if he had ever raced in competition.

"She's pulling into that lot ahead," Dana said.

"I see her. It looks like a day care center."

The young woman hurriedly left her car and ran into the building. A moment later she returned, carrying a small child wrapped in a blanket. Matt parked behind her car, blocking her escape.

Holding his badge, he said, "Get in the backseat of my car. We're going for a ride."

When she noticed Dana in the passenger seat, she nodded and complied. Matt then drove to the park and cut the engine. Turning halfway in his seat, he scowled at her. "When's the last time you saw Rob Turnsby?"

She shook her head and hesitated. "I-I haven't seen him in weeks."

"Why's that?"

"He's on a business trip. He said he would send money for the baby as soon as he could, but I haven't heard from him."

Dana gasped. "That's Rob's baby?"

"Yes, we're going to be married."

Poor little fool.

Matt asked if she knew that his wife had recently died and she acknowledged that she did. She hadn't known about her until a friend showed her the obituary. When asked if she ever sold alternative medicine supplements door-to-door, she said, "No. I've worked at the convenience store since I graduated from high school last year."

Matt appeared as surprised as Dana. "So you've never received any support from him?"

"No, sir. I live at home with my parents."

"Why haven't they gone after him for support?"

Her lower lip quivered and she began to cry. Between sobs she said, "They think the baby is Jimmy's."

"Jimmy who?"

"My high school sweetheart. He was killed in Iraq."

They both took a deep breath and exhaled in concert.

Matt retrieved a business card from his wallet and handed it over the seat. "I want you to call me if and when you hear from Rob Turnsby. I may be getting back in touch with you later. Understand?"

She nodded and the tears continued to slide down her cheeks.

He drove her back to her car and waited while she strapped the baby in an infant seat. Dana then drove her home and he followed. When they left her parent's home, he said, "How about dinner. It's been an exhausting day."

"I'm too overwrought to eat. Can I take a rain check?"

"You bet. I'll take you back to the motorhome."

Chapter Eighteen

Dana slumped into her recliner chair when Matt dropped her off. She rested her eyes for a few moments before retrieving the diary from her oversized purse. She had to know whether her sister knew about the other women. The next entry was written in late February:

I couldn't sleep so I got up just after 2:00 to look out my bedroom window. The freshly fallen snow is beautiful with the full moon highlighting it. It's almost like daylight. I noticed tire tracks leading to the road from my car stall in the garage. Has Rob taken my new car out for a drive? Why didn't he ask me to go with him? I went to his room and his bed had not been slept in, again. Where has he gone and with whom? I can't go on like this.

Dana swore aloud before continuing:

I know I should talk to Angela or Dana about this but I'm too embarrassed and humiliated to admit that I made such a huge mistake. Angela warned me not to marry him but I wouldn't listen. I was so in love with charming Rob Turnsby. I should have known that he was only in love with my divorce settlement. How could I have been so stupid?

Her cell phone rang and she was elated to hear from Sarah. "I talked them into letting me leave the hospital day after tomorrow," she said.

"That's great news, Sarah. I'll be up to see you in the morning."

"How's the investigation going?"

"I don't want to discuss it on my cell. You never know who's listening. I'll fill you in when I see you." Sarah understood and Dana went back to her reading. Matt called a few minutes later, asking if she had acquired an appetite.

"After the Linda Johnsbury interview, I don't think I'll ever be hungry again."

"Come on, Dana. No sense both of us eating alone."

"Aren't you tired of my company by now, Agent Brown?" Before he could answer, she said, "I've got a lot of reading to do. I'll see you in the morning." She hung up without another word.

The next twenty pages contained only descriptions of Georgi's ailments and her indecision about seeking a divorce. Weary of reading, she rose from her chair and opened the refrigerator. There wasn't much food left. She needed to grocery shop. Maybe she should return to the store where Sharon worked. Grabbing her purse and coat, she peeked through the entry curtain to make sure that Matt wasn't lurking outside. No one seemed to be in the area so she quietly closed and locked the door. Her rental car was waiting under an overhead light.

Why didn't I park it on the other side of the motorhome? When she reached to unlock the driver's door, she noticed someone standing on the fringe of light behind the car's rear bumper.

"Going somewhere, Miss Logan?" The voice was deep and unfamiliar, his face shadowed by an oversized hood.

Her hand trembled and she dropped her keys.

"I suggest you go back inside and stay there."

"Matt?"

He said nothing more as he disappeared into the darkness.

Unsure whether it had been Matt, she hesitated before unlocking the car. Suddenly angry, she quickly opened the door. Backing from the space, she drove onto the street. She kept an eye on the rearview mirror and saw that no one had followed, but she knew Matt's tactics. When the Lucky Inn's lighted sign loomed to her right, she pulled in and ordered a cheeseburger and coffee, although she wasn't hungry. Cars passed by but she didn't see his white sedan. If the man in the RV Park wasn't him, then who?

Someone was obviously trying to scare her off the case. Was Rob still hanging around, unable to leave the country? She recalled that he had planned his escape months ahead of time. Maybe the hooded man was one of his relatives. Sheriff Turnsby? Anything was possible.

A car honked behind her and she realized that she was still parked at the take-out window. Pulling ahead, she parked in one of the lanes. A car pulled in beside her. When his window slid down, she recognized his scowling face. He was motioning her to roll down her own window.

"I see you're finally hungry," he said.

"Stop following me."

"I meant what I said about placing you in protective custody."

"I don't appreciate you trying to scare me back at the motorhome."

Matt shook his head. "That wasn't me, Dana." His door opened and he quickly reached in to unlock hers through the open window. He then slid in beside her.

Handing him the cheeseburger and coffee, she told him what had happened.

"I was afraid of that. You're lucky he didn't kill you, like the housekeeper. Now you know *why* I've been what you seem to think is overly protective."

"Why is this happening, Matt?"

"I assume there's a lot of money involved. By the way, have you finished the diary?"

"Not yet."

"Then let's go back to the motorhome and take turns reading the rest of it aloud. I'm not leaving you alone, if I have to sleep on the floor."

Ten minutes later she picked up the diary, surprised there were only a few pages left. They could finish it off by ten o'clock and Matt could go home, wherever that was.

She read the next entry aloud as he made himself comfortable on the couch.

I'm going to hire a private detective. Laura stopped by again today and I ordered a relaxant because I'm having trouble sleeping. She's such a good listener that I told her more than I should about my problems. She's very sympathetic and gave me the name of a good investigator that her sister hired to "get the goods on her husband," as she called it.

Dana wondered aloud who the PI was. "Probably some friend of Laura's. Anything to trick Georgi out of her money."

"You may be right. Tomorrow we need to find out which of the girlfriends actually called herself Laura."

"But aren't you surprised that they're all still here in town?"

"Maybe not. We've still got two women to locate and there may be more. Turnsby seems to have a harem. One of them might have left the country with our suspect."

Matt took the diary and read the next entry, dated a week later.

I'm not feeling well. The capsules that Laura delivered make me nauseous. Maybe I should just take half the recommended dosage. At least I'm sleeping better. Rob has been coming home earlier to look in on me. He's back to his old charming self. What shall I do? I haven't heard from the investigator. I gave him a $5,000 advance and he said he would call during the day as soon as he has some information.

"They were milking her for all they could get," he said. "I wish your sister had named the investigator."

"How many are in the area, Matt? There can't be that many."

"I doubt he was a licensed PI. He was probably just some con artist friend of Laura's, whoever she is."

"Do you think she was one of the women we interviewed today?"

"It certainly wasn't Linda. I'll reserve my opinion until after I talk to the others tomorrow. In the meantime, let's finish the diary:"

I received a call from the investigator today. He said that he needs more money to expand his operation. He needs to hire an additional man so they can watch Rob's every movement 24 hours a day. So far he has nothing to report. I told him that I would think about it and get back to him tomorrow. He insisted that he call me in the morning. If Laura had not recommended him, I wouldn't consider giving him more money, but I'm desperate so I wrote another $5,000 check from my savings account.

"I thought my sister was smarter than that."

"Desperate situations often overrule common sense, Dana. Listen to this:"

I've been noticing the way the housekeeper looks at Rob. It's as though she wants to devour him. Am I being paranoid? Women don't throw themselves at men unless they get some encouragement. Why would Rob be interested in a crude woman who can't even speak proper English?

"Good question," he said. "Have you noticed that Turnsby's women so far have limited educations and low-end jobs?"

"Yes, his insecurities are showing. Georgi must have made him feel inferior although she would never deliberately do that to anyone."

"Back to the diary:"

I've decided to close out everything except the business checking account. I've got to stop Rob's free spending. The construction company hasn't turned a profit for some time. He's never home although he says he's busy working. I no longer believe anything he says.

Matt looked up from the diary, saying, "This is one of the things I've been looking for:"

I've consulted my lawyer in San Francisco. I'm changing my will and leaving the bulk of my estate to my sister Dana and niece Kerrie. I'm also leaving small gifts to Angela and a couple of other friends. My trusted lawyer has the routing number to my offshore account. If anything happens to me, he'll get in touch with Dana and Kerrie. I'm so glad that I took his advice about the house title. Rob reluctantly agreed to a postnuptial agreement as a condition of receiving additional money for the business. I've paid for everything, including the property taxes, so no matter what happens to our marriage, he can't take my beautiful house away from me.

"Looks like you're a rich woman, Dana Logan."

"I don't care about that. I just want to see Rob behind bars."

Matt turned the page:

"I'm getting weaker every day. I stopped taking all the pills and I'm still not getting any better. Sometimes I wake up choking. The doctor can't find anything wrong with me and I'm afraid to eat anything the housekeeper prepares. I tried to get rid of her but she said that Rob hired her and only he can fire her. Rob says I'm being silly and that there's nothing going on between them. I need to get away from here. I'm going to call Angela and my sister tomorrow. I know they'll help me. I desperately need some rest so I'm going to take a sleeping pill.

"That's all she wrote," he said, laying the diary aside.

The torrent of tears she had been holding back since her sister's death overwhelmed her. Matt got to his feet and held her in his arms. "We'll find the bastard, Dana. I promise you that. And when we do . . ."

Chapter Nineteen

True to his word, Matt spent the night wrapped in a blanket on the motorhome couch. Next morning he was red-eyed and stiff. Dana felt guilty that she hadn't offered him Sarah's bunk.

"Nothing here but coffee for breakfast," she said.

"No problem. We'll stop by the kiosk before we go to the hospital."

"Then what, Matt?"

"The coroner will be back in his office this morning. I'll grab a quick shower and get over there for the autopsy reports while you're visiting your friend."

She insisted that she was capable of driving, but he was adamant. When her friend was out of the hospital, he would consider leaving them alone. Unless, of course, they wanted to be held in protective custody.

They rode in silence to the kiosk and said few words when he dropped her off at the hospital. Her visit with Sarah was pleasant but Linda Johnsbury and her baby were on her mind. Rob had not only killed Georgi and Tonya, he had run out on his own child.

"My kids left early this morning," Sarah was saying. "They both have jobs . . ."

Dana nodded but wasn't really listening. She wondered about the women they had yet to interview. Were they also young innocents like Linda? Or were they women who didn't care whether a man was wearing a wedding ring?

"Dana, you're not listening to me, are you?"

"I'm sorry. I can't help thinking about Rob's girlfriends."

"Do you think one of them helped him kill your sister?"

"I wish I knew. Not knowing is making me a wreck."

"It seems the investigator is doing a good job."

"He's trying."

"He's a nice looking man and seems devoted to you."

"I just happen to look like his favorite actress."

"It's more than that. I've seen the way he looks at you. He reminds of me of Sheriff Grayson."

"Don't go there, Sarah. This case is already painfully similar to the murders in California."

"Complete with an amorous lawman."

"Matt will be back soon. Don't you dare say a word–"

Sarah pressed her thumb and index finger together and ran them across her lips. Smiling, she said, "Enjoy the admiration while you can. All too soon we'll be elderly and no one will pay us any mind."

"Let's solve this case before we worry about amorous men."

There was a knock at the door before Matt walked in. Grinning, he said, "Turnsby's cousin, the coroner, isn't a great fan of his. In fact, he told me about another woman who isn't on our list."

"What about the autopsies?"

"Your sister died of asphyxiation. Her throat closed and she choked to death."

Dana bit her lip. "That's what nearly killed Sarah. What caused it, Matt?"

"There were so many chemicals in her system that the coroner is still running tests."

"What about Tonya Beardsly?"

"Her injuries suggest that she was hit by a car from behind. The body was so badly mangled by the dogs that it's hard to come to a definite conclusion."

"He must have run her over with his pickup truck."

"I don't think so, unless it was a small truck. The impact injuries were mainly to her back and legs. So our next order of business is to find the other women and check out what they're driving."

They left the hospital at 10:30 and drove to the auto parts store where Kim Yankton worked. They found her behind the service counter, a dishwater blonde in her mid-thirties. Wide-hipped and wearing no makeup, she bore little resemblance to the rest of Rob's harem. She also denied knowing him.

"Witnesses will swear that the two of you have a relationship," Matt said, displaying his badge.

"They're lying. I don't know anything about him."

"Oh, come on, everybody knows him. How long have you lived in this town?"

"Too long," she said, slamming down her clipboard.

"He promised to take you away from here, didn't he?"

"Who told you that?"

"Was it a trip to Burmuda in May?"

"New South Wales," she said angrily. "He promised to take me to see my grandmother. She's not well."

"When's the last time you saw him?"

"A couple of weeks ago. He said his wife was dying and that we would finally be together."

"Did he ask you to sell vitamin supplements to his wife?"

The woman's mouth opened in surprise. "I told him I wouldn't do that."

"How long ago did he ask?"

"Five or six months ago."

"What make and color of car do you drive, Kim?"

"A white stepside Chevy pickup."

"I see. Well, don't leave town. I'll be in touch."

"This case is getting more convoluted by the minute," Dana said as he opened the car door for her. "Who's next?"

"Dawn Talson. She's a hotel waitress."

"Rob's certainly an equal opportunity womanizer, isn't he?"

Talson was on her day off and refused to unlatch the chain from her apartment door. When Matt showed her his badge, she reluctantly let them in. She was a very young, long-haired blonde, with a bicycle parked along her living room wall.

The place was a mess. A suitcase was sitting near the door and she looked as though she were preparing to leave.

"Let me guess. You're meeting him in Bermuda?"

She denied knowing Rob Turnsby, but after a few minutes of questioning broke down and cried. A horn sounded out front and Dana opened the door to find a cab waiting.

"You're not going anywhere, young lady. You're under arrest on suspicion of murder." He then read her rights.

Speechless, Dana watched him cuff the young woman and lead her out to the car. After she had been booked and fingerprinted, she was led to a jail cell.

"Do you really think she was going to meet him?" Dana asked when again seated next to him in his car.

"She would have told me if she were going somewhere else." He smiled. "We're getting closer to finding him. Let's wrap this up with the name the coroner gave me. I'll come back to question Dawn Talson later."

Their next stop was at the home of Rob's secretary, Melanie Shamera, an attractive, fortyish brunette. When asked if she knew where her boss had gone, she said that she hadn't seen or heard from him in several days.

"When did he tell you he was closing down the business?" he asked.

"Three days ago. He was waiting for us when we came to work. He said he was laying everyone off."

"Did he say why?"

"Some contracts didn't come through."

"I noticed a new little, white step-side pickup out front? Is it yours?"

"I–uh–was given use of it when I worked for Rob."

"He gave it to you for extra services rendered, didn't he?"

The secretary paled but said nothing.

"We can talk here or at the jail."

Melanie told them that she and her boss had been involved in a long-term affair but that she had no idea where he'd gone. She hastily wrote a list of employees' names and phone numbers for Matt. She also denied taking part in the prescription and alternative medicine schemes.

Matt handed her his card and told her to contact him if she heard from Turnsby.

"Who's last on the list," Dana asked when Matt's car left the curb.

"Katie Bannatt, a pharmacy clerk at the hospital."

"She must be the one who–"

"Yeah, she might be the one who gave Turnsby the prescriptions."

"And nearly killed Sarah."

"A good possibility."

Chapter Twenty

"I didn't know Mr. Turnsby was married. He never came in with his wife."

"Everybody in town knew he was married to the mystery writer."

"Well," she finally admitted, "I think he did say that he was getting a divorce."

"That's what he told all his women, but you're old enough to know better."

She shrugged and haughtily lifted her chin. Katie Bannatt wasn't a natural blonde and she definitely wasn't young.

"When did he ask you to give him medicine without a prescription?"

"Never. I'd lose my job and probably go to jail."

"I can arrange that," Matt said.

She appeared so insulted that Dana wondered whether she was actually involved with their prime suspect.

"Did he ask you about any medications that might cause certain problems?"

"As a matter of fact he did. He said his wife needed some information for a novel she was writing."

"Such as?"

"It was several months ago and I really don't recall–"

"Did he ask you about a prescription that could cause a patient's throat to swell enough to cause death?"

"Yes, I told him that certain sleeping pills could cause the problem. And that any number of prescriptions can cause swelling of the throat and tongue if the patient is allergic to the ingredients." The angular woman turned her back to busy herself with a scoop and capsules.

"If you think of anything else, give me a call." Matt placed his card on the counter and told her not to leave the county. He then took Dana's arm and they returned to the car.

"Why didn't you arrest her?"

"I'm putting a tail on her and a phone tap to see if she gets in touch with Turnsby. There's a chance she's telling the truth and that he got his prescriptions online."

"What about Sarah?"

"It's probably a coincidence. The doctors think it was an allergic reaction to Tumeric and Ibupropin. In any event, I warned the pharmacy manager to keep a close eye on Bannatt although I doubt she had anything to do with your friend's medical problems."

"Sarah almost died of an infection. Couldn't it have been caused by something from the pharmacy?"

He thumped his palm against the steering wheel. "I'm trying to unravel one thread at a time, Dana. There are enough of them in this case to make a king-sized basketball."

She sighed. "All right, Matt. Who's next?"

"We'll start with the first name on the employee list. He glanced down and read the name, Joe Marly, the construction supervisor. "If he hasn't found another job, he might be at home."

Marley *was* home and not in the best of moods. Lanky with receding hair, his dark eyes bulged above a red bulbous nose. He was more than willing to voice an opinion of his former boss.

"The guy's an idiot," he said. "He doesn't know the first thing about running a construction company. If it wasn't for Morris and me, it woulda gone down the tubes a long time ago."

"He built a nice home for his wife," Matt said.

"*He* didn't build it. It was mostly subcontracted work with me supervising. His wife paid for it. She also kept pumping money into the business to keep it afloat."

Dana tensed but kept her thoughts to herself.

"Did he say anything about his wife to you and the other employees?"

"Yeah, I don't trust a guy who bad-mouths his wife. A man's supposed to protect his wife, not trash her to other people."

Their next stop was at the home of construction foreman, Morris Walkins. Tall and paunchy, he spoke in a loud voice, which made Dana wonder if he were hard of hearing.

"Oh, he's a ladies man, all right. They was always comin' out to the jobsite to see 'im. Some of 'em was so young that I figured the guy for a pedophile."

"Did he ever say anything that would lead you to believe he would kill his wife?"

Walkins chewed his lower lip. "I wondered about that after hearin' him talk to one of his lady friends. I can't remember exactly what he said but it sounded like he was expectin' her to kick off any time. I noticed him smilin' when he said it."

"Did you ever meet his wife?"

"Yeah, real nice lady. My wife reads her books."

* * *

"How many more are on the list?" she asked over dinner at the local steakhouse.

"Just two. Lawrence, the plumber and Catagon, the electrician. "We'll work them in tomorrow."

"What about Dawn Talcon?"

"Why don't I take you back to the hospital to spend some time with your friend while I interrogate her."

"Good idea. Why do I feel that we're forgetting something?"

"Probably because there are so many loose ends. We'll tie them up as soon as possible."

* * *

"You look exhausted, Dana. Are you getting enough sleep?"

"Not much. All the interviews keep running through my mind like a bad movie."

"Tell me what you've learned today."

Dana filled her in on the people interviewed. "I should have been taking notes" she said. "I'll start a journal tonight so we can discuss everything that's happened, once you're out of here."

"I won't rest easy until I'm back in the motorhome."

"Nor will I, but I don't think you're in any danger. It's me they're after. Georgi left nearly everything to Kerrie and me."

"Who are you referring to, Dana?"

"Rob and whoever he's working with. I don't think he's smart enough to plan everything on his own."

"I'm surprised the agent allowed you to come here alone."

"He's stretched so thin that I'm surprised he hasn't called in reinforcements."

"Maybe he has. I know he won't let anything happen to you."

"He's not invincible, Sarah, and we *can* take care of ourselves."

"I'm afraid I won't be much help for a few days."

"We've still got your trusty baseball bat and I'm thinking of buying a gun."

"You think we'll need one?"

"I'll ask Matt when he gets here."

Visiting hours were over when he finally appeared, haggard and disheveled. His expression said the interview with Dawn Talcon had not gone well. He shook his head when she asked about it.

134

"She insisted she was planning a trip to her sister's home in Billings, not to meet Turnsby. I called and her sister verified her story. So I took her to the airport."

"One suspect scratched from the list."

"I'm still not convinced."

"You're a suspicious man, Agent Brown."

"That's my job, Ms. Logan. Are you ready to leave?"

"Yes, and tomorrow I'll be bringing Sarah home from the hospital."

He closed his eyes and slapped his forehead. "I forgot. I've got two interviews in the morning."

"No problem. I'll drive over by myself."

"Not a good idea."

"Then follow me here before you do your interviews."

He agreed and they left the hospital. When he dropped her off at the motorhome, he said, "I shouldn't leave you alone."

"I'll be fine. I'll use the baseball bat if someone tries to break in." She then asked his advice about a gun.

"Let me think about that one," he said. "I'll be back at eight in the morning."

When he left she unpacked her laptop and began her journal. Predating it to the day she and Sarah arrived, she wrote every detail she could remember, including the meal that Tonya Beardsly had prepared. Had it only been five days? It seemed an eternity.

In a separate section she listed all the people involved. She described them and their characteristics in as much detail as she could remember. *Georgi could have written an entire mystery novel with this cast of characters, if only she had known about them.* Closing her eyes, she envisioned her sister sitting at her computer. That was another loose end. She needed to discover her password and find her latest manuscript, which had to be on her computer.

Which password would Georgi have used? Mystery? Novelwriter? Diary? GTurnsby?

She wrote down every password she could imagine. One of them had to work. She would try them all when they returned to her sister's house.

A scratching noise distracted her. It seemed to be coming from the bedroom in the back of the coach. Quietly leaving the dining booth, she tiptoed toward the sound. It was well past ten and she knew that her shadow could be seen on the shade. Lying on her bed, she carefully lifted a corner of the curtain and peered out. Unless someone was crouched low behind the motorhome, no one was out there. She may have imagined it, but she thought she heard the noise again. This time it sounded as though someone were using a saw. Baseball bat or not, she wasn't going out to investigate. Instead she moved forward to the driver's seat and reached to blow the horn. Three long blasts should do it. Pulling aside the drapes covering the windshield, she saw outside lights coming on from the other RVs. It wasn't long before someone knocked at the door.

"Miz Logan, is something wrong?"

He sounded like the manager but she grabbed the bat for protection. Unlocking the door, she told him what had happened.

"Let's have a look," he said, flashing his light along the motorhome.

She followed him around to the back of the coach where they discovered a partially severed water hose. The manager said it appeared that someone had used a serrated knife.

Matt was right. She *was* in danger. As soon as she was back inside, she dialed his number. He must have been sleeping because he fumbled and dropped his phone. When she told him what had happened, he sounded alert. He would be right over.

Chapter Twenty-One

Matt inspected the motorhome himself. He wondered aloud if the culprit thought the hose was connected to the propane tank. "I'm glad the bottles are in a locked compartment," he said. "Whoever did this is either trying to scare you, or is serious about causing bodily harm. That's why I'm placing you in protective custody."

"I can't allow you to do that, Matt."

There was enough reflected glow from his flashlight that she noticed his look of surprise. "You're not making this easy for me, are you?"

"Use me as a decoy," she said. "I'm sure there's at least one lawman in this town who can guard the motorhome at night, without falling asleep. I'm willing to pay his wages."

"All right. I'm doing this against my better judgment. I'll see if I can locate an off duty officer."

"You won't regret this, I promise."

"Always the amateur sleuth," he grumbled as he took her arm and helped her up the steps.

It was a long night. Dana slept fully clothed in the recliner chair, waking whenever she heard the slightest noise. Officer Murray was out there, somewhere, quietly keeping an eye on the coach. Her cell phone and Sarah's bat were close at hand as well as the largest butcher knife from the small kitchen. She wondered how Sarah was going to react to all the weaponry and extra security. She fleetingly thought they should allow Matt to place them in protective custody, but they'd been in worse situations in California. They would get through this and help Matt find Georgi's killer.

When Matt arrived just before eight that morning, she was exhausted and fuzzy-brained. He didn't appear to be in much better shape, but managed a weak grin. After a quick cup of coffee, he followed her to the hospital. "Take no chances," he warned. "I'll stop by as soon as I'm finished with the interviews."

Dana hurried into the hospital where she found Sarah ready to leave. Except for her hospital pallor, she seemed her old self. They carefully hugged and the nurse wheeled her patient to the elevator. Somewhat edgy, Dana scanned both directions in the hall and inspected the elevator before she would allow the wheelchair to enter.

With the nurse's help, Sarah squeezed into the passenger seat of the rental car. "Couldn't you find something bigger–?"

"I'm glad you reminded me, Sarah. We'll stop by the rental agency and see if we can swap for a larger car. I've been driving for days with my knees under my chin."

A burgundy minivan was setting on the lot and they talked the agent into exchanging it, although the van had not yet been detailed. Promising to clean it themselves, they made the deal and Dana loaded several items from the trunk of the car.

"Agent Brown won't know this car is ours," Sarah said.

Nor will anyone else. "Won't he be surprised? Are you feeling well enough to go for a ride?"

"Yep, I feel like a caged lion that just escaped the zoo."

"We're going to Georgi's house to check out her computer."

"You think it's safe?"

"I brought the bat. We'll be fine."

Dana first drove to the discount store to have the house key duplicated. Matt had returned it that morning but she knew he would demand it back when he discovered she had used it. She wasted no time driving to her sister's home. It wouldn't be long before he found them.

She carefully checked the grounds before opening the entry door. No one seemed to be in the vicinity. She helped Sarah up the stairs and insisted that she lie on the office couch while Dana tried her luck at guessing Georgi's password. All the words on her list were rejected and she searched her memory for alternatives.

"Type in her name," Sarah suggested. "Or try DanaLogan or sisterDana or your home address in California."

"None of them work."

"What about pets' names or childhood toys?"

Dana remembered Georgi's favorite toy, a large teddy bear she kept on her bed. What had she called it? She typed in HermieBear and waited. "Sarah, you're a genius."

Scrolling through the file names she clicked on Diary of Murder. It had to be her latest manuscript. "Listen to this:"

I know my husband is planning to kill me. I can read it in his eyes. It's only a matter of time until he has the courage to end my miserable life . . .

"She wasn't writing about her own life, was she?"

Dana shivered. "I hope not. This may be pure fiction, but what if Rob read the manuscript and decided to validate the plot? Maybe he didn't know that she already mailed the book to her agent."

Her cell phone rang and she saw that it was Matt calling. She hesitated. If she didn't answer, he would put out an APB on both of them. "Dana Logan here," she said.

"My last interviewee won't be available until this afternoon. Where are you, by the way?"

"With Sarah. I just got her tucked into bed." She did a finger cross.

"Stay put and I'll see you in about an hour, after I interrogate my next witness."

She wanted to ask which witness but let it pass. "See you then," she said and hung up.

"You should have told him where we are, Dana."

"He's already spread too thin. We need to help him crack the case."

"I hope you know what you're doing."

Dana continued to read as Sarah dozed off. Scrolling quickly, she skimmed the pages until she arrived at chapter five:

I found the travel vouchers in his brief case. He's planning to leave with one of his women. The dates on the vouchers are April 5th. They're going to Barcelona . . .

That's two days from now. But Spain? Is this still pure fiction or did Georgi incorporate the facts into her fiction? She closed her eyes and felt a migraine coming on. She hated to wake Sarah but they had to reach the motorhome before Matt did.

She managed to help Sarah off the couch, down the stairs, and into the van. Checking her watch she realized that nearly an hour had passed since Matt's call. She was cutting time too close. Her phone rang several moments after Sarah had settled in her bunk.

"Where's your car and whose minivan is parked in your space, Dana?"

She knew he wouldn't be happy they had swapped vehicles, without telling him. She was right. He lectured her for at least ten minutes on the dangers of going off on her own. Thank heavens he didn't know where they'd gone. She was beginning to feel like an errant child.

"Enough, Matt. How about filling me in on what you've learned."

"I wish I had something concrete to tell you but–"

"Have you interviewed Sheriff Turnsby?"

"No, he's my afternoon appointment."

"I doubt Rob's brother will tell you anything worthwhile."

"Maybe, but remember his cousin the coroner doesn't like him. His brother may also have it in for him."

"Are there any employees left to interrogate?"

"None that I can find. They're a mobile bunch. They go from job to job, one town to another, wherever there's work to be found."

"And Rob's girlfriends? Have you located more of them?"

"No, but we've got a variety to choose from. I'd like to get your impressions of each one of them."

She motioned him to be seated. "I'm flattered that you consider my opinions of value."

He sighed heavily. "I've got so many angles to consider that I can't sort them all out alone. I thought you'd want to help."

She smiled. "I do and I'll be glad to give you my impressions. Let's start with Sharon Zumwell. She says she only dated Rob a few weeks before she dumped him. I believe her that it happened over six months ago. I think we can scratch her from our list."

"You're probably right."

"Amanda Smelton, in my opinion, is out for whatever she can get. I wouldn't put it past her to get involved in Rob's prescription and alternative medicine schemes." She noticed that he was taking notes. "Linda Johnsbury is a definite victim. She's too young and vulnerable to have been involved in a murder plot during her pregnancy."

"What about Kim Yankton?" he said, looking up.

"I think she's a definite suspect along with the secretary, Melanie Shamera, and the pharmacy clerk, Katie Bannatt."

"So you've narrowed them down to the last four I interviewed? What about Dawn Talson?"

"She's the dark horse, Matt. I think she's a possible."

Grinning, he said, "I'll run background checks on all of them. I know you're much better at determining a woman's character than I am."

141

"I'm surprised that you'd admit that, Agent Brown."

He sighed but said nothing.

"Now, about the gun—"

"Not a good idea."

"My late husband taught me to use a revolver *and* a rifle," she said. "I've even fired a nine millimeter Glock."

He lowered his eyes when he said, "A dog would be much safer."

"A dog?"

"Yes, a retiring police dog would be better protection."

"But, Matt, we would trip over a dog in the motorhome."

"Bert is still very agile and could be trained to stay under the dining booth when you're not using it." He rose to leave. "I'll bring him with me when I return this afternoon."

Chapter Twenty-Two

Bert was a handsome, eight-year-old German Shepherd, who bonded immediately with Sarah. For some reason he shied away from Dana. As Matt promised, the dog soon learned to lie under the dining booth after he was fed and petted.

"I do feel safer," Sarah said when Matt had carried in a 40-pound bag of dog food. Dana directed him to the coach's passenger seat, saying "It's getting a bit crowded in here."

"Bert's worth his weight in firearms," he said, "and I won't have to worry so much about the two of you."

She handed him a cup of coffee and urged him to sit for a moment. "Have you heard anything about Rob?"

"I'm afraid not."

"What about the tracking devices built into vehicles these days?"

"He must have disabled the one in his pickup."

"I've been reading about the microchip invasion, electronic sniffers in everything from shampoo bottles to clothing and car keys. I'm horrified at the invasion of privacy although I can see where it *would* help track down criminals, like Rob."

"I'm looking into it," he said, checking his watch. "It's almost time for my appointment with Sheriff Turnsby." Before he left, he taught them basic canine signals, which the dog instantly obeyed. Sarah quickly picked them up and wore Bert out practicing them. The German Shepherd seemed happy to retire beneath the dining booth.

Dana wished Matt luck with his interview. When he left, she said, "I need to make a copy of Georgi's manuscript to read on my laptop."

"What if Matt calls or stops by again?"

"We'll say that we needed groceries, which we do, by the way."

"What if there are microchips in our shoes?"

"We can't worry about that now, Sarah. The chips are in everything, including license plates and credit cards. Let's get over to Georgi's place."

She was glad they had swapped cars and that Bert was so obedient. The dog stayed at Sarah's side as they climbed the stairs to her sister's office. Dana started a CD copy of the manuscript while Sarah reclined on the couch, with Bert on the floor beside her. They were both startled when the dog barked and ran to the door.

"Someone's here." Dana checked the CD, relieved that it had finished loading. Quickly removing it from the tray, she slipped it into her purse and shut down the computer.

"We have every right to be here, Sarah. Don't panic. Bert will protect us."

Sarah was sitting on the edge of the couch, a hand on her chest. They waited, listening as Bert whined and pawed at the door. It seemed an eternity before the door slowly opened and a familiar face peered inside. Bert turned to look at Sarah, who slowly lowered her hand. The dog sat, his eyes trained on the intruder. Thank heavens Matt had taught them hand signals.

"What are you doing here?" the woman asked.

"I might ask you the same thing."

"I saw a strange car outside and heard a dog bark, so I decided to check it out."

"How did you get in?"

Rob's former secretary said a key to the house was in Rob's desk at the construction office. She still had her key to the office. "Rob called and asked me to pick up some papers from his desk here at the house."

Dana left her chair. "Rob called? From where?"

"I have no idea. He said he would call back later to give me a mailing address."

"Did you get in touch with Matt Brown, the investigator."

"Not yet."

Dana wanted to strangle the woman. "Rob's a murder suspect and you could be arrested for aiding and abetting his escape."

"Murder?" Melanie Shamera stepped around the dog and walked into the room. She was obviously shaken. "Rob said his wife died from an overdose of sleeping pills."

"He lied."

Dana offered her the desk phone. "I suggest you call Agent Brown."

The secretary turned to leave, but Bert growled and blocked the woman's path.

"Call him now before you're in over your head," Dana said.

She hesitated. "I'll use my cell phone."

They listened as the secretary made arrangements to meet with Matt at her home.

"If you knew what we do about Rob Turnsby, you would avoid him at all costs," Dana said. "He's a sociopath who ruins lives. I'm certain he killed my sister."

She nodded and Sarah signaled Bert to allow her to leave. Dana wondered whether they could get downstairs in time to follow her. Sarah surprised her with her agility. They were able to reach the van before Melanie disappeared. "Keep an eye on that small pickup," she said as she backed down the circle drive. "She might just lead us to Rob."

"Shouldn't we call Matt?"

"Not enough time. We've got to keep her in sight."

Sarah coughed and held a hand to her throat.

What am I doing? She's in no shape for a car chase. Dana slowed the van and allowed the pickup to disappear. "Call Matt and tell him what happened. I'm taking you back to the motorhome."

"Are you sure?"

"Absolutely."

Sarah phoned Matt and ended the call with an apology. She was much better at smoothing wrinkles than Dana. "He's on his way," she said. "He's going to try to intercept her before she gets to town."

"Good, let's stop at the store for a few groceries. I plan to spend the afternoon reading Georgi's manuscript while you take a nap." Bert seemed to chuff his approval.

* * *

It was half past four when Matt called to tell them he had followed Melanie Shamera to an abandoned warehouse south of town. She hadn't called him on her cell so she was about to be arrested when she returned to the pickup. He was calling because he couldn't get through to the sheriff's office. Would they keep trying and ask for backup? Rob Turnsby could be in the area. Dana relayed the message to the county dispatcher and hoped that the sheriff would follow up on it. Why did he have to be Rob's brother?

She found reading difficult because she was so worried about Matt. Maybe they should drive to the warehouse to offer assistance. Bert could make short work of Rob if he tried to escape, unless he used a gun. Sarah vetoed that idea. Matt could take care of himself. She took her own laptop from the bedroom cabinet and suggested researching each of Rob's girlfriends.

"It'll cost a fortune to get complete histories on all of them, but I guess you can afford it now, Dana."

"Not quite yet but I'm willing to spend the entire inheritance on locating Georgi's killers."

"You think there was more than one?"

"I'm sure Rob had help. He seems to be totally inept in everything he does, except for charming the pants off women."

"A common gigolo."

"How true that is." Dana checked her watch again. It was nearly 6:00 p.m. How was Matt faring at the warehouse? And why didn't he call?

Chapter Twenty-Three

They finished their chicken soup and Dana rebooted her laptop. Disappointed that Georgi's manuscript had not revealed a clue to her death, she thought her sister may not have known what was happening before she finished the book. It was nearly seven o'clock and they had not heard from Matt. He wasn't answering his phone so something must have happened to him.

"I'm going down there, Sarah. Will you be all right here alone with Bert?"

"I'm fine. We're going with you."

"Are you sure?"

"You bet. I'm not missing out on any more excitement."

They grabbed a heavy flashlight, Sarah's bat, and Bert's leash. A light snow was falling and they dressed appropriately. The windshield of the minivan was already coated with snow and the closer they got to town, the heavier the white stuff fell. Swirling in hypnotic patterns, the snow caused Dana to blink her eyes. The road was slick and she slowed to 20 miles per hour, hoping no one was following. She knew Sarah was just as frightened but neither said a word.

They saw faint lights ahead and Dana hoped that it was the outskirts of town. "Call the sheriff's office and ask if they've heard from Matt," she said.

Sarah dialed but reported the circuits busy. "It must be the storm."

Which street should they take to find the warehouse? "We can stop at the kiosk," Dana said, "to ask directions."

"Fine with me. Coffee sounds good."

The kiosk was closed, but a nearby café was still open. Bert stayed to guard the van as they sloshed through the snow. *This is a really fine idea*, Dana thought as they entered the café.

"You must mean Warehouse Road?" the waitress said when they asked. "Take the next street to the left and follow it out of town to the railroad tracks. Turn right and it's about a mile down that road. But I wouldn't advise you to go there tonight in this storm."

"I wouldn't advise anyone to go there," Dana said when they returned to the van. She tried dialing Matt's number. This time it rang through to his mailbox. She left a message and sat watching the snow, undecided what to do. The storm was getting worse.

"Try the sheriff's office again, Sarah."

"I'm getting a recorded message that says they're closed. I thought they never closed."

"The dispatcher's probably taking a coffee break."

"What shall we do?"

"Find Matt."

They turned left and headed south out of town as Dana kept an eye on the overhead compass. A faint pair of tire tracks led the way and she was convinced that her prayers had been answered. "Watch for any signs of a railroad track," she said. I'm not sure whether we turn right on this side or the other side of the tracks."

"I guess we'll have to get out and look."

"You can get lost in a storm and freeze to death."

"That might happen anyway, Dana, if we get stuck in the snow."

"We can't turn back now."

"Look," Sarah said, "a railroad crossing sign."

She slowed the van to five miles per hour. "Watch on your right for a road."

Sarah rubbed the window with her sleeve. "Uh-oh, I think we passed it."

Backing up was out of the question. The van wasn't a four-wheel drive vehicle. If she backed off the narrow, two-lane road they could be stuck until the spring thaw. "We can't just sit here."

Check the odometer," Sarah said. "Then drive until we find another road where we can make a U-turn. We can drive back until we reach whatever mileage the odometer recorded."

"Great idea *if* we can *see* another road. Otherwise, we'll keep going until we run out of gas. And speaking of gas, we have less than a quarter of a tank."

"Maybe there's an emergency kit in the back with a flare."

"What good is a flare? There's no one out here to see it."

"I can walk behind the van with Bert, holding the flare until we find the side road. I'll light the flare and you can back up slowly until you reach the road. It's not far, maybe a hundred feet.

"What if you get off the road?"

"I'll follow our tire tracks."

Unconvinced, Dana climbed between the seats and crawled to the back of the van where she found a black case against the side wall. Instead of a flare, there was a large flashlight that nearly matched their own.

"I have a better idea, Sarah. *You* back the van and I'll carry the flashlights."

"But I'm not very good at–"

"Back slowly and don't turn the wheel. Keep your eyes on the left mirror and follow the lights. If you get off track, I'll wave the flashlights up and down. You can then stop and pull ahead." Dana was adamant. Sarah was in no shape to be stumbling around in a snowstorm. She should have stayed behind in the motorhome.

Her friend at last consented and lightly gripped the wheel. Dana knew she was nervous, but her plan had to work. The accumulation of snow was at least six inches and they knew what could happen if the van left the road. They would be marooned until someone came along. With their luck, it would be the sheriff or her former brother-in-law.

Dana wrapped a wool scarf around her head and neck and pulled on heavy gloves. The moment she left the van, she was pelted with wind-driven snow. Head down, she opened the van's side door wide enough to slide inside, when she needed to, then made her way around to the back. Squinting to locate the tire tracks, she walked a few yards and stopped to wag the flashlights on the van's left side. She prayed that Sarah wasn't so nervous that she would floorboard the van.

Waving the flashlights, she noticed that the van didn't seem to be moving. Shading her eyes against the snow, she continued to swivel, making certain she was still in the tracks. She had taken several dozen steps when she lost her footing and fell. Sarah opened her door to yell, "Dana?"

Regaining her footing, she yelled "Keep coming." The van spun its wheels and didn't move. Plowing back through the snow, she crawled into the open side door, thankful the snow was blowing from the north. Shivering, she pulled the door closed, saying they needed something to use for traction. She could see nothing in the van that would work until Bert licked the side of her face and pawed at the blanket on the seat.

Stroking his head, she said, "Bert, you're a genius."

Gathering the blanket, she told Sarah to back slowly without stopping. She then left the van to stretch the blanket behind the rear wheels. Teeth clattering, she started back down the road, stopping a few yards from the van to signal Sarah. "Keep coming, keep coming, "she yelled as she watched the taillights grow brighter.

Now if she could only find the side road. The wind seemed to have picked up and it was nearly impossible to see the tracks. The snow was filling them in. If the van stopped again, they would have nothing left to generate traction, unless they used their coats. She didn't want to consider that possibility.

Shielding her eyes, she crouched to make sure that she was still following the tracks. Exhausted and shuffling her feet, she stubbed her toe on something hard like a railroad track. The road had to be on the other side. The van was close and she had to move faster. It was then she glimpsed a road sign on her right, and continued walking past, counting another fifty steps. Motioning Sarah with her flashlights to continue backing up, she hurried around to the van's passenger side to climb in through the open door.

"Keep going," she yelled. "I'll tell you when to turn onto the road. Shift into a forward gear before the van completely stops." She prayed they wouldn't drop the transmission in the process. "We're passing the road sign. Shift fast into a forward gear as smoothly as you can. *Now.*"

Sarah made a frightened sound that reminded her of the "Three Stooges." The van jerked forward and Dana directed her to turn right. She then slid the side door closed and climbed into the passenger seat. If she had miscalculated where Warehouse Road was located, this could be their last trip together.

Chapter Twenty-Four

"I don't see any delineator posts, Dana. How are we gonna stay on the road?"

"There are tire tracks. Look closer." The slight indentations in the snow wouldn't last and she prayed they would make it to the warehouse before they disappeared. Someone had obviously gone down the road not long before them. She hoped it had been Matt.

The snow seemed to be lessening or maybe it was wishful thinking. Sarah checked the odometer and reported that they had traveled half a mile. The wind seemed to be picking up and they discussed the possibility that a ground blizzard could finish them off. The thermometer was down to fifteen degrees.

"I'll call the sheriff's office again," Dana said. "If they don't answer, I'll call 911."

"I doubt we'll be able to get through in this storm."

"There's a telephone book in the pocket behind your seat. I'll keep dialing until I reach someone." She punched in the number but could get no signal.

The tracks curved to the right and Dana wondered if they left the road. They couldn't stop because they might lose traction, so they decided to follow the tracks up the slope, which leveled off onto a plateau. Whoever made the tracks must have known where they were going.

Dana held her breath when a large building came into view. It had to be the old warehouse. The snow had all but stopped and she noticed a vehicle parked outside what appeared to be a loading dock. When they pulled alongside she recognized the car. It belonged to Matt.

"He must be inside," Sarah said.

"I'll try calling him again." She punched in the numbers but could hear nothing but static. She then opened the passenger door. "Stay here while I look around."

"Bert and I are coming with you."

"All right, but be as quiet as you can."

Sarah lifted a finger to her lips, warning the dog not to bark. The two women then climbed the steps to the loading dock. Each carried a flashlight as a possible weapon. A small dilapidated door creaked open and they swept the interior with their flashlights. Snow had sifted in through holes in the roof, drifting into mounds on the floor. There didn't appear to be anyone around but Matt had to be there, somewhere. Dana quietly called his name.

Sarah released Bert from his leash and he bounded off into the darkness. Before long they heard him growl. "Bert," she called. "Where are you?"

The dog barked from a corner of the building. Playing their lights along the lower walls, they spotted him sniffing something on the concrete floor. Dana's heart nearly stopped when she noticed something that resembled a body. *No, it can't be.* Her flashlight moved over the man and up to the gash on his brow. A pool of blood surrounded his head, which had frozen to the littered floor. She could hear Sarah's voice but her words made no sense.

Matt can't be dead. She was unable to find a pulse so she began CPR.

"He's gone, Dana."

"No." she cried. "He can't be. Call 911." She then felt a hand on her shoulder.

"There's no cell service in here."

She knelt on the cold floor. Wetting her finger, she held it under his nose. She thought she felt his breath but soon realized that it was the wind whistling through the cracks in the walls. Matt *was* dead.

"We can't just leave him here, Sarah." She reached to wipe her tears.

"He's too heavy for us to carry. We'll have to leave him here until the paramedics arrive." Sarah started off across the building with Bert in tow.

"Where are you going?"

"I saw a canvas tarp near the door when we came in. We can cover him with it."

Tears stung her eyes as she stroked Matt's hair, realizing for the first time how much he meant to her. Arrogant, stubborn man that he was, his death, added to Georgi's, was more than she could bear. She then remembered the diary and hoped it was still in Matt's briefcase. They needed the information he had collected from his interviews to solve the murders. Feeling like a criminal, she felt in his pockets for his keys. When she found them, she kissed his cheek, said her goodbye, and walked back to the cars. She passed Sarah returning with the tarp and told her that she would meet her at the van. If her friend guessed what she was planning, she would no doubt object.

They followed their own tracks back to the main road. The snow had stopped entirely and the moon was peeking through departing clouds. Dana felt a deadly calm settle over her, as though she were having an out of body experience. They still had not been able to reach anyone by phone so they decided to drive straight to the police station in town. Hopefully no one in charge was vaguely related to Rob.

Wind was picking up and a ground blizzard was brewing. The windshield wipers moved so fast that it was difficult to see the road. When she set them at a lower speed, blowing snow blocked her view. If they made it back to town, she would track down Turnsby herself. She was a rich woman now and could hire the best investigators in the world. If it took every penny of her inheritance, she would spend it on capturing the killers.

"Are you all right, Dana?"

"I'm fine. I'm just trying to decide how to track down Rob and his accomplice."

"I'm with you all the way, but please consider carefully what you're doing. We could be Rob's next victims."

"He must have killed Matt."

"I was thinking the same thing. Maybe Rob didn't have enough money to leave the country after your sister closed the bank accounts."

"That must be why he killed her."

* * *

They arrived at the police station just before midnight, unsure whether anyone was on duty. When they pushed through the heavy door, they noticed a young man seated at a desk, ready to nod off. When told what had happened, he referred them to the sheriff's department.

"No one's answering the phone." Sarah held up the cell. "We've been trying to call them for hours."

"We need paramedics," Dana said, slamming her fist on the counter.

"But you said the officer's dead."

"Is this your first night on the job, young man? Whoever killed him is getting away and the coroner won't be happy about receiving a frozen body. I suggest that you call them *now.*"

Sarah looked up at her in surprise. She must not realize how much hatred Dana had acquired during the past few days. Gripping her arm, she said, "Calm yourself. This young man will do the best he can. Won't you, dear?" she said, turning to him.

Sarah the peacemaker.

Grumbling, he returned to his desk to pick up the phone. They listened as he called the hospital and ordered an ambulance.

"You also need to contact the sheriff," Sarah said, smiling sweetly.

He frowned as though insulted. "You don't have to tell me how to do my job, ma'am."

Dana half turned, saying, "You see what we're up against, Sarah? No one wants to cooperate. We need to call Matt's headquarters in Cheyenne."

"Cheyenne?" the young man said, his jaw dropping. "You don't need to call them in. We can handle it."

"I don't think so." She took Sarah's arm and led her back to the van, where Bert was patiently waiting. "I don't think we can get in touch with Matt's superiors until later this morning, but they need to know what's happened. Hopefully they'll send in reinforcements as soon as possible."

"Let's get some sleep, Dana. It's been a very long day."

I don't think I'll ever sleep again."

Chapter Twenty-Five

Dana slept fitfully until dawn when she arose and dressed. Sarah was snoring softly in her bunk and she didn't want to disturb her. Tiptoeing to the front of the coach, she retrieved keys from her purse and gave Bert a treat to keep him quiet. She then made her way to the van. Matt's briefcase was under the seat and she carefully opened it. The diary was in a folder and a number of briefs were neatly filed.

Dana hurriedly flipped through them. Handwritten copies of the interviews were difficult to read because he had been left-handed, but she intended to read every word. Shivering because she hadn't worn a coat, she decided to take the briefcase into the motorhome. She was worried about returning the files to the authorities without them arresting her for theft.

Bert was waiting on the landing. He looked hungry so she quietly fed him. The dog would always remind her of Matt and she wondered whether the police would take him back. They should probably move to another RV park.

Gathering a legal-sized note pad and pens, she settled herself in the dining booth. Spreading the contents of the briefcase in stacks on the table, she first read through the interviews with Rob's girlfriends. There was nothing new there because she had been present. The sheriff's interview was the one she was looking for. She found it under the autopsy reports. It was brief and antagonistic, as she had feared. Sheriff Turnsby might have killed Matt and turned off the phones, hoping that she and Sarah would die in the storm. They needed to move to a more secure location.

"What about Georgi's three-stall garage?" Sarah said moments later. "There's a door high enough for the motorhome."

Dana smiled. "That would give us a chance to thoroughly search Rob's office."

"We'll need dark blankets to cover the windows, or we'll have to retire at sundown so nobody'll know we're there."

"The blankets are a good idea but we can stay in the motorhome in the garage," Dana replied. "Hurry and get dressed. We need to get out of here."

Within half an hour they had disconnected the utilities, paid the bill, and driven out of the park. They then took the only road out of town leading to Georgi's subdivision, hoping they wouldn't be spotted by any of the Turnsby clan. Dana knew it would not be long before the police were looking for Matt's briefcase.

The garage was locked so they went through the house to use the automatic door opener. Dana held her breath as she drove the motorhome into the garage with little overhead room to spare. The minivan pulled in beside the RV and they quickly closed the doors.

"Time for breakfast, Sarah. Georgi's cupboards are nearly bare so we'll be dining in the garage."

"Fine with me. My stomach's running on empty."

Later, after Dana called the Division of Criminal Investigation in Cheyenne, they sorted through the papers in Rob's office. Stacking them in relevant piles, they discovered several dozen unpaid bills. "I'll have to pay these," she said. "I don't want creditors ruining Georgi's good name."

Sarah totaled them on the calculator. "There's over a hundred thousand dollars' worth of bills here. What was your brother-in-law doing with the company's money?"

"Probably spending it on himself and his girlfriends."

"If he was embezzling, why didn't he put some away."

"Rob's mind was obviously on other things."

"He probably didn't know the bank accounts were closed until it was too late." Sarah indicated shelves filled with various electronic gadgets. "I'll bet he plans to come back for these."

"I'm sure he will but we'll be ready for him."

"What about the sheriff?"

"He'll probably get a court order to search the house," Dana said. "I've got to call Georgi's lawyer and transfer the title of the house into my name as soon as possible. I'll do that now."

"Good idea. I'll make a list of all these overdue accounts."

They worked the rest of the day before remembering blankets to cover the windows. Leaving Bert to guard the house, they drove to a Casper discount store. While shopping they spotted one of the women who had dated Rob. She was hurriedly collecting household supplies.

"Looks like she's setting up housekeeping, Dana."

"I wonder with whom?"

"You don't think it's with Rob, do you?"

"Nothing would surprise me."

Dana returned to the van while Sarah stood in line at the checkout counter. She watched everyone leaving the store, including the blonde who tossed her bags into a white, step-side pickup. Sarah arrived before the woman left the parking lot and they trailed behind. The truck turned right on Curtis Street, crossed over railroad tracks and eventually turned onto a side street to park in the driveway of the second house on the block. Dana drove past as Sarah recorded the house number.

"She doesn't know you," Dana said, "but if Rob's there, you'd be in trouble if you go to the door. We'll come back later and watch to see if he's around."

"Which one is she?"

"Kim Yankton, the blonde who works at the parts supply store."

"We won't have to worry about hanging blankets on the windows tonight. We'll be sitting here on stakeout."

When they returned to the house a note was stuck to the front door. "It's illegal to leave an animal unattended in a house overnight." It was signed by the sheriff.

"He's on to us, Dana. Bert must have barked when the doorbell rang."

"I'll call him and explain. He probably would have gone in, but was afraid of the dog."

"I wonder why Rob didn't give him a key?"

"He probably did but Bert discouraged him."

"I wonder what he's after."

"Bank records, Rob's electronic toys. Who knows?"

"Maybe the prescription bottles."

"I didn't think of that. I wonder what Matt did with them?"

"If he didn't mail them to Cheyenne, they must be in his car."

"I wonder if someone from the DCI has arrived yet from Cheyenne?"

"If they have, they'll be looking for Matt's briefcase, Dana."

She sighed. "I'm ready to turn it over to them."

"What about the diary?"

"Fortunately, there's a copy machine buried under all this rubble. We'll run a duplicate copy before I hand it over."

"Good thinking, Logan."

"Let's get it done, Cafferty, before the sheriff returns with the dog catcher."

Chapter Twenty-Six

They took Bert and the briefcase with them on stakeout. If the sheriff broke in, Dana planned to file a complaint. They turned on the yard lights and knew their neighbor would be watching if someone pulled in the driveway.

"We should probably trade the van in for another car," Dana said, while they waited across the street from Kim Yankton's house. "Someone will be turning us in as stalkers."

Sarah yawned and checked the time on the dashboard clock. "It's 10:45. If Rob doesn't show up soon, I'm afraid I'll fall asleep."

Dana encouraged her to take a nap. She might have to take one herself later. Bert was already napping on the backseat and they both felt much safer with him along. While they waited, she thought about all the interviews she had read in Matt's briefcase. She was surprised that no one from the DCI had contacted them. Maybe the sheriff had somehow waylaid them or distracted the new agent who had come to investigate the murders.

So many questions filled her mind that she couldn't sleep, if she wanted to. Why would Rob hang around the area where he had committed three murders? It couldn't have been lack of money. He could have sold Georgi's sports car as well as business equipment, and any number of items in the house. But why would he leave his wife's jewelry and cash behind in the freezer? Georgi must have hidden them there so he couldn't dispose of them? Or had the housekeeper held out on him because she didn't trust him?

Bert chuffed from the backseat and she glanced at the house across the street. The front door had opened and a vague light was visible. Two shadows left the house and moved toward the detached garage. She couldn't tell whether it was a man and woman or two men. Kim Yankton was tall and a little broad in the beam and these two appeared to be wearing heavy, dark clothing, like pea coats and watch caps. The garage door opened and a small car backed onto the street.

"Sarah," she whispered, without taking her eyes from the suspects. "I'm going to follow the car that's leaving the garage. Are you awake?"

Sarah didn't answer so she was on her own. She waited until the car reached the corner and turned right before starting the engine. It was a short distance to the intersection and she caught sight of them stopped at the signal. Pulling within three car lengths, she noticed the vanity license plate: ROBT. Arrogant creep. He couldn't resist flaunting himself on everything he owned. Dana wondered if his initials were embroidered on his underwear.

She followed them to the road, which led out of town to the railroad tracks. They must be returning to the scene of the crime. She wondered whether Matt's body had been picked up the previous night or whether it still lay on the warehouse floor. Shivering, she pulled into a service station and called 911. When the dispatcher answered, she said, "Rob Turnsby, who murdered his wife, housekeeper, and the DCI agent is on his way to the old warehouse where Matt Brown's body was found. You need to get in touch with the DCI agent who came here today to investigate."

"Who *is* this?"

"Dana Logan, sister of the murdered wife."

"The sheriff is out of town–"

Dana hung up on the dispatcher. No sense trying to explain about Sheriff Turnsby. She would have to confront him soon. She then thought of Matt's cell phone. Maybe the DCI agent, who replaced Matt, had retrieved his phone. She dialed the number. After four rings it went to his voice mail. The sound of his voice brought tears to her eyes.

The gas gauge read empty so she quietly left the van and pumped the tank full. Bert had his nose pressed against the glass and she blew him a kiss. She heard his sharp bark and regretted her display of affection. Why did he like Sarah and not her? Maybe it was her cologne.

Sarah was still asleep and she wondered about her hearing. How could anyone sleep through a dog's bark? She then remembered that her friend was exhausted and still recuperating from her ordeal in the hospital. No sense going back on stakeout. It was close to midnight and they all needed sleep. Thank heavens they had covered the windows with blankets before they left home. It was *her* home now. She wondered if the house was paid for or whether a foreclosure notice was in the mail. Hopefully Georgi had paid her personal bills. There was so much that she didn't know.

Few cars were on the road and she was startled when a red light filled the van's interior as she pulled into her driveway. A large man in uniform stepped from his car and opened her driver's door. He motioned her to leave the van. When she did, a bitterly cold wind whipped snow into her eyes and chilled her to the bone.

"Dana Logan?"

"Yes."

"You're under arrest for the murder of Matt Brown."

"That's ridiculous. Every minute of my time can be accounted for."

"So you say."

"You must be Sheriff Turnsby. I've been expecting you."

Obviously surprised, he merely grunted.

"I'm shocked that the DCI hasn't arrested you yet for involvement in the murders of not only my sister, but Tonya Beardsly, and Matt Brown.

He laughed and reached for his handcuffs with his free hand. She then noticed that he was holding a gun.

"There are people who will testify that I was nowhere near the crime scene when Agent Brown was killed. You should also know that I mailed all of his investigative work to DCI headquarters in Cheyenne. She raised her hand to shield her face from the blowing snow."

"Be careful," he growled. "I can shoot you for resisting arrest."

Dana shook her head, determined not to show her fear. "I have a very snoopy neighbor who is watching us at this very moment. She'll testify that I've been home all day and the time I left this house last night. Your cousin the coroner will also testify as to the time of Matt Brown's death. By the way, can anyone testify to your whereabouts?"

He hesitated. "I'll be back. Consider yourself under house arrest." The sheriff turned and left, his tires skidding on the ice.

Dana noticed the lights disappear when the drapes closed in the house across the road. She was trembling when she got back into the van. Thank God they had turned on all the yard lights before they left.

"You handled him very well, Logan. He was obviously trying to intimidate you."

"He'll be back unless someone arrests *him*."

"I wonder why we haven't heard from the DCI?"

"I'm not sure, Sarah, but they're going to hear from me when the office opens this morning."

"Let's get some sleep. Bert can stay in the room with us tonight."

"I think we'd better sleep in the motorhome. It's harder to break into."

Chapter Twenty-Seven

Bert's loud growl woke them at 3:15 that morning. Groaning, both women turned over in their bunks and tried to go back to sleep. Dana then realized the dog might be warning them of an intruder. Slipping quietly into her robe, she tiptoed into the coach's living room where she peeped through the wooden blinds. She could see nothing in the garage, although the outside yard lights shot spikes of light around the door's edges.

Bert chuffed beside her and she reached to quiet him. He didn't shy away, she realized with relief, so he must be getting used to her. Forsaking her favorite cologne may have been the reason.

The sheriff had probably returned to break into the house. It might even be Rob returning to haul away everything he could. No matter who it was, she wouldn't try to stop him. Everything pertaining to the murders was stored in the motorhome. He could take whatever else he wanted. She hoped that whoever it was wouldn't think to look in the garage. Just in case, Sarah's bat was resting against the entry door. She would use it if he tried to break in. Then Bert could finish him off or hold the burglar at bay.

Dana tiptoed back into the bedroom to wake Sarah, who was sleeping soundly. Whispering in her friend's ear, she told her about the possible break-in and that they should be prepared. She removed the blankets and pillow from her own bed and told Sarah to lie on them between the bunks. She then took Sarah's bedclothes and spread them on the living room floor in the unlikely event the burglar tried to shoot his way into the motorhome. Positioning herself near the door, she cradled the bat in both arms. Bert would let her know if he entered the garage.

They'd had little sleep in the past 48 hours and Dana dozed off with Bert by her side. Sometime later, he nudged her neck with his cold nose and quietly chuffed. Instantly awake, she whispered, "Good boy," and rubbed his ears. She then crawled to within inches of the door with the bat held at the ready. She heard men's voices and closed her eyes to listen.

"You think they're in the motorhome?" one of them asked.

"Why would they stay in the garage? They probably went to a hotel."

"The van's still out front."

"Maybe they wanted to make it look like somebody's here."

"Yeah, they coulda took a cab."

She held her hand around Bert's muzzle and shushed him in his ear. The dog shook his head but seemed to understand. She then heard someone rattle the locked door.

"There should be a bar on that shelf. We can pry the door open."

"They've got a dog with 'em. He'd be barking by now if they were in there."

"Yeah, you're right. Let's go."

Dana resisted the urge to peak through a window to get a look at them. She thought she recognized the sheriff's voice but wasn't sure. The other man didn't sound like Rob and she wondered who he might be. Her heart was pounding so hard that she couldn't breathe. She would deal with *who* they were in the daylight. First she had to contact the new investigator.

Sarah was already asleep and she hoped she had missed the excitement. Dana rolled up in the blankets and went back to sleep on the floor, with one hand on Bert's collar. If they returned, she would be prepared.

When she awoke several hours later, her cell phone was ringing. Scrambling to reach it before the caller hung up, she banged her knee on the dining booth and cried out in pain. Sarah sat up dazed from the bedroom floor and looked as though she were going to scream.

"Grab the phone on the night stand," Dana said, hobbling into the bedroom. By then the phone had stopped ringing. The number wasn't available. The screen simply said, Private Caller. She wondered whether it belonged to the investigator.

"He'll call back. Let's get some breakfast."

When she told Sarah about the intruders during breakfast, she insisted that they leave. They may not be as lucky next time.

"What do you think they were after?" Sarah said. "The money and jewelry in the freezer?"

"Maybe, but why all the murders?"

Dana called DCI headquarters in Cheyenne and told them what had happened. Where, she asked, was the new investigator? She was told that he had arrived yesterday morning from Casper, and that Matt's body had been delivered to the coroner. When asked about Sheriff Turnsby, she was told that he was under investigation.

"Who's the new investigator and when's he going to contact us?"

"Chad Ryley, with two Ys. They have no idea what his schedule is."

"Swell, what's *our* schedule?"

Dana thought for a moment. "Why don't we stay put and wait for Ryley. In the meantime, we can conduct people searches on the Internet." Sarah nodded and they slid from the booth and went into the house. The place was a mess. Cushions had been ripped open and thrown on the floor, which was also littered with Georgi's beautiful paintings and artifacts. Rob's office was back to its original state and the electronic gadgets were missing. When they made their way up the stairs to her sister's office, Dana expected to find similiar chaos. Georgi's books were scattered on the carpet and the file cabinet was on its side, but the drawers were locked again. Had Matt locked them the last time he was there?

"I guess they couldn't pry them open," Sarah said.

"Thank heavens for that."

One of the desk drawers was open with its contents scattered.

"They must have been in a hurry or they would have made a more thorough search."

"What were they looking for?"

"I wish I knew. Let's get started on the web search. We'll clean up the mess when we're finished."

Dana used her sister's computer to scroll through various locator sites. She settled on one that promised complete criminal background checks. Taking her credit card from her wallet, she signed on and paid for the service. The first name she typed in was Robert Turnsby in the state of Wyoming. They were shocked when his nationwide criminal record filled the entire screen.

"Look at this, Sarah: His record dates back to his eighteenth birthday. Wait a minute. There's an asterisk that says he also has a juvenile record that can't be listed. Juvenile records are permanently sealed unless the child is certified as an adult for a crime such as manslaughter."

"I wonder if he served time in reform school."

"I doubt it. His father was probably a judge." Dana scrolled down the long list of offenses. "When he was nineteen, he was charged with possession of a controlled substance and, soon after, arrested for assault. All charges were dropped. No community service or a fine levied. I wonder if all the victims were bought off."

"That explains a lot. If Rob got away with all that, he must think he can get away with murder."

Dana winced. "Literally, Cafferty." She printed the list and clicked back to the name page. She typed in William Turnsby but got no response. She tried Willard and Wilbur.

The latter brought up the sheriff's background, which also filled the screen. They discovered that he was four years older than his brother, and had definitely been on the wrong side of the law.

"How did he get to be sheriff with a record like that?"

"Look at the dates and locations. His family either sent him away or he left town on his own. Here's a drug charge in Illinois when he was eighteen. He spent three years in prison under the alias, Daniel Strathmore."

"How did he get away with that?"

"It was nearly thirty-five years ago, before electronic record keeping. I guess anyone can buy a new identity in the big cities."

"But how did this Internet company find out?"

"You've got me there. You can't even slice a few years off your age anymore. Everything's out there in cyber space."

"I wonder if somebody in the police records room sold the information to the Internet company?"

"Nothing would surprise me, Sarah."

After the printout, they began with the list of Rob's girlfriends. Sharon Zumwell had no criminal record and had lived her entire life in Wyoming. Amanda Smelton had moved from California where she had two shoplifting convictions as a teenager. There were quite a few addresses listed so she had moved around a lot. There was also a box full of family names listed as her next of kin.

"If I'm right," Dana said, "she grew up in a large family below the poverty line. She's looking for someone with money."

"No wonder she latched on to Rob."

"Then she's a definite suspect."

Dana printed the file and went on to the next name: Linda Johnsbury. She could find no listing for the 19-year-old and her baby. "She's probably listed under her parents' names, Dana. Do we know their first names?"

"No, but I doubt that she's anything more than an innocent victim."

Chapter Twenty-Eight

Kim Yankton was another story. She had transferred from the girl's reform school in Sheridan, to the women's prison at Lusk. Shoplifting, drugs, and burglary charges filled an entire page. They could find no other offenses when she reached the age of 25.

"Looks like she straightened up her act," Sarah said. "But that doesn't mean there's no larceny left in her soul."

"Or substance abuse. It seems to be rampant among the younger generation."

"Let's add her to our suspects' list."

There were no Dawn Talsons listed. She must have recently moved from her parents' home and the information hadn't been updated. Matt had more or less dismissed her, but Dana wasn't so sure. She added her name to the list.

Rob's secretary, Melanie Shamera, was next. Matt's last phone call had been made while following her to the old warehouse. Had she killed Matt or helped Rob corner him in the building? She forced herself to concentrate on the screen.

Melanie's criminal record was nearly as long as the Turnsby brothers. Most of her offenses were drug related although she had taken part in several burglaries. She also spent time in the women's prison at Lusk.

"She's our prime suspect, Sarah, although Rob seems to have attracted other women with criminal records."

"Kindred spirits."

"Right. There's one name left, Katie Bannatt."

When the name came up, there was little to go on. There was no criminal record and the pharmacy clerk had lived her entire life in Wyoming. Maybe she had been telling the truth about her relationship with Rob. He had probably befriended her just to get information about certain drugs. How strange, especially since all the information was available on the Internet. He probably couldn't resist practicing his charms on any available female.

"What now, Logan?"

"I'll clean up this mess while you supervise."

Several hours later, while vacuuming up the last of the debris, Dana discovered a key. When she showed it to Sarah, she suggested trying it in the entry doors. That would explain how the burglars gained access to the house. She was right. The key opened the back door. Rob must have given it to the burglars, telling them to retrieve his electronic gear. Dana then remembered their conversation in the garage. She was sure they were also intent on murdering the two of them.

"Why us?" Sarah asked.

"Maybe Rob wants the house back."

"There's got to be more to it than that?"

"He must be desperate by now. He owes creditors over a hundred thousand dollars and his bank accounts have been closed. I doubt there was much money left in the construction account, if any."

"Then we're in real danger." Dana's cell phone rang. It was Chad Ryley, the DCI agent. He agreed to meet them at the house within the hour. The Cheyenne office had filled him in on the burglary and he would be taking them into protective custody. She suggested hiring bodyguards and Ryley said they would discuss the matter later.

"How does he sound?"

"Like a play-it-by-the-book kind of agent."

"Nothing like Matt Brown?"

"I'm afraid not."

"We'll work around him, Dana. Let's search the Internet for protection agencies. If we've already hired someone, he'll be less likely to take us in."

They climbed the stairs to Georgi's office and Dana booted the computer. She found an agency in Casper that furnished her with costs for 24-hour protection. They didn't, however, provide inside bodyguards. Dana scribbled $30 an hour on a notepad and Sarah added them up, along with travel expenses, for a grand total of $6,048 a week or roughly $25,000 a month.

"They call it custom protection, Sarah. Their agents are former police officers, military police, and special forces members."

"That's a lot of money, Dana."

"How much are our lives worth?"

She shrugged. "We'd better wrap this case up in a hurry."

Dana shut down the computer and called the protection agency again to arrange for immediate surveillance. An armed guard in an unmarked car would be there within an hour, with two men working twelve-hour shifts. Sarah suggested they also install electronic eyes around the property.

"Birds and blowing objects can set them off. The way the wind blows here we wouldn't get any sleep."

"How about surveillance cameras?"

"That's an excellent idea. We can pick some up this afternoon at one of the electronics stores in Casper. I'm sure we can hire Mr. Musgrove, the yard man, to install them." She picked up the phone and called.

Chad Ryley arrived a few minutes later, and they were surprised by his appearance. Rail thin and several inches shorter than Dana, he wore steel rimmed glasses that seemed too large for his face. His smile was wide and they liked him at once. When he asked to see the damage, Dana apologized for disturbing possible evidence by cleaning up the mess. She then showed him the key.

"So you think it was an inside job?"

She explained the circumstances and Ryley simply nodded. She then told him that she had hired 24 hour protection, but he wasn't convinced that they shouldn't be taken into custody. Although he approved of the police dog, he vetoed Dana's request for a gun.

"I'll have a talk with your guard," he said and turned to leave.

"What about Matt Brown's evidence? Did you find the prescription bottles in the trunk of his car?"

"I'm not allowed to discuss that with you, ma'am." He opened the front door. "I'll be in touch."

Dana's face crumpled. "Why did they have to kill Matt?"

Her friend took her arm and led her up the stairs. "Let's get back to work on the criminal reports. The answers have to be right here in this house."

Chapter Twenty-Nine

They read the criminal reports, deciding that every suspect was linked by drug abuse. Was it possible they were involved in trafficking? Plenty of drugs were in the news, including young men in the petroleum industry who worked on drilling rigs. Dana heard that some had been arrested for manufacturing methamphetamines at remote drilling sites. Drugs had also been smuggled into the Indian Reservation in the northern part of the state. She wouldn't put it past the Turnsby brothers.

"Melanie Shamera is the most likely of Rob's girlfriends to be involved in drug smuggling," Sarah concluded.

"I agree. She could have been an accomplice in all three murders as well. The small pickup she drives is possibly the one that killed the housekeeper."

"She's not a blonde, Dana, and she's not that young."

"Kim Yankton must be *Laura* although she's not that young either."

"Georgi may have considered her young."

"That's true, but she described Laura as a young, bubbly blonde. I don't recall any of them as bubbly."

"It might have been an act."

"Maybe, but we need to get a closer look at all of them." Dana left her chair. "I have an idea. Let's take a drive."

She hesitated when she backed the van from the garage. A car parked on the edge of the property had a man crouched behind the wheel. How obvious was that? Their first guard?

Why didn't he come to the door to introduce himself? Chad Ryley must have already talked to him and left. She decided to ignore his presence as she pulled onto the road. Glancing in the rearview mirror, she noticed that the car was following. What if it wasn't the guard? She checked her watch. It had been exactly an hour since she had called the agency. It had to be him. Maybe he was an off-duty cop who lived in the area.

When they reached the discount store, Dana bought a surveillance system and seven gift baskets. While standing at the checkout counter they noticed a man watching them. Was he their guard? He followed them into the parking lot and Dana did an about-face to confront him.

"Keep walking," he said as she approached. "I'm here to protect you." The big man wearing dark glasses brushed past her to unlock his car. He obviously didn't want to be seen in their presence.

"Come in the house for a cup of coffee," she said to his back. "We want to meet you."

"Against the rules, ma'am." He opened his car door without looking at them. "I need to keep my distance."

"My gosh, Dana. We're in the middle of James Bond movie."

"We'll do it their way. Come on, let's go."

They bought groceries on their way home and he was there. They knew he was following them and discussed whether they felt safer. They decided they did, but why did he have to be to so standoffish? He reminded Dana of her former brother-in-law.

"I remember a couple of celebrity women who fell in love with their bodyguards," Dana said. "I guess it's the agency's way of protecting them?"

"Protecting who?"

"Either party. The agency could probably be sued if a guard was distracted long enough for a crime to be committed." Dana punched the garage door opener and they eased in beside the motorhome.

Sarah picked up two bags of groceries. "Where are we staying tonight?"

"We could sleep in the house, but despite the guard, I feel safer in the motorhome."

"Shouldn't we let him know where we'll be?"

"No, he made it quite clear there will be no contact."

"With our luck the snoopy neighbor will turn him in as a stalker."

Dana groaned. "I didn't think of that. I'd better talk to him."

"Wait until dark. It'll be harder for the snoopy neighbor to see what's going on."

"If I do it now, she'll know that we're aware of his presence."

"Get his cell phone number while you're at it. Somebody might break in out back without him noticing. By the way, is he just going to sit in his car or will he patrol on foot?"

"That's a good question to ask him, Cafferty." She took a notepad and pen from her purse and left the house. She knew the guard wouldn't be happy to see her, but she was paying his salary. That made her his boss.

"I need to talk to you," she said when he rolled down his window. When she told him about the neighbor, he groaned. "It's not a good idea to just sit out here and listen to music," she said. "These houses are sitting on five-acre lots. That makes any strange car an instant attraction." She told him about Sheriff Turnsby and that he would probably arrest him on a stalking charge.

"I think you should call your office and tell them the situation," she said. "There's got to be better way." Before he could answer, she asked for his cell number. She then returned upstairs to Georgi's office.

"Do you think this will work?" Sarah asked.

"It's worth a try, if you're feeling up to it. I can't do it because I was with Matt during the interviews."

"What shall I say?"

"That each woman is one of the lucky gift basket winners in the city directory contest. Their names were chosen from among a list of working women."

"But what if they call the city to see if I'm for real."

"Few people look a gift horse in the mouth, as the old addage goes." Dana booted up the computer and began to compose a color brochure which sang the praises of working women. Fortunately, Georgi's color printer had good resolution. When she was finished, she printed business cards on stock from her sister's desk drawer.

"Who is Agnes Smith?"

"You don't want me to use your real name, do you?" She went to work on a script for her to memorize.

"I don't know if I can remember all this. My memory's not what it was."

"You can practice on me. You'll soon be reciting it in your sleep."

The funeral director called while Sarah was memorizing her talk. Georgi's body had returned from the coroner's office and he wanted to reschedule the cremation and memorial service. Dana told him she'd have to contact her sister's friends and allow them enough time to fly in from San Francisco. Rummaging through her purse for her sister's phone book, she found Angela's number. She then left a message on her answering machine.

Sarah looked up from her script. "Have you told Kerrie yet about your sister's death?"

Dana groaned. She had forgotten to call her daughter, or maybe she had subconsciously blocked it from her mind. Kerrie would be devastated that her favorite aunt had been murdered.

She wasn't at her desk at the magazine office, so Dana left a message in her voice mail.

"Now what?"

"Let's practice your script, Agnes Smith. We may not have much time before the killer and his accomplices leave the area."

Chapter Thirty

Dana parked halfway down the block from the Lucky Inn, where Sarah left the van carrying a gift basket. She shook her head when she returned. "It's not Amanda Smelton," she said. "She's about as bubbly as a hibernating fish."

"How'd it go?"

"I was nervous but I remembered every word."

Dana smiled. "I'm proud of you, Cafferty. But it's strange because Amanda was quite flirtatious when Matt interviewed her."

"She's definitely not bubbly with women, even after winning a gift basket. Who's next on the list?"

"Sharon Zumwell."

When they arrived at the market, Sarah was back in less time than it took Dana to check her list. "Sharon doesn't work here anymore and her boss doesn't know why she quit her job."

Surprised, Dana said, "I already crossed her off our suspects' list. I hope nothing has happened to her." She drove around the block to the small house behind the store. Sarah got out and knocked. When no one answered, she peered through a window.

"Looks like the house is still lived in. Maybe she got another job."

"I hope you're right but I'm worried about her." Dana picked up her cell phone and punched in Chad Ryley's number. When he didn't answer, she left a message.

"No one's answering their phones today, are they?"

"Let's get on to the next suspect, Dawn Talson. Hopefully she's back from her trip to Montana."

Matt had questioned Talson at her small apartment on the other side of town. She worked as a waitress, but Dana couldn't remember where. Retrieving her notebook, she found the notes she had taken from Matt's files. Dawn worked at the Colton Hotel Restaurant. They would try there first.

Sarah returned from the hotel with the basket, sadly shaking her head. "She also quit her job and hasn't been seen since she flew to Montana."

"Good grief, is Rob taking all his women with him?"

"He does like a harem, doesn't he?"

Katie Bannatt was next. Sarah wore a frown when she left the hospital pharmacy, minus the gift basket.

"That woman nearly ripped the basket out of my arms."

"No bubblies."

"Absolutely none. I don't know what Georgi's husband saw in that person."

"Probably nothing more than her knowledge of the pharmaceutical business."

They pulled into the parking lot of the convenience store where Linda Johnbury worked. Dana explained again about the baby. She also said that she didn't think the teenager was involved in the murders. Sarah seemed sympathetic but insisted that no one should be above suspicion. When she returned from the store, she was smiling. "I found a bubbly suspect."

"Maybe she's just an excitable kid."

"Dana, she gushed like a geyser. She even asked if she would be on TV."

"Oh, dear. We'd better hurry with Yankton and Shamera before the word is out."

Melanie Shamera was at home. Her small, white company pickup was parked out front and she promptly answered the door. Twenty minutes passed before the door opened again.

Sarah sighed as she seated herself in the van. "She likes to talk more than I do."

"Good. Did she gush when you handed her the basket."

"No, she just set it aside and started complaining about her former boss."

"Rob?"

"Yes.

"Wonderful. What did she say?"

"Rob is a two-timing sneak. He ordered her to pick up some papers from his home desk and take them to the old warehouse where we found Matt. She said no one was there."

"She didn't notice Matt following her?"

"She claims she saw no one, and hasn't heard from Rob since. She thinks he ran off with another woman."

"She's either lying or . . . why would she tell you all that, a perfect stranger?"

"I have that kind of face. People will tell me anything."

"I hope she doesn't suspect that you're involved in the investigation."

"If she does, she doesn't care. She's obviously a woman scorned."

"So he used her and left her for someone else."

"We have two missing girlfriends so far. I wonder which one–?"

"Kim Yankton is our last gift basket recipient. Let's get over there before the store closes."

Sarah returned from the store grinning like a beauty contestant. "Miss Bubbly was thrilled to win the basket. I was afraid that she was going to climb over the counter to kiss me."

"She must be *Laura*."

"I agree."

"What took so long?"

"I had to track her down. The other employees thought it was a joke that she won."

"I wonder why."

"One of the clerks said that she does as little work as possible, and that she's on the verge of getting fired."

"No wonder she and Rob got along. Two of a kind."

"What now, Logan?"

"We'll go home and I'll write a report for Chad Ryley based on what we've learned so far."

"Is our guard still following?"

"I haven't seen him since we left Melanie Shamera's house."

"Don't tell me the sheriff waylaid him."

"I think we'd better get home before dark and lock ourselves in the motorhome." Dana picked up her phone to call Chad Ryley. He was the only lawman she trusted.

Chapter Thirty-One

Another unmarked car occupied the edge of property when they pulled into the circle drive. Dana got out of the van and walked over to introduce herself. The man behind the wheel rolled down his window when he noticed her approach. He wore sunglasses although the day was overcast.

"What happened to the other guard?" she asked.

"You lost him in traffic. He was due to go off duty anyway."

"So he just left us unprotected?"

The crew cut, smaller man merely shrugged.

Checking her watch, she said, "Your agency is no longer needed as of 0800 hours tomorrow. Tell your supervisor to send me a bill." She turned and walked away.

"Who's going to protect us," Sarah asked when the garage door closed behind them.

"We're going to buy a gun."

"There's probably a waiting period, Dana."

"We'll soon find out."

Bert barked from the backseat and they realized it was past feeding time. After they had all eaten a quick meal, they would drive back to Casper to find a suitable weapon. It was half an hour before closing when they entered the gun shop. A spindly, elderly man behind the counter recommended a Glock 9mm. After he jotted down her driver's license number and placed a call to a state office to check on her record, he sold her the gun, ammunition and a cleaning kit.

He asked whether she wanted targets for firing practice and she declined. She would test the pistol's accuracy somewhere in the Wyoming outback, with an empty can or two.

It was well past dark when they returned home with a car following close behind. They hoped it was their guard. Sarah punched the garage door opener and they drove straight in. They then decided to check the answering machine before they settled in the motorhome for the night. There was still no message from Chad Ryley, the state investigator.

"You don't think they killed him, too?" Sarah asked as she watched Dana take the Glock from its case and aim at the draped windshield.

"Nothing would surprise me."

"Then why did you fire the guards?"

"I was mad, and it may have been a mistake. They just seem so ineffective." She loaded the gun and placed it in the nightstand.

Sometime after 2:00 a.m., Dana heard the dog chuff and was instantly awake. Fumbling in the dark for the gun, she palmed it and crept into the kitchen. Sliding into the dining booth, she carefully laid the Glock on the table and separated the horizontal blinds with her thumb and index finger. The garage was dark but she could see streaks of light from the yard. She gasped when something hit the concrete floor. Bert was beside her and she reached to prevent him from barking. She then noticed a muted light moving about the garage as though someone were searching for something. Where the hell was their guard?

Sarah slid into the booth opposite her and reached to look through the wooden blinds. Bert quietly stood at the door, ready to attack as Dana picked up the gun, hoping she wouldn't have to use it. The dog was the best bodyguard they could hope for.

A sudden clanking noise startled them as the overhead door began to rise and yard lights flooded the garage's interior. They were afraid to look through the blinds and alert the burglars to their whereabouts. What was happening? They heard men's muffled voices and the sound of a vehicle moving in beside the van. The yard lights went out and there was total darkness. She could hear Sarah's frightened breathing and hoped that she wasn't hyperventilating.

"Load the stuff and let's get out of here," someone said. The male voice sounded familiar but she couldn't quite place it. She reached across the table to cover Sarah's hand. Her own heart was beating like a kettle drum.

"A light just went on upstairs in the house across the road," someone said.

"I'll take care of it," a graveled voice replied.

Dana cringed. She hoped they wouldn't kill the snoopy neighbor.

An engine started and the garage door was closing. Hopefully no one had stayed behind. She exhaled slowly. Behind her Bert chuffed quietly, which she hoped meant that everyone had gone.

"What just happened?" Sarah whispered.

"Whoever it was retrieved something from the garage."

"Where's our guard? Is he one of the gang?"

"If he were, those men would have known we're here. They might have tried to kill us."

"Along with the snoopy neighbor?"

"I hope she's still alive." Dana felt guilty that she had told the sheriff about their neighbor, although it had probably saved their lives. They sat in the booth for over an hour, trying to decide what to do. It wasn't safe to investigate in the dark so they decided to wait until daylight. Dana tried calling Chad Ryley but her call was again routed to his voice mail. What could have happened to him?

They slept a few hours until dawn. Dana then left the motorhome to look out onto the road. It was snowing and the unmarked car was still parked on the edge of the property although there didn't seem to be anyone in the driver's seat. According to her instructions, he should still be there for another hour. She wondered how early the agency opened for business. She was going to tell them what she thought of their service.

Taking a quick shower while Sarah prepared breakfast, she dressed in heavy sweat clothes and running shoes. She needed to learn what had happened to their guard as well as the woman across the street. If she were still alive, she might have seen what had taken place a few hours earlier.

Bert accompanied her when she left the house half an hour later. She noticed no tracks in the skiff of snow as they made their way to the unmarked car. Brushing snow from the driver's window, she looked inside. Lying across the seat was the guard she had talked to earlier. Blood was seeping from a wound in his forehead. The door was locked so there was nothing she could do for him. She quickly dialed 911 and requested an ambulance. She then hurried across the road. No one answered the door at the neighbor's house. Undecided what to do, she tried Chad Ryley's number again. Still no answer.

Dana closed her eyes, wishing that it were all a bad dream. Bert startled her when he barked from across the street. Before she reached her house, she heard the wail of an ambulance in the distance. They could not have responded that quickly. What was going on? She turned to look back at the house across the road and saw a curtain close on the top floor. Why didn't her neighbor answer her door?

Chapter Thirty-Two

When the ambulance arrived, both women left the house to ask about the guard's condition. They were only told that he was still alive. The paramedics hooked him up to IVs and whisked him away to the hospital, leaving them with many unanswered questions. As soon as they returned to the house, Dana called the protection agency and reported what had happened. When asked if she wanted to continue the service, Matt's face floated through her mind. Hesitating, she said no. She didn't want any more men needlessly injured or killed.

"There are still too many loose threads, Dana."

"That's what Matt said. We've got to investigate them one at a time."

"What about Georgi's memorial service?"

"I haven't heard from Angela or any of Georgi's other friends. The funeral director will just have to wait."

The phone rang several minutes later. "I'll be darned," Dana said, checking the caller I.D. "It's Angela."

Dana told her as little as possible and asked that she notify the rest of Georgi's friends. When she hung up, she said, "As soon as Angela gets back to us, we'll schedule the memorial service."

"What about Kerrie?"

Dana gasped and decided to scroll through her cell phone messages. "She tried to call after I shut off the phone last night. I didn't want anyone to know we were in the motorhome."

She dialed her daughter's work number and Kerrie picked up on the first ring. When told of her aunt's murder, she said nothing for several moments. She must have covered the phone with her hand because Dana knew she was crying.

"I'll come right away," she said at last.

"Wait until we can schedule the service. You don't want to jeopardize your job."

"Job be damned. I'll get another. It sounds as though you need me."

"It's too dangerous, honey. I'd rather you didn't come just yet."

"That's exactly why I *am* coming. You need my help."

"We have guards," Dana said, crossing her fingers.

"I'll catch a flight out this afternoon." Kerrie hung up immediately after telling Dana she loved her.

She didn't want to place her daughter in danger, but remembered her help in the past. Kerrie was a very capable young woman as well as a good writer. She had obviously inherited the family's communication genes, although unlike her Aunt Georgi, nonfiction was her forte.

"Kerrie's coming?" Sarah asked with a broad smile.

She nodded, worried that her daughter's arrival would only complicate matters. Although she had earned a brown belt in karate, she could be brave to the point of recklessness. She was certainly no match for a gang of murderers.

Sarah had drawn a circle in the middle of a legal pad. She then drew lines from the center as investigative threads, adding the names of each suspect at the end of each line.

"Before we start on your threads," Dana said, "we need to get in touch with Chad Ryley." She called his cell number but he still wasn't picking up. She then called the Cheyenne office and was told that Ryley had not reported in since leaving Casper.

"He's dead, Dana. I know he is."

"I hope you're wrong. Jim Smith, an investigator from Gillette, will be arriving today."

"I hope he's not the next victim."

"I know," Dana said frowning. "Who's our first thread?"

"Rob Turnsby."

"Did you give his girlfriends each a thread?"

She nodded. "Let's not forget the sheriff."

"Right, he's the most dangerous. I'll list him first."

"I think we should fax the sheriff's rap sheet to Cheyenne, in case they don't have it."

"Good idea, Cafferty. We'll then figure a way to trap him."

"Kerrie can help with that. Her past experience in crime reporting is invaluable."

"We do need all the help we can get."

Angela called several hours later. She and two friends booked a flight leaving the following day. Dana immediately called the funeral director and arranged for the memorial service to be held the day after their arrival. The funeral director asked if she would be present during cremation. She declined, but arranged for Georgi's ashes to be placed in a marble urn. She would decide where to place the urn when Kerrie arrived.

Her daughter arrived at the airport in Casper that afternoon. It had only been a month since Dana had seen her, but it seemed forever. After hugs all around, they left town and headed for the interstate. Kerrie took notes while Dana told her what had happened since their arrival in Wyoming. Investigative reporting was obviously still in Kerrie's blood.

"The first thing we need to do is interview the sheriff," she said.

"About what?"

"The mysterious deaths that have happened here this month."

"You think he'll talk to you?"

"If he's told that I'm from a news magazine, he'll talk."

"Especially to a beautiful, young reporter."

Ignoring her mother's compliment, she said, "I brought my camcorder."

"Good, the sooner the better. I wouldn't be surprised if the sheriff is the ring leader of a drug cartel."

Dana gave her the sheriff's office number and Kerrie called for an appointment. Told that he was unavailable, she left her cell phone number. If he didn't call soon, she would go to his office and insist on an interview.

"We need to switch cars again," Sarah said. "Sheriff Turnsby will recognize the van."

Dana drove back to the rental agency where four cars sat on the lot. They chose a burgundy SUV with tinted windows. When the paperwork had been filled out, they settled Bert in the back and transferred Kerrie's luggage.

"It's beginning to feel like musical cars," Sarah said once they were back in the garage.

"I guess we'll stay in the house now that Kerrie's here."

"I think it's safe enough. The burglars got what they wanted last night."

Kerrie asked to read Dana's notes as well as the suspect profiles collected from the Internet. When she finished reading, she shook head. "This is the most convoluted case I've ever seen. You're right, we need to start with the Turnsby brothers. It seems they're heavily involved in drugs and murder. I wish you hadn't fired the guards, Mom."

Dana sighed. "I don't want to be responsible for any more deaths. And that reminds me, we need to call the hospital and ask about the last guard. I don't even know his name."

Sarah called the hospital and reported that he was still alive, but that only relatives would be told his condition.

"It must have been the sheriff who wounded him," Dana said. "Otherwise, he wouldn't have been caught off-guard. . . Sorry for the unintended pun."

"If that's the case, he's still in danger, Mom. They'll finish him off so he can't identify his assailant."

"And since it happened in the county, it's under the sheriff's jurisdiction." Dana immediately called the protection agency and told them the situation. They needed to place a guard in the hospital to protect one of their own.

"I'm going to the sheriff's office now before this gets any worse," Kerrie said.

"We're going as backup," her mother insisted. "We'll park down the block and sit in the back so we won't be recognized. If you're not out in an hour, we'll come in after you."

They laughed when Bert woofed his approval.

Chapter Thirty-Three

They sat in the back seat with Bert several hundred yards from the sheriff's office. Silent for most of their wait, they were absorbed in their own fears. Dana checked her watch again. It had been nearly an hour since Kerrie went inside. Five more minutes and she'd follow. She then saw her daughter hurrying down the road toward them. Flushed and breathless, she opened the driver's door and slid inside. Starting the engine, she said, "Let's get away from here before I tell you what's happened."

Her mother gave directions to the park and they stopped on the far side, out of sight of the Lucky Inn. Kerrie then turned in her seat to say, "The sheriff hasn't been in his office for three days. I talked to a young deputy who thinks he was arrested by state authorities, or is on the run."

"Why are they after him?" Sarah asked.

"Suspicion of heading a drug cartel."

"I knew it." Dana said. "That's why those men were searching the house and garage. Drugs were hidden there."

"Apparently so. I also interviewed the dispatcher. Sheriff Turnsby threatened to harm her children if she told what she knew."

"How in the world did you get her to talk?"

"I promised I wouldn't mention her as a source for my article. And she thinks the sheriff will only return in handcuffs."

"Did they tell you who else is involved?"

"They're both scared, Mom. I had a hard time getting anything out of them, but I reminded them that the drug ring is ruining young lives. They also know that they will eventually have to testify in court."

"Did you ask about Rob?"

"Yes, he's definitely involved. The deputy overheard an argument between him and the sheriff. It seems that Rob demanded more money. He was told that if he valued his life, he'd better be satisfied with the status quo."

"His brother told him that?"

Kerrie nodded. "He was also told to keep his women in line. The deputy thought he meant they were using the drugs instead of delivering them. So their drug use was deducted from Rob's share of the profits."

"No wonder he was so desperate when his money tree was chopped down."

"And the reason he killed Georgi," Sarah said.

The sun was setting when they arrived at the rural subdivision. It was time to make arrangements for their guests. Dana sighed with relief that Kerrie had learned such vital information. Now, if only the DCI investigators would get in touch. What had happened to them?

The yard was dark when they pulled into the circle drive. Dana hurriedly turned on the outside lights once they were safety inside the garage. When she checked the answering machine, a message awaited from Mr. Musgrove. He would install the surveillance cameras the following afternoon. It was too late to return his call and Dana hoped he wouldn't arrive before they returned from the airport. She also wondered if the cameras were necessary now that the drugs had been removed from the garage. Sarah would insist on them.

Curious about their neighbor, Dana glanced across the road. The house was dark. Was the neighbor a member of the drug ring? It made sense that she was reporting their whereabouts to the sheriff. That would also explain why she never answered her door, although she had earlier talked to Matt. Maybe it wasn't the same person he had interviewed. One of Rob's missing girlfriends might be living there now to watch their every move. She couldn't spend any more time thinking about it. There were house guests to prepare for.

* * *

The plane was late. There had been a delay in the San Francisco to Denver flight, forcing the small commuter plane to wait for them. Two friends accompanied Angela and they all appeared to have emerged from the pages of a fashion magazine. Dana hung back, uncomfortable in her sweat suit, but Kerrie immediately charmed them. Had she really given birth to this amazing young woman who seemed to be able to handle every situation with grace?

They all piled into the SUV and headed back down the highway. Sarah had prepared an elegant dinner, which only needed to be heated and served. The four bedrooms were ample and all that remained to be done was to take part in the memorial service the following day. Dana wondered whether any of Rob's relatives would be present.

* * *

The chapel was small and tranquil. No organ music played and flowers were nearly nonexistent. Dana was embarrassed by the lack of elegance that Georgi deserved. She should have talked to the director in person. There had obviously been a lack of communication. She heard one of Georgi's friends say, "We must be in the wrong place."

In tears, she apologized for the mistake. She then spotted *him* standing near the door at the back of the chapel. How dare he sneak in for the service? "Rob," she yelled, and he immediately turned and left. Kerrie went after him but was blocked at the door by the funeral director.

"Let him go," he said. "Can't you see how the poor man is suffering?"

"Is he responsible for this mismanagement of service?" Dana demanded.

The man shrugged and said nothing.

"Are you aware that there's a warrant out for his arrest for the murder of my sister?"

"Nonsense," he said. "Rob wouldn't kill–"

Dana stepped around him and followed Kerrie to the exit. When they reached the street they watched the sports car leave the curb. Kerrie whipped out her cell phone and called 911 to report Rob's whereabouts. They then returned to the chapel to confront the director. Dana insisted that he move the service to his best chapel and he grudgingly complied. Rob, he said, had chosen the chapel and paid the bill. No wonder it looked like a pauper's sanctuary.

"I'm surprised he was here," Sarah said in that soothing voice of hers.

"I am, too. Maybe he's not as evil as we thought."

"His brother has probably dominated his entire life."

"That and Rob's desire for wealth and power."

The funeral director beckoned them into another room. Richly carpeted and filled with flowers and organ music, it met Dana's expectations. The service went well with everyone reciting a short eulogy. They then returned to the house. Angela and her friends would be leaving the following morning, so they spent the evening talking about how much Georgi meant to them. No one could understand why she married Rob.

"Did she ever talk about Rob's relationship with his brother?" Dana asked no one in particular.

Jenny, a slender brunette, remembered a conversation with Georgi. She had said that she couldn't understand why Rob was afraid of his brother. Dana knew that Will Turnsby was four years older and larger in stature, but there had to be another reason for his behavior.

"The sheriff must have forced his brother into the drug ring," Kerrie surmised. "You said he wasn't a good businessman, so he needed money. He then charmed the women in his life into dealing drugs for him."

"But who committed the murders?" Sarah wanted to know.

Dana frowned. "Probably not Rob. He's too much of a wimp."

"The sheriff and his henchmen must be responsible."

The others agreed. Angela then asked if they were in any danger.

"The surveillance cameras are working and Bert's on guard," Dana assured her. "I've also got my Glock handy and I know how to use it."

"I doubt they'll return," Kerrie said, refilling her drink. "They got what they came for the other night. There's no reason to harm any of us."

Angela lifted her glass. "Here's to our beloved Georgi."

"Hear, hear," the others said.

"Without her our lives would have been less friendly, less comforting, less beautiful." Tears streamed down her face as she sipped her wine.

Chapter Thirty-Four

Their guests left on their scheduled flight at 9:30 the following morning. It had been a pleasant yet bittersweet visit. Kerrie and Sarah said they also felt a void when Georgi's friends left, and the best way to fill that void was to immediately jump back into the investigation. She asked Sarah to try Chad Ryley's cell phone number once they left the airport. His calls were still being routed to his voice mail, so she called the Cheyenne office. When she hung up she said that Ryley had still not been heard from and that Jim Smith, the Gillette investigator, was on his way to the house.

Dana couldn't help worrying. Parking outside her home was a dangerous practice. She hoped Agent Smith wouldn't join the growing list of casualties. The governor needed to send an army of investigators to round up the drug ring.

"There's a red light behind us, Dana. You'd better pull over."

She'd set the cruise control but had increased speed when she thought of Agent Smith. Dana prayed the patrol car didn't belong to Sheriff Turnsby. When he stepped from his car she recognized the uniform of a highway patrolman.

"You're nine miles over the speed limit," he said when she rolled down her window "That's much too fast for existing weather conditions."

She apologized and told him that a DCI agent was waiting for them at home. He was investigating her sister's murder as well as at least two others. He eyed her skeptically until Kerrie left the car to talk to him. Before long he was back in his patrol car and leading the way.

"How did you manage that?" her mother asked.

"Professional courtesy."

An unmarked car was parked in the circle drive. Dana immediately left the SUV to make sure Jim Smith was still alive. The patrolman also left his car and walked over to talk to the agent. They had obviously been communicating by police band radio.

"Please come in for coffee," Dana said to both men. The chilling wind had picked up and was blowing snow in swirls around them. Thank goodness they didn't have rules against entering houses. When they had settled in the spacious kitchen, both officers admitted they were on the lookout for Sheriff Turnsby as well as his brother Rob.

"We're worried about Chad Ryley," Dana said. "What could have happened to him?"

"We're also looking for him," the investigator said, his brown eyes trained on Dana. "No one's seen him in the past two days."

He reminded her of an aging western movie actor whose name she couldn't quite remember. She hoped he was as good with his gun.

"Sheriff Turnsby," Sarah insisted. "He must have killed him like poor Matt Brown."

"I hope not, ma'am," the patrolman said, rising from the table. He thanked them for the coffee and left.

The DCI agent asked for any information they had that might help with his investigation. Dana retrieved copies of the Internet reports along with the notes she made from Matt's files. She then told him about the missing prescription bottles and her impressions of Rob's girlfriends. Kerrie also filled him in on her interviews with the deputy and dispatcher. Obviously impressed with their work, he gave them his cell number and said he would be in touch.

When he left, Sarah rose to clear the table. "I hope he doesn't disappear like Chad Ryley."

"He looks quite capable," Dana replied. "A lot like Matt."

"But not nearly as handsome as the highway patrolman."

Sarah turned back from the sink. "Is he single, Kerrie?"

"Unfortunately not."

When the phone rang, Dana picked up, hoping the call was from Chad Ryley. All she heard was someone breathing. Shivering, she hung up, wondering whether the call had been made to frighten her. The phone I.D. said Private Caller. Checking the surveillance screen she noticed that two of the cameras were inoperable. She immediately called the installer. When he didn't answer, she assumed that he was out clearing snow. Shaking her head, she thought, *No, he can't be part of the drug ring. I'm getting downright paranoid.*

"We need to go through everything in Georgi's file cabinet," she said. "With three of us, it shouldn't take long. We might find a clue to help in the investigation."

The drawers were locked so Kerrie retrieved a crow bar from the garage to pry them open. Dana then withdrew all the folders and separated them into three stacks. They then began reading. Moments later Sarah found a photograph of Georgi and Rob standing outside a cabin.

"They're smiling so it must be theirs. I wonder where it's located?"

Dana left the desk to have a look. "Keep searching. Maybe there's a map. That could be where Rob and his brother are hiding."

There were several photographs taken of the area. Maybe Rob's cousin, the coroner, knew where the cabin was located.

She went back to the desk to call him, but was told he was in another part of the county. She left a message for him to call.

Kerrie was reading one of her aunt's manuscripts and was apparently enthralled. "Listen to this:"

They buried their cache in an old shed some twenty feet from the cabin's north wall. She told them about the shed when they were first captured. She thought it would save her husband's life, but they took it mercilessly . . .

"Cache of what, Kerrie?"

"I'm not sure. Part of the manuscript is missing. Do you think Aunt Georgi overheard her husband talking to his brother about burying drugs near the cabin?"

"She may have been so frightened of the sheriff that her only recourse was to include the information in her work, hoping the right people would read it and help to break up the drug ring."

"Do you think she was afraid the sheriff would kill Uncle Rob?"

"Maybe she knew more than anyone thought. Your aunt was a very intelligent woman. I'm surprised she didn't include the information in her diary."

"She was probably afraid that someone in the house would find the diary and destroy it," Kerrie said.

"You could be right."

Sarah was searching through a file when she found a hand drawn map of the road leading to the cabin. "I wonder if your sister drew this," she said, holding it for them to see.

Dana took it from her and compared it to the topo map she discovered in one of the folders. A few minutes later, she drew an X on the map, saying, "I believe it's here."

"Then we need to call Jim Smith and let him know."

Dana called the number and got a voice recording. Why didn't the investigators keep their phones in service?

"I hope nothing has happened to him."

"Already, Mom? I wouldn't think so."

Sarah got to her feet. "You're not thinking of going to the cabin, are you?"

"The thought has entered my mind."

"Don't even consider it, my friend. It's too dangerous."

"Why? We have Bert and my gun."

"The whole Turnsby gang might be there."

"If we leave before dark, we can check to see if anyone's in the cabin. From a distance, of course."

Sarah sighed in resignation. "Let's Google it. Then we can print out some Map Quest directions."

Dana rebooted the computer. Twenty minutes later she pulled the map and directions from the printer. "It's a 40-minute drive from here, which means we should leave by 3:30 this afternoon. That should place us within a short hiking distance from this plateau above the cabin just about twilight," she said, tapping the map. "If there are lights on in the cabin, we'll know someone's there."

"And a good chance no one will be able to see us," Kerrie said.

Sarah reluctantly agreed. "First we need to trade the SUV for a four-wheel drive vehicle."

"Are you serious about this, Mom?"

"Very serious. If something has happened to Agent Smith, I don't trust anyone else with the information. It might get back to the sheriff."

"Okay," Kerrie said. "If we don't hear from the investigator by two o'clock, we'll trade cars and dress like lumberjacks."

"We need to go today before they leave the area," Dana said. "I think a run to Casper to buy what we need is in order."

Dana tried to call the investigator a number of times that day but he wasn't answering his phone. She left him several messages, including the news that they would be reconnoitering the cabin. That alone should prompt an immediate response. As much as she dreaded driving up the mountain in their Hummer trade-in, she began getting ready for the trip. Kerrie and Sarah followed suit. Their newly purchased gear had already been loaded into the back of the H2, and Sarah packed a picnic basket in case they were stranded. Dressed in hiking boots, jeans, sweaters, and sheepherder coats, they snapped a wool jacket around Bert. Dana then stowed her gun in its case on the console and Sarah's bat accompanied their survival gear.

They stood briefly in the garage looking at one another as if questioning the wisdom of their plan. Before anyone could talk the others out of going, Dana climbed into the Hummer and punched the garage door opener. A minute later they were on their way.

Chapter Thirty-Five

"Good thing the Hummer's equipped with a tracking device," Sarah said as they started up the mountain.

Kerrie snorted. "We can be tracked by satellite wherever we go, whether we want to be or not."

Dana checked the rearview mirrors. "Unless the rental car agent is a Turnsby relative, I doubt anyone knows we've switched vehicles."

"Don't forget the nosy neighbor across the road, Dana."

"I think whoever lived there has vacated the premises. There weren't any lights in the house last night. I've been worried that whoever lived there has been replaced by a gang member."

"Take the next road to the left," Sarah said, holding the printout in her lap.

The sun had partially dropped behind a stand of pine trees when Dana checked the mileage. There were still thirteen miles to go. When they left the pavement, she noticed that the side road had not been recently plowed. Slowing the H2, she negotiated several snowdrifts that stretched across the narrow road. A number of tire tracks were visible, some as wide as their own. She doubted that hunters were there in April, and it wasn't the time of year for tourists, so the tracks must have been made by gang members.

"Are you sure we should be doing this, Dana?" There was a tremor in Sarah's voice.

"We'll be fine. Your job is stay in the Hummer and man the phones. We can't have a cell phone ringing while Kerrie and I are out on the ridge overlooking the cabin. If a state investigator calls, give him directions and ask him to come as soon as possible."

They reached the ridge just before dark and doubled back into a grove of trees. Kerrie picked up the heavy flashlight while Dana withdrew her Glock from its case. She also reached for a pair of binoculars. Bert would stay behind to protect Sarah and the Hummer. A few minutes passed before Dana decided that it was dark enough to conceal them. Unfortunately, the snow would showcase them in their dark clothing. They should have worn white.

Quietly opening and closing doors, they crept single file back to the road. They had estimated that the ridge was several hundred yards ahead and they moved in that direction. Slogging through ankle deep snow, they moved cautiously away from the road to where they hoped the ridge was located. The fading sun streaked the sky ahead of them and they noticed an opening in the trees, which led to a precipice. Kneeling on the edge, they looked down on an unlighted valley. Not a flicker of light was visible.

"Could we have made a wrong turn?" Kerrie whispered in her mother's ear.

"I don't think so," Dana whispered back. "Maybe they covered the windows with blankets."

"They could have moved to another location."

"As remote as this place is, why bother?" Dana raised the binoculars to her eyes and carefully scanned the area. They then heard a vehicle approaching on the road. Both women flattened themselves on the ridge, hoping they wouldn't be seen. Releasing the breath she had been holding, Dana glimpsed headlights starting down the slope. She followed its lights as it curved down the road and stopped about an eighth of mile below them. Truck doors slammed and the headlights went out several moments later. Before long, dim light filtered through the trees. Cabin lights? No wonder she hadn't been able to spot the building. It was surrounded by thick stands of pine trees.

"The entire gang didn't arrive in that pickup," she whispered to Kerrie. "I wonder if we can creep down there and listen to what they're saying."

"Not a good idea, Mom. The rest of the gang might be coming in behind them. If we're caught on the road–"

"You're right. We'd better go home and call the DCI first thing in the morning, and give them directions to the cabin."

They followed their tracks back to the Hummer. The impressions they made were so deep that Dana wondered whether gang members had seen them. If they had, the two of them were in danger. She signaled her daughter to stop. They could angle off to their left and make their way through the trees to where they had parked. She prayed no one had noticed the black H2 parked among the trees.

Moving silently in the direction they thought was in line with the H2, they soon realized they were lost. They needed to find the road and make their way back. The sky was overcast and snow could resume at any time. Chilled, Dana rubbed her arms. Some detectives they were. They could freeze to death before they found their way back. Sarah must be worried out of her mind.

"Let's retrace our steps back to the precipice," Kerrie said. "We can follow them back to the road."

"Good idea. If anyone was following that pickup, they should have reached the cabin by now."

Kerrie led the way. When they reached the ridge, they knelt on the edge to listen. Dana had just motioned her daughter to leave when they heard a scream. It sounded as though it came from the cabin.

"It could have been a wild animal," Kerrie whispered. "Maybe a mountain lion."

"It sounded like a woman's scream." She gripped Kerrie's arm and motioned for her to follow. They stepped in their own tracks, which were easy enough follow. Within minutes they spotted the Hummer. Dana stopped when she noticed a dark object on the ground near the front fender. They found Bert lying on his side. When Dana touched his head, her hand was wet with blood.

"Sarah."

Dana rushed around to the passenger side and opened the door. The seat was empty.

"Looking for someone, ladies?" An average-sized man wearing a dark hood was standing near the rear of the Hummer. The object in his hands resembled a club.

"What have you done with my friend?" she demanded, groping for the gun in her pocket.

Kerrie gripped her mother's arm, whispering, "Wait."

"She's visiting *my* friends at the cabin," he said laughing.

So it was Sarah they heard screaming. "What are they doing to her?"

"See for yourself." He pointed his club in the direction of the cabin. "Come with me."

"And if we don't?"

"There won't be anything left for you to identify."

"We'll follow you," Kerrie said, "after we tend to our dog." She helped Dana lift Bert into the Hummer and cover him with a blanket. He still seemed to be breathing.

"Let's go," he said, waving his club.

He must have seen the gun case, Dana thought. *And why does Kerrie want me to wait before I draw my gun?*

"It must be awfully crowded down there by now," Kerrie said casually.

"Not really. Some of our people are making runs."

"Deliveries, you mean?"

"You're pretty smart for a good-looking babe," he said. "We'll have to get better acquainted."

"It's a little difficult when you're waving that club around."

Dana held her breath as Kerrie moved in closer. Were her karate skills good enough to disarm him? She then realized why her daughter hadn't wanted her to use her gun. It would alert the others at the cabin. Her fingers curled around the Glock in her pocket. She needed to distract the man so that Kerrie could disarm him.

"You slimely bastard," she said. "I won't let you near my daughter."

"Your daughter?" he said, absently lowering the club.

Kerrie moved toward him in a blur of motion, kicking him in the chest and knocking him onto his back in the snow. While he gasped for breath, Dana grabbed the club and angrily took revenge for what he had done to Bert. The club was wrenched from her hands before she could hit him again.

"He's out, Mom. Grab the rope in the back of the Hummer. We'll tie and gag him before he comes to."

"He must be the one who killed Matt," Dana said before stumbling off through the snow.

"Hurry. We've got to save Sarah."

After carefully tying and gagging him, they left him there on the ridge. It would serve him right if he froze to death, Dana thought, resisting the urge to push him over the edge. At Kerrie's suggestion, they rolled themselves in snow to disguise their dark clothing for the trek down to the cabin. Dana was still so enraged that she no longer felt the cold.

Chapter Thirty-Six

They were thankful for the thick stands of pine trees, which blocked the cabin's view of the road. Dana carried the baseball bat, following Kerrie with the club. Her gun would be used as a last resort. They walked in the tire tracks to minimize evidence of their existence. When they approached the cabin, they slid their feet to make a snowy trench rather than leave footprints. Hiding behind a nearby spruce, they heard voices and crouched beneath a window to listen.

"Jack shoulda been back by now. You think the other women got themselves lost?"

"Good riddance," a familiar voice said. "They'll freeze to death and we won't have to look for 'em."

"You'll never find them," they heard Sarah say. "They're too smart for you."

Men's laughter echoed from the cabin walls. "*You're* not very smart, are you, Grandma? You didn't even put up a fight."

"I just got out of the hospital," she said, her voice on the verge of tears.

"If you don't cooperate, we'll put you in the morgue."

"The attorney general's office is sending men up here, as we speak," she said.

More laughter. "And how are they gonna find us?"

"We faxed them a map."

"You're lying, old lady."

"How do you think we found the cabin?"

No one spoke for several moments. Someone then said, "We'd better get out of here, Will."

"Don't be stupid." The voice had to belong to Sheriff Turnsby. "A major shipment's arriving in the morning."

"Not if it's intercepted by the law," another man said.

"You're probably right. If you're lying, old woman, we'll come back to feed you to the bears."

"I have no reason to lie."

"Load up everything and let's get out of here."

"What about the old lady?"

"Tie her up and leave her for the coyotes. She won't last long."

"Jack'll finish her off when he gets back. He likes swingin' that club."

They heard more laughter and the sound of slamming doors. Scurrying back into the trees, they waited. After what seemed an eternity, the cabin door opened and the occupants departed. Carrying large boxes, they deposited them in the pickup bed.

Dana prayed that Sarah was the only one left behind. The cabin door had been left open, so the sheriff was cold-blooded enough to carry out his threat. If wild animals didn't get Sarah, she would certainly freeze to death. She gritted her teeth and waited for the sound of the pickup to fade away. When the taillights disappeared, they entered the cabin. Sarah was tied to a wooden chair, her eyes closed as though she were praying. There didn't appear to be anyone else around, but they weren't taking any chances. Cautiously, Dana whispered in her ear. "We're getting you out of here."

Kerrie found a knife in a kitchen drawer. When the ropes had been cut, they helped Sarah to her feet. Tears streamed down her cheeks as she said, "I overheard them say they were going to a hideout in South Dakota."

"We're so sorry we left you–"

"It was exciting, Dana, but I don't think my heart can stand much more."

She gave her a hug.

"You two stay here," Kerrie insisted. "I'll scout up ahead to make sure they're gone." She left before they could protest, and was back within half an hour, carrying a knapsack and leading the dog on his leash.

"Jack's still on the ridge but they nearly destroyed the Hummer. The tires are flat and the windows broken. Hopefully they didn't damage the engine."

Sarah carefully hugged the German Shepherd, who didn't seem to recognize her. "I guess we'll stay in the cabin until help arrives," she said, rising from her chair to retrieve a first aid kit to bandage Bert's head. He must have only received a glancing blow, Kerrie said, because the Hummer's fender had taken the brunt of Jack's attack.

Sarah looked up from her nursing stint. "There's got to be a way to attract some help."

"I'll climb to the top of that upper ridge in the morning," Kerrie said. "Hopefully I'll be able to get out on my cell." Taking sandwiches from the sack, she said, "Let's have some dinner."

Kerrie went back to the H2 for blankets and they huddled together near the stove. There was still a good supply of wood behind the cabin. It would be a long night to think about freezing to death if no one found them.

"We might be able to drive the Hummer back as far as the main road on its rims," Kerrie said. A snow plow would find them eventually, if they didn't succumb to hypothermia.

Bert whined at the cabin door at daybreak and Kerrie let him out. "It's snowing," she whispered to anyone who might be awake.

Dana groaned and sat up. They couldn't bring themselves to sleep on the dirty sheets in the cabin, so they slept on cushions on the floor, wrapping themselves in blankets.

They helped a groaning Sarah to her feet when she woke an hour later. Dana then made coffee and they ate granola bars as they discussed their possible fate. They decided to retrieve everything from the H2 before it snowed again.

"We should have dragged Jack down here last night," Dana said. "He must have died during the night."

"If he had managed to untie himself, he would have used the club on all of us," Kerrie said. "He was a killer, Mom. You did mankind a favor."

"But–"

"No buts. We'll check on him when we go back for our stuff."

They left Bert with Sarah and climbed back up the slope. When they reached the ridge, they looked for Jack but could find no sign of him. He might have untied himself or an animal dragged him off. They found no evidence of either happening, and there didn't seem to be any extra tracks in the snow.

"He probably came to last night after I brought Bert to the cabin," Kerrie said, looking about. "He could have stepped in existing tracks and spent the night in the Hummer."

"Then he could be anywhere, waiting in ambush."

"I think we'd better go back to the cabin, Mom."

Sarah had her bat ready when she tentatively opened the door. The bat was no match for Jack's club, Dana thought, and decided they needed a code. Three short knocks, a pause, then two more.

"It was too cold to spend the night in the Hummer," Sarah said. "The keys were still in the ignition but the heater wouldn't have kept him warm with the windows broken."

"He may have found something to board up the windows."

"Or he has his own cabin not far from here."

"It's the middle of April," Kerrie said. "How cold can it get this time of year?"

"Flowers are already in bloom at home," Sarah said wistfully.

"We need the rest of the supplies, Kerrie. I'll shoot him if I have to."

"We also need to get a message out on one of our cell phones." She checked hers again to make sure there was no service in the area.

"I wonder how the drug ring managed to get messages here?"

"A two-way radio, maybe?" Kerrie looked around the cabin.

"They must have taken it with them."

"Or they had a cell booster or satellite phone."

"With our luck we'll have to send smoke signals."

"That's not a bad idea, Mom. We could set fire to a pile of wood and hope that a forest ranger notices the smoke."

"What about Jack the clubber."

"One of us will stand guard with the gun. Bert will certainly let us know if someone's in the area." Kerrie reached down to pet the injured dog.

"Okay, let's get started."

The only open area was on the ridge. It took several trips to carry enough wood to make a good-sized fire. They then broke small, dry inner limbs from trees for kindling. Dana lit the pyramid-shaped wood pile stuffed with newspaper found in the cabin while Sarah stood guard with the gun. Bert never left her side. A slight breeze was blowing, which helped fan the flames. If it snowed again, the blaze would soon be smothered.

"Keep breaking branches," Dana said. "We can't use up our entire supply of wood for the cabin. We may be here a while." She then thought of the cabin furniture. If they could wrench the cabinets loose, they would also burn.

As they watched, smoke sailed upward toward the east. It made a good deal of smoke and they hoped that sparks wouldn't ignite the trees.

"Not much chance of that," Sarah said. "There must be an inch of snow on most of the branches."

Bert's growl was a definite warning. Scanning every direction, they decided to immediately return to the cabin.

"What about the supplies, Mom?"

"Later," Dana said, taking the gun from Sarah. "Jack is probably still holed up in the Hummer."

When they reached the cabin, Dana led the way, gun in hand. Pushing the door open, she peered through the crack to make sure no one hid behind the door. Jack must still be near the ridge waiting for them to make a mistake.

Chapter Thirty-Seven

Kerrie tossed more wood into the stove. Huddled around it, they discussed their options. Hiking out to the main road wasn't practical and Jack was an ever present danger. They could no longer split up, which prevented Kerrie from climbing the upper ridge to try her cell phone signal. Sarah was in no shape to make the climb. They decided to walk out to the road together to check on the fire. The smoke was only a thin wisp and they knew they had to add more fuel to the embers. What could they burn without depleting their supply of wood?

"There's an old shed out back," Kerrie said. "There must be something there."

"What if Jack's hiding in the shed?"

"We've got a gun, a club, and a bat. And don't forget Bert."

They checked for footprints in the snow. "Animal tracks," Sarah said, when they noticed small indentations leading to the shed.

"Probably a rabbit." Dana withdrew the gun from her pocket. "We may have to skin one and cook it for dinner. Our food supply is pretty meager."

"Could be a wolf or coyote," Sarah said, hanging back. "I don't think they taste good."

"Only one way to find out." Kerrie reached for the shed door and flung it open. The storage building was empty.

"They must have kept their drug cache in here. It's to the north of the cabin, as Aunt Georgi wrote in her book."

"The shed's pretty rickety." Dana pushed on the outer wall. "We can knock it down and burn the boards. If only we had a hammer."

"This club makes a good battering ram." Kerrie set her feet wide apart and swung at the door. When it fell from its rusty hinges, she swung again. Sarah then joined in with her bat. Before long they had a large pile of rotting wood, which they carried up the slope. The fire was still smoldering but had all but burned itself out.

Dana patrolled the perimeter with Bert and the gun while they carefully stacked the wood, which made a good bonfire. Someone had to notice the smoke. It was their only chance.

It was time for another trip to replenish the wood when they heard the sound of an engine. It could have been a forest ranger but they weren't taking chances. Sarah immediately grabbed Bert's growling muzzle and they hid behind the nearest pine tree. A red pickup stopped on the road and pulled into the clearing. Dana peered around the tree in time to watch Rob Turnsby and Amanda Smelton leave the truck.

"I wonder who set the fire?" they heard him say.

"Probably that crazy man, Jack."

"Yeah, it could have been him. I asked Will to get rid of the creep."

"Well, let's go down to the cabin and get cozy."

"We'd better throw some snow on the fire before we go."

"It'll burn itself out. You can't start a forest fire in all this snow."

"Yeah, I guess you're right. Let's go."

When the truck left, Kerrie said, "We can steal the pickup when they go inside the cabin."

"If he leaves the keys," her mother said.

"He's so anxious to get *cozy* that I'm sure he'll leave them. Be ready to go when I get back." Kerrie took off in the direction of the road.

Dana knew it was useless to argue. Flattening herself on the ridge, she watched as Kerrie made her way down the road toward the cabin.

Sarah reclined beside her. "What if they notice our things in the cabin?"

"Hopefully they'll think they belong to other gang members. If not, Kerrie's going to be in trouble." *And we'll have to rescue her.*

"At least we know that Amanda's the blonde who drove Georgi's car, and probably called herself Laura."

"That's not important now. We've got to protect Kerrie and get ourselves out of here." Dana slid back from the ridge and helped Sarah to her feet. They were brushing snow from their clothing when they heard a man's voice. Bert growled but cowered when he saw him.

"Going somewhere, ladies?" This time he held an even larger club. His head was bandaged and his nose badly misshapen. She knew he was going to repay her for his head injury, and reached in her pocket for the gun.

"Jack, how nice to see you again," she said, forcing a laugh to cover her fear. He looked as though he were preparing to strike.

"Nice," he repeated, lifting the club.

Dana fired from her coat pocket, hitting him in the chest. Jack crumpled like an imploded building. She knew he was dead but felt only numb. How could this have happened? She had killed a man. Suddenly her heart was pumping in her throat and she felt as though she would lose her lunch. Sarah rushed to her side and hugged her.

"You had to do it. He would have killed us both."

"I know, but—"

"They must have heard the shot at the cabin."

"I hope Kerrie's out of sight."

"Help me drag him behind the tree."

They quickly covered him with snow and kicked enough to cover the drag trail they had made. Dana then crawled back to the precipice to check on Kerrie. The pickup truck was still parked on the road and two people standing nearby were looking in her direction. They had to be Rob and Amanda, but where was Kerrie? The couple got into Rob's pickup, which began to turn around.

Dana slid back from the edge and motioned Sarah and the dog to follow. When they reached the road, they hid behind the nearest pine tree and waited, hoping their new tracks wouldn't be noticed from among the many others. They soon heard the sound of an engine. Her gun pointed skyward, Dana thought of the man she had already killed. She wouldn't hesitate to shoot Rob, if need be. She wasn't so sure about Amanda. No matter how misguided she happened to be, Dana doubted that she had taken part in a killing. On second thought, if she *were* Laura, she had killed Georgi with her pills.

The truck stopped and a door slammed. She heard snow sloshing as someone walked toward their tree. Nudging Sarah and Bert around to the back side of the giant evergreen, she held her breath and listened.

"A lot of tracks," she heard Rob say, "but nobody's here. It was probably crazy Jack shooting rabbits."

"Let's go back to the cabin," she heard Amanda say.

The pickup door slammed and the truck sounded as though it were turning around. Before long the engine noise faded. Dana closed her eyes, inhaling deeply.

"What's become of Kerrie?" her friend whispered.

Dana bit down hard on her lip as they made their way back to the ridge. The sun was setting and she dared not use her binoculars. Kerrie was down there somewhere. If she didn't return with the pickup soon, they would go after her.

Chapter Thirty-Eight

A light snow was falling as darkness descended on the ridge. Bert was whimpering, probably more from hunger than the cold. Her own stomach ached and she knew that Sarah was always hungry. The light breeze chilled them despite their heavy clothing. What to do? Kerrie still had not returned.

Dana decided. "I'll make a quick trip down the hill to find Kerrie. Take Bert back to the Hummer. There must be some food left in the back."

Sarah started to protest but simply nodded.

Already covered with snow, Dana slid most of the way down the hill and quickly hid in the trees near the cabin. She heard a woman's laugh and the sound of clinking glasses. They must be toasting their successful drug sales, she thought bitterly. What have they done with Kerrie?

A gloved hand gripped her lower face and a voice whispered in her ear. "Sorry to be so late, Mom, but I'm waiting for them to go to bed."

"Why?" she breathed.

"He's got the truck keys in his pocket."

"Why don't we just march in there with my gun and take the keys away from him?"

"He has his own gun in a shoulder holster. You're not a quick draw artist, are you?"

Dana shook her head. "No, but I had to kill Jack"

"I was afraid of that. I would have gone back to check on you after I heard the shot, but they came out of the cabin. I caught a glimpse of you on the ridge after they went back inside, so I knew you were all right."

"Too bad I didn't know that about you."

Kerrie changed the subject. "I could hot wire the truck if it wasn't locked."

"It's strange that he would bother to lock it here."

"Maybe he was afraid that monster with the club would steal it."

"Crazy Jack? Yes–well–now what, daughter?"

"Go back up with Sarah. I'll get the keys *and* his gun while I'm at it."

"How will you get inside?"

"I found a key under a rock near the back door. Isn't that where everyone hides spare keys?"

"Please come back with me. I don't want you risking your life."

"I'm quite good at self defense, Mom. And they won't be expecting me."

Dana knew better than to argue. "Be careful. We'll be in the Hummer, trying to stay warm." They embraced and Dana handed Kerrie her gun before starting up the hill. She found Sarah and Bert huddled in the H2's back seat, wrapped in a blanket. Sarah warned her of broken window glass and offered a bag of trail mix. When Dana closed her eyes and tried to meditate, her body ached, her brain refusing to concentrate on her mantra. It wasn't long before she heard Sarah softly snoring beside her. She could sleep through a tornado. Try as she might, she could not help replaying various scenes in her mind of Kerrie sneaking into the cabin. What if she tripped over the lovers in the dark? Gritting her teeth, she quietly opened the door and closed it. If Kerrie needed help, she would be waiting outside the cabin. She prayed that Sarah wouldn't wake up and discover her missing, and that Jack didn't have a twin brother.

When she got back to the road she saw headlights coming around a distant curve. Quickly retreating to the Hummer, she watched as a small, white pickup drove past. The road was becoming a regular highway.

Kerrie.

Hurrying back down the road, she followed tracks to the edge of the ridge and again reclined in the snow. She noticed the pickup pull in behind Rob's truck and the lights go out. She couldn't chance sneaking down there without being seen. A full moon was rising over a mountain peak and reflected snow made visibility brighter than twilight. A moment later she watched the small pickup quickly back in a half circle and head back up the road. It wasn't long before she heard voices yelling. Had Kerrie stolen the truck?

The small truck passed by before she got to the road. It then pulled off into the area where they had parked the Hummer. She managed to get there as Kerrie was helping Sarah into the truck.

"Hurry, Mom, Rob will be up the hill soon with his gun." She grabbed Bert and helped him into the bed of the pickup. The seat would be more than crowded with the three of them. "There's no time to grab our gear."

Dana pushed in beside Sarah and the pickup lurched forward. Kerrie turned off the headlights and drove back to the road. They had not gone far when headlights filled the interior of the cab and they heard what sounded like a bullet hitting the truck. They ducked and their pickup swerved on the icy road. Headlights grew brighter as Rob's truck gained speed behind them.

"We can't outrun him, Mom. What shall we do?"

"Drive on the wrong side of the road. How much gasoline do we have?"

"Three quarters of a tank."

"If I remember right, a curve's coming up soon. There's a small logging road off to the left about halfway in the curve. I'll tell you when to slow down." Thank God there was enough reflected light for them to see. She wondered whether Rob could see the small, unlighted, white truck on the snowy road. She doubted it. That's probably why he hadn't fired another shot.

The curve was coming up and Kerrie drove on the left edge of the road. "Let off the gas," her mother said, "and don't touch the brake. If we miss the road we'll make one of our own. I doubt that big truck of Rob's can fit between the trees like this one."

The pursuing truck was nearly on them when Dana told her to make a hard left.

"I can't see, Mom. The mirrors are blinding me."

"Sharp turn to the left *now*." Branches scraped the side of the truck as it bounced and landed hard on the logging road.

"Make sure it's in four-wheel drive," Dana said. "And don't stop for anything."

"They kept going," Sarah shouted, "but they'll turn around and come back."

"Let's get as far away as we can."

"I'm glad I was the designated driver for most of our ski trips," Kerrie said, maneuvering the small truck between snowdrifts.

"What if we get lost, Dana?"

"Lost is better than shot. By the way, where's the map?"

"In my purse. I was so sleepy that I left it in the Hummer."

"Okay, we'll find a high point and try our cell phones. With the sheriff headed for South Dakota, it should be safe to call his department for help. If not, the highway patrol."

"Still no headlights behind us, Mom. Maybe they can't find the side road."

"Someone up there is looking after us," she said, "but let's make sure we can't be found."

Some twenty minutes later, they were surprised to find an area devoid of snow. Massive pine trees were clustered so close to the narrow road that both sides served as a partial canopy. The road was now little more than a trail. Rob would scratch his prized red truck if he tried to follow them any farther. Kerrie drove carefully uphill on the edge of the trees until they reached a small summit. Shutting off the lights, she decided that it was a good place to test for cell service.

After few minutes of moving about, she quickly got back in the truck. "I see headlights coming down the road."

Dana opened her window and craned her neck to look behind the truck. The lights were still quite a distance away so there was time to drive down the hill to hide. They then climbed back to the summit to watch. Lying in snow was becoming a habit, Dana thought, as she watched the headlights approach. They disappeared when the truck reached the canopied area, and Dana held her breath as she waited for the Dodge to continue down the road.

A coyote yipped and they could hear Bert's sharp retort. Sarah quickly slid back out of sight to quiet the dog. A moment later they noticed headlights retreating back down the road. She had been right. Rob was more concerned with his own truck than the one that had been stolen. It was probably a gift to one of his girlfriends. If so, two of them now rode with him and were giving him hell.

Kerrie was punching in numbers without success. "No cell service here," she said.

"I wonder if we can sneak back to the Hummer and grab our gear before we head back to town."

"Do you think it's safe?"

"It's light enough that we can creep along looking on both sides of the road, in case they're lying in wait."

"I'll ride in the truck bed with Bert and do a 360-swivel while you drive," Dana said. "We can escape into the trees if we spot him. I don't think he could follow us far in the trees."

"Unless we get high centered in deep snow."

Sarah remembered ski poles in the truck bed. They could periodically test the snow's depth, if necessary. Agreed, they returned to the truck and slowly backtracked down the road. Kerrie volunteered to ride in the back with Bert while her mother drove. She would tap the top of the cab to switch drivers if she spotted Rob's truck, or got too cold.

The moon had crested and was beginning to sink into the western sky when they reached the main road. Quietly leaving the truck, they walked a short distance in both directions to make sure no one was parked in ambush. They then drove slowly back to the Hummer. Dana parked a short distance away while Kerrie led Bert to sniff around the H2. She then unlatched the tire carrier and opened the overhead door. She motioned Bert to jump inside.

Chapter Thirty-Nine

Kerrie drew her mother's gun when Bert growled and yelped in pain. A struggle within the Hummer was taking place as she carefully crawled into the storage area. Before she could determine who or what had attacked Bert, a huge cat leaped through one of the broken side windows.

"Stay," she demanded before the dog could follow. "You're no match for a mountain lion." Hurriedly grabbing Sarah's purse and an armful of gear, she called Bert to accompany her. Dana was sloshing through snow toward them.

"Grab what you can fast and let's get out of here," Kerrie said. "They may have heard the commotion at the cabin."

Within minutes they were headed back to town. "Thank heavens that cat was hiding in the Hummer. It probably prevented anyone from taking our gear."

"Crazy Jack may have lured the cat in there to scare us away," Kerrie said. "You should see what it did to the seats, Mom. I hope you've got good insurance."

"We can afford the repairs, dear."

"Do you think that's why Rob's still around? Hoping to get rid of us so he can collect Aunt Georgi's money?"

"Most likely. Matt Brown, the DCI agent, wanted to place us in protective custody."

"It's either that, Mom, or we fortify the house."

"I tried that with the guards and surveillance cameras."

"And Bert," Sarah said. "I'm for hiring more guards with police dogs."

"I doubt that Rob went back to the cabin after the truck was stolen," Dana said. "He may have followed his brother to South Dakota."

Kerrie checked the dashboard clock. "It's nearly 2:30. How many patrolman are on the road at this hour? We can call them later this morning. Maybe Agent Smith will finally answer his phone."

"In the meantime," Dana said, taking the phone from her purse, "I'll call 911 now that we're on the main road. She punched in the numbers and waited. A sleepy voice answered and she repeated details of their plight several times before the dispatcher understood them through the static. She would report the call to the temporary sheriff when he reported for work later that morning.

"Isn't there anyone on duty to capture criminals?" Dana asked.

"We're short-handed this month with the sheriff and two deputies leaving."

You've got to be kidding. "Fine, I'll call the highway patrol before they get away."

"Don't take it out on the dispatcher, Dana."

"You know I hate incompetence and this goes way beyond anything I've ever experienced." The patrol number was listed on her phone and she punched it in. There was more static before the signal disappeared. "Wouldn't you know that we're in another 'no service' area?"

It was 3:32 in the morning when they pulled into the circle drive. They had forgotten to take the garage door opener from the H2, so Dana unlocked the door and made her way to the garage. When they left the small pickup, she said: "Someone trashed the house again. I think we'd better stay in the motorhome."

"Uh-oh," Sarah said, "Look what they've done to it." The tires were flat, windows broken, and the sides of the coach were badly damaged. Someone had obviously been angry, Dana thought, or just plain sadistic.

Cringing, Kerrie said, "Looks like we'll be staying in a hotel."

"I haven't checked the upstairs yet. We'll look after Bert searches the house. Someone might still be here." She held her Glock at the ready.

When the German Shepherd finished his inspection, they climbed the stairs to Gerogi's bedroom, which was also a mess, as was her office. Rob's bedroom, however, had not been touched.

"I guess we know who's behind this catastrophe," Sarah said.

"But who wants to sleep in the madman's bedroom?"

"No one," her mother said, "Let's have a look at the other rooms."

The two bedrooms opposite each other at the end of the long hall were in pristine condition. At least they could get some sleep. Kerrie suggested they take photos of the mess to show the investigators before they started cleanup the next morning. As tired as they all were, they could easily sleep until noon.

Dana's cell phone rang at seven that morning. Groping, her eyes still closed, she dropped the phone, disconnecting it. Whoever it was could call back. Realizing it might have been an investigator, she checked the message screen, which said *Private Caller.* No phone number was listed. Groggy from lack of sleep, she wondered whether the caller had been Rob or one of the burglars. She tried Jim Smith's cell number and then Chad Ryley's. Both phones went directly to voice mail. Furious, she resisted the urge to throw the phone against the wall.

Sarah sat up yawning. "What's wrong?"

"We're still in danger. I've got some phone calls to make." She hurried to Georgi's office for a phone book and looked up the protection agency number. When the answering service picked up, she left a message for someone to call immediately when the office opened. She needed two guards for the day. Dana then called Mr. Musgrove and was surprised when he answered. He was on his way to repair the surveillance cameras and would be there in fifteen minutes. She asked him to pick up an additional surveillance system on his way.

Finally, some progress.

"I hate to do this to you, Sarah, but we've got company coming in fifteen minutes. Time to get dressed and make coffee." She then woke Kerrie, promising an afternoon nap. Checking her watch, she decided that the state office should be open and she called the number. When she had filled in one of the agents, she was told that under the circumstances, they would have to take them into protective custody.

"Not on your life, young man," she said. "I've hired guards and my house will soon be an armed fortress. Your department needs to catch the criminals and forget about us right now. I'm faxing you a copy of the map to the cabin. I suggest that you call in the National Guard to track down your agents."

"They're accounted for, ma'am."

"Then where are they?"

"I'm sorry," he said. "That's confidential."

Furious, she hung up on him. *One giant step backward.*

Sarah tapped her shoulder. "French roast or cappuccino?"

"How about a paisley straight jacket? I'm one step away from a padded cell."

Chapter Forty

"No wonder you couldn't see anything," Mr. Musgrove said. "Somebody taped the cameras."

"I wonder why they just didn't break them," Dana replied.

"Probably so they could be used later. I'm afraid I'll have to reinstall them on the second floor."

"Do whatever's necessary."

The security company returned her call and she ordered two guards. Since they didn't provide bodyguards, she asked for someone who did. The manager recommended a retired local police officer, whom she immediately called. Jeff Mailey was available and agreed to arrive before noon.

"That should do it," she told the others. "I'll ask Mr. Musgrove to replace all the outside lights before he leaves. Have I forgotten anything?"

"We need to buy a car, Mom. The rental agency will never rent us another."

"Good idea. Why don't we call the Brink's Company and ask if they have an armored car."

Kerrie laughed. "I was thinking more along the lines of a sleek, black limo."

"I'm afraid your inheritance has gone to your head, dear. I was actually considering a sleek, black VW. "

"Try shoving Bert into the back seat–"

The doorbell rang and a sheriff's deputy awaited them on the porch.

"Dana Logan?" he asked.

"Oh, good, you've come to file a burglary report. We've been waiting to clean up this mess until you got here."

"No, ma'am. I have a warrant for your arrest?"

"On what charge?"

"Auto theft."

She laughed. "Who's idea of a joke is that?"

"No joke. I have two other warrants here for a Sarah Cafferty and Kerrie Logan."

Dana beckoned him inside. "If my friend, Matt Brown, were still alive, I'd know who put you up to this."

The young officer looked at the vandalized living room and stuttered, "I-I'm not authorized to file a burglary report."

"Who sent you here to arrest three dangerous car thieves, without backup?" Dana demanded.

"I got a call from the Division of Criminal Investigation."

"Are you sure? Because if you're not, you need to sit down and listen to what has happened so far." Dana swept a broken picture frame from the nearest chair. She then turned him over to Kerrie, who obviously had him mesmerized. When she finished, he went back to his patrol car to retrieve a burglary report form. He filled it out before he left, apologizing for his mistake.

"He didn't even look at the pickup, Dana."

"He'll be back. It will give him a chance to see Kerrie again."

Their bodyguard arrived two hours later. They liked him on sight and Bert took to him immediately. Jeff Mailey was a medium-sized man with gray hair and a nice smile. He would occupy Rob's room because the balcony overlooked the courtyard. The arrangement would work just fine. Now, if only the new outside guards would stay alive. Maybe one of them could discover who was staying in the house across the road.

Sarah flirted with their bodyguard throughout lunch and Dana worried that she would keep him distracted. She did manage to question him about Sheriff Turnsby and his entire department.

"All I know about Turnsby is scuttlebutt. But I do know that somebody slipped up when they hired him. He has a criminal record."

"We know," Dana said. "We need something concrete to connect him and his brother Rob to the drug ring operating in this area."

"Well, ma'am, there's a snitch who used to fill me in on such things when I was on the police force. He could still be around."

"I'm willing to pay him whatever he wants for information leading to the Turnsby brothers' arrests."

"In that case, I may be able to help. He'll tell anything for a price."

"Please find him. We have an outside guard to protect us while you're gone."

Their bodyguard returned just before dinner, his usual smile missing. His former snitch had left town.

They ate Sarah's roast beef in near silence. After dinner, Dana showed him Rob's girlfriends' criminal records, and asked his advice.

"APBs should be out on all of them," he said. "Do you know if that's been done?"

"No, but maybe I should call their homes tonight to see if any of them are still around. Then we'll have a good idea who the drug runners are. We already know that Amanda Smelton is involved and that the pickup truck we took was either driven by Rob's secretary or Kim Yanton." Yankton and Smelton are both blondes and could have called themselves *Laura*.

"Yankton was the bubbly one," Sarah reminded her.

"And the secretary, Melanie Shamera, was the one Matt Brown followed to the old warehouse."

"At least you've narrowed them down to three," he said.

"But why are the authorities keeping us in the dark?"

Their bodyguard shrugged. "Departmental policy, I guess."

"What do you recommend, Jeff?"

"Leave the investigation to the police and stay safe here at home."

"Dana can't do that," Sarah said. "She's got to be on top of everything."

"I don't have much contact with the police department these days," he said, "but I have a friend who still works there." He took a phone from his pocket and walked into another room.

"He's the best," Sarah said, smiling.

"Don't distract him," Dana warned, taking out her own phone. "He's our best resource." She then gathered the computer printouts and dialed a number. When Sharon Zumwell didn't answer, she called Linda Johnsbury. Her mother answered. Linda had not been home for two days, and she had reported her disappearance to the police. Dana could hear a baby crying in the background and was relieved that Linda had left her behind. Kim Yankton didn't answer her phone, but Melanie Shamera picked up on the first ring.

"Did you get your pickup back?" Dana asked.

"Who is this?" She sounded frightened.

"Dana Logan. I heard that your pickup truck had been stolen."

"Not mine. It's parked out front."

"Have you heard from Rob?"

"Uh–not recently."

"His other friends are missing, Melanie. I suggest that you don't answer your door or the phone. It might be best to stay with a friend."

"I don't know why you're warning me, but I'll consider taking your advice."

"When you're in a safe place, call the police and tell them everything you know about the Turnsby brothers. If you're involved in any way, turning state's evidence could save your life."

Dana heard a click at the other end. She then called Amanda Smelton's number. The recorded message said her phone had been disconnected. She was surprised when Dawn Talson answered. When she learned it was Dana, her tone was sarcastic.

"Still playing detective, I see."

"Just making sure you're all right. Rob's other girlfriends seem to be missing."

There was silence on the line. When she asked who, Dana mentioned Linda Johnsbury. Dawn gasped. "I told her not to get involved."

"Involved in what?"

"Nothing."

"The drug ring, you mean?"

"How'd you know?"

"Everyone knows, Dawn. You need to get in touch with the police and tell them everything before *you* turn up missing." She heard a catch in the young woman's voice before she replaced the receiver.

One more call. Katie Bannatt was home and irritated to hear from Dana. "I told you I don't know anything about Rob Turnsby's business," she said. "And furthermore–"

"His other girlfriends are missing."

She gasped. "You don't mean–?"

"They could be in serious danger. I suggest that you call the police and tell them everything. And don't answer your door tonight for anyone."

Katie Bannatt hung up without another word.

Chapter Forty-One

It had been a long, sleepless night. It seemed that she had just dozed off when the phone rang on her nightstand. The clock radio said 7:00 a.m. *Who could be calling this early?* She checked the I.D. which said *Private Caller*. When Dana answered, she heard heavy breathing and immediately replaced the receiver. Someone was definitely trying to frighten her. She angrily grabbed her robe and hurried downstairs to the kitchen. Kerrie was already there, eating a bowl of cereal.

"We should hire a housekeeper-cook, Mom."

"Like Tonya Beardsly?"

Kerrie frowned. "I wonder who killed her? Was it Rob, her husband, or one of Rob's girlfriends?"

"It could have been the sheriff or one of his henchmen."

"But why kill someone who had already been fired?"

"To keep her quiet?"

"Do you think that's what happened to the other missing girlfriends?"

"A good possibility," a male voice said from the kitchen door. Jeff Mailey appeared glum. "I just heard from my friend at the PD. Linda Johnsbury's body was found floating face down in the North Platte River early this morning."

Dana sat down hard on the nearest stool. "Oh, no. Did she drown?"

"They think she was strangled."

Dana cradled her head in her hands. The Turnsbys had struck again. Why in heaven's name couldn't the police find them? Rob's other women had probably suffered the same fate, unless he decided to keep one alive.

"I need to call them back," she said, "before it's too late." She picked up the phone and called Dawn's number. When she told her that her friend Linda had been killed, there was a silence on the other end. Dana then heard her sobbing.

"It's my fault Linda's dead," she said at last.

She waited for her to continue.

"I introduced her to Rob but I never dreamed that he would get her pregnant."

"Do you think that's why he killed her?"

"I don't think it was him, but it's possible."

"Was Linda part of the drug ring?"

"Not at first, but Rob made her do some deliveries before the baby was born. He said nobody would suspect a pregnant teenager."

"She wasn't doing drugs while she was pregnant, was she?"

"Yeah, and I guess that's why her little girl has something wrong with her."

"And I was feeling sorry for Linda."

"She was a good person before she met Rob . . . Just a dumb kid."

Dana sighed. "Are you willing to testify against the drug ring, Dawn?"

"Can you promise me immunity?"

"I don't know if I can do that, but I'll certainly try. . . Why don't you ask the police when you call about protective custody?"

"I don't trust them."

"Why?"

"The sheriff said all lawmen are like him. I was afraid the deputies would tell him what I said and they would kill me, too."

"He lied to you, Dawn. He's the only bad lawman I've ever known."

Several moments passed before she said, "Please help me. I'll tell the police everything I know if they'll give me immunity."

"I'll do whatever I can," Dana promised her. "I'll pay for the best lawyer possible to represent you."

"You'll do that for me?"

"You were foolish to get caught up in the drug ring, but I know the circumstances. With your help, we'll see that they're all arrested. We can't allow them to destroy any more lives, like Linda's.

"I feel so bad."

"I know you do, Dawn. What can you tell me about Katie Bannatt and Melanie Shamera?"

"I don't know Katie, but Melanie's pretty tough. She's the one who ordered the drugs and set up the deliveries. I do know she's bitter because Rob told her she's too old, like his wife.

Dana gasped.

"I'm sorry. I know she was your sister, but Rob was always saying awful things about her, like he didn't want to sleep with her anymore–"

"I know what a monster he is, Dawn, and I can't thank you enough for helping me track him down. I'll do what I can to get you immunity, but you need to contact the law for protective custody as soon as possible."

"I will. Thank you."

Dana hung up just long enough to call Melanie Shamera. After she told her about Linda's death and the other missing women, she said, "I can help you."

"How?"

"Dawn Talson is turning state's evidence. I'll hire the best criminal lawyer possible to get you both immunity in exchange for your testimonies."

"You don't need me if Dawn is giving us up."

"I think we do. You can testify about the drug origins and she'll tell the authorities about the deliveries."

Melanie said nothing.

"By the way, were you involved in the murders?"

"No. I didn't find out about them until recently. Rob never asked me to help him kill anybody."

"What about the state investigator, Matt Brown?"

"I knew nothing until I read about him in the newspaper."

"He followed you out to the old warehouse."

"I didn't see anyone. I just left the packet of papers on a shelf in that ratty old office, and left."

"But Matt said your car was parked at the loading dock."

"Rob told me to leave my truck there and take the one parked out back. There's a rough dirt road behind the warehouse that leads into town. It's a half mile shorter than the gravel road, and it was beginning to snow."

"Did you pass a car on your way to town?"

"No, I didn't see anyone."

"Was the sheriff around at that time?"

Melanie thought for a moment. "He had picked up some packages from the office that afternoon. He said he was going to deliver them himself."

"Drugs, you mean?"

"Yeah, meth and weed."

"Do you know who killed him, my sister, and the others?"

"I didn't have anything to do with that. It was probably the sheriff and his stooges."

"Not Rob?"

"Are you kidding? He's a coward."

But he's still an accomplice to murder. "Who was Laura?"

"Kim. She bragged about how easy it was to fool Rob's wife."

Dana gripped the edge of her chair in anger. "I'm going to hire the very best lawyer I can find. I want you to tell him everything you know. Turning state's evidence is the only way to save your life, Melanie. Unless, of course, you want to spend more time in prison."

"No," she said, sounding frightened.

"Call the police right now and ask for protective custody. I'll send the lawyer to the county jail for both you and Dawn."

She then tried calling Katie Bannatt again but she didn't answer. Hopefully she had already turned herself in.

Chapter Forty-Two

Dana asked her new bodyguard to check on Rob's surviving girlfriends. "I hope they've been taken into custody," she said.

"As far as I know only two of them called the station."

"Which two?"

"Shamera and Talson, I believe."

"So Katie Bannatt didn't take my advice. She's either deeply involved or she was telling the truth about her lack of involvement with Rob."

"Or somebody got to her before she could call," Jeff said. "I don't want you ladies going anywhere on your own. From now on, we stick together."

"I promised I'd hire a lawyer to get them off on state's evidence."

"Staying alive is the most important thing you can do. You'll need to testify against the gang once they're arrested. And I can help you find the best criminal lawyer in the area.

Why didn't we know about you sooner? She thought, remembering the other guards.

"By the way," he said, "is there anything you haven't told me about this case?"

Dana thought for a moment before remembering the private phone calls. "Can your PD friend trace them?"

"I'll give him a call," he said and left the room.

Kerrie had remained silent throughout the conversation. She seemed troubled. "We were lucky on the mountain,

Mom. We had no idea how vicious the gang members were. They could have killed Sarah before they left the cabin. I wonder why they didn't."

"I've been wondering the same thing. Remember when one of them called her 'Grandma?'"

Her daughter nodded.

"She may have resembled his own grandmother. Even killers have soft spots."

"They did leave the door open so she'd freeze to death."

"They also knew that we were on the mountain and could possibly rescue her."

"And yet they killed the mother of Rob's baby."

"I guess I'll never understand the psychotic mind, Kerrie. I don't understand how anyone can kill, maim, and destroy lives for power and money."

"You'd be surprised how many people will."

Dana shivered. "Let's check the surveillance system and make sure everything's in working order. As good as Jeff is, he can't be everywhere at once." Dana glanced out the bay window. Their outdoors guard was still on duty. She also noticed that the drapes were slightly open at the house across the road.

"Someone's in there," she said. "I wonder if it's one of Rob's girlfriends or a gang member placed there to watch us."

"I'll check," their bodyguard said. "I'm glad you told me everything that's taken place."

They watched as he walked across the road and rang the bell. He waited several minutes on the porch before returning.

"Whoever's there is hiding," he said. "I'll call the sheriff's office and request a deputy to check it out."

Within twenty minutes a deputy knocked on the door with his night stick, but no one answered. They watched as he slowly circled the house. A few minutes later his patrol car drove across the road into Dana's circle drive.

"Kerrie, I believe that's *your* deputy." Dana said.

She smiled. "It sure looks like him."

As Dana predicted, he had returned to check on the stolen pickup in their garage. He then lingered a few moments to talk to Kerrie.

When he left, she said, "They're short-handed at the sheriff's department. It seems that two of the deputies quit not long before the sheriff left town. Do you suppose they're members of the drug ring?"

"Or victims. Maybe they knew too much, like Tonya Beardsly and Linda Johnsbury."

Jeff asked, "Did he mention their names?"

Kerrie gave him the names and he left the room to call his friend at the police department. When he returned, he said, "I've been invited back to work at the PD. They think I'm hot on the trail of suspects."

When Dana gasped, he said, "Don't worry, ma'am. My job is right here."

"Then let's wrap up this case, Mr. Mailey."

"It's not going to be easy. The PD isn't the primary investigative team, so my friend has to go through proper channels. I did learn that the state checked out the mountain cabin and found the body of Jack Jones, which is probably an alias. I'm afraid that you're going to be interrogated about his death."

His cell phone rang and he left the room to answer it.

"Dana." Sarah called excitedly as she descended the stairs." I just saw two people leave in the black sports car from the garage across the road."

"Men or women?"

"One of each, I think."

Dana picked up the phone to call the highway patrol. Hopefully they could intercept Georgi's car before it reached town. Cringing, she remembered a similar call that resulted in Matt's death.

"We need to follow that car." she said, "A patrolman might not be available in time." She told Kerrie to find their bodyguard.

Within minutes they were on their way, the guard following Jeff Mailey's inconspicuous sedan. As an added precaution, Dana called the sheriff's department, hoping the young deputy would retrace his route. Their bodyguard said both directions needed to be covered, so they were traveling south toward Cheyenne. When they crested a hill nine miles south of town, a black car appeared on the horizon. Jeff estimated the distance to be less than a mile "Hang on," he said, stepping down on the accelerator.

Dana hoped that Jeff and their guard were armed. She wondered whether they could make a citizen's arrest if a patrolman failed to arrive in time. The distance between them and the sports car decreased and Jeff asked that she retrieve a pair of binoculars from the glove compartment. They needed to check the license number. He then called his friend and repeated the four digits and county number.

"They're southbound on Interstate twenty-five," he said, "about twelve miles from town." He then told him the nearest mile marker.

When he hung up, he said, "Carl's going to relay the information to all law enforcement agencies in the state. We'll stay on them until they're apprehended."

"Then what, Jeff?"

"A road block will be set up. We're assuming they're armed and dangerous."

The sports car passed a large truck and accelerated. Jeff followed suit. He said he didn't think the car's occupants would suspect they were being followed by a plain white sedan. There was too great a distance for them to recognize anyone in the car.

"Unless they have binoculars," Dana said.

"The ones you used are high powered. I doubt they have anything comparable."

"A patrolman's coming up behind us," Sarah said, craning her neck. "I wonder why he doesn't have his red lights on."

Jeff checked his mirrors. "The patrolman doesn't want them to know he's around. He's now in position to assist in an arrest once the sports car gets to the road block."

"A lone officer would be risking his life if he tried to stop them," Kerrie said. "I once wrote a news report about a young officer who tried that in California. He was gunned down as soon as he reached the car."

Jeff grunted as he pulled back into the right lane, as did their following guard. The patrol car pulled between them and was nearly tailgating the sedan.

Chapter Forty-Three

"A road block'll be set up about halfway between off ramps," he said. "The patrolman behind us is radioing the mile markers to the officers ahead. When the sports car gets close, they'll pull onto the highway and flip on their overhead lights."

Sarah asked, "What if they try to run the road block?"

Their bodyguard laughed. "That only happens in the movies. Unless they're driving an armored tank, they could get themselves killed. The officers will be in attack position with their weapons drawn. Only fools would try to run the block."

"Only fools get mixed up in drugs and murder," Dana replied.

They followed the sports car in silence for several miles before they noticed flashing lights. The patrol car behind them suddenly roared into the left lane, lights rotating and siren screaming.

As they approached the police barrier, Jeff slowed the car and pulled off the pavement onto uneven ground. "Stay in the car," he said, getting out and drawing his gun. He then ran to assist the patrolmen. Disregarding the order, Dana slipped from the car and followed. She could hear Sarah screaming her name but continued down the roadway, which gradually sloped into a wide ravine. The sports car was upside down on its roof. Steam shot from the radiator and she could smell the stench of gasoline. She expected flames to erupt at any moment. *How,* she wondered, *could anyone survive the rollover?*

Several officers were cautiously approaching the car from every direction, their guns drawn. Dana gasped when a hand gripped her arm and dragged her back from the edge of the ravine. "It's not safe, Mom. There may be a shootout."

"Well, at least we know that some of the gang has been captured." Hesitating, she followed her daughter back to the car where they waited for more than an hour for their bodyguard to return. Traffic was light but those who drove past slowed to gawk at the accident.

When they noticed Jeff Mailey moving back up the roadway toward them, his head was lowered as though he were examining the pavement. His pant legs flapped in the breeze and his face wore a deep scowl. Once seated in his car, he said, "The man survived the rollover but the woman didn't. He's been taken into custody."

"Who?" they asked in concert.

"Rob Turnsby and Kim Yankton."

"Oh, my Lord," Dana said. "I wonder if they were on their way to meet the sheriff."

"There were drugs in the trunk of the car, so they were probably on a delivery run. Turnsby claims the woman owned the drugs and that he knew nothing about them."

"Of course he did. That coward never took responsibility for his own actions. Why not blame a dead woman?"

"They'll interrogate him about the other gang members. If he's as spineless as you think, he'll soon crack and spill everything he knows."

"Thank heavens." Dana closed her eyes and rested her head against the seat.

"They must have been hiding in the house across the road all this time, Mom. I wonder what happened to the people who used to live there."

"I don't know, dear. I hope they weren't murdered like the others."

"It's a shame what happened to the sports car," Jeff said.

"Good riddance." Dana opened her window and took some deep breaths. "Georgi probably never got to drive it. . .Let's go home. I'm exhausted."

"Yes, ma'am. Looks like I'm out of a job."

"Not as long as the sheriff and his gang are still at large."

"I'm sure they'll be rounded up soon. One of the patrolmen said DCI agents are on their trail."

"No wonder they haven't been around," Sarah said.

They spoke little during the drive back to the house. Weary, they settled in the living room to decide their next course of action. Their bodyguard advised against anything other than rest.

"Every law enforcement officer in the state is on the lookout for the sheriff and his gang," he said. "And I understand that the FBI has been called in. Our state officers are a great bunch of men. Unfortunately, one rogue sheriff can taint their public image."

"He was a rogue from the time he was born, Jeff. I wonder how he fooled the county into hiring him."

"He may have hacked into their system and substituted a glowing report for his criminal rap sheet. Who knows these days? Anything's possible."

"Speaking of officers," Dana said. "We should visit our wounded guard in the hospital."

Jeff lowered his gaze to the floor. "I hate to tell you this, ma'am, but the guard didn't make it either."

Dana groaned. "How many bodies does that make so far?" Spreading her fingers, she counted Georgi, Tonya Beardsly, Matt Brown, Linda Johnsbury, Jack Jones, Kim Yankton, and the guard. "Seven people died needlessly and who knows how many others will be killed before the gang's arrested."

Sarah patted her back. "We can be thankful our names aren't on that list. It could have happened on the mountain or in the motorhome that night in the garage."

"But why us? Unless Rob doesn't know that Georgi changed her will. The estate wouldn't have gone to him no matter what happens to us."

"I wonder if he knew that the house title was only in her name." Sarah said.

"Georgi's lawyer said that Rob signed a quit claim deed for the house so she'd loan him more money for the business. The lawyer advised her to do just that."

"I'm surprised we haven't heard from a Turnsby lawyer, Mom."

"I think both Rob and the sheriff know he doesn't have legal recourse, which is why they've been trying to scare us out of the house."

"The phone calls and vandalism. That makes sense, Dana."

"If it's true, we're still in danger."

Jeff informed his police friend of Dana's suspicions. When he finished his call, she asked, "Any word yet about Rob's interrogation?"

"It seems he got himself lawyered-up. Some big-time Denver attorney arrived before they could get anything out of him."

"That figures. His brother, the sheriff, must have put up drug money to keep Rob quiet. Now what can we do?"

"Not much unless you've got some information you haven't told me."

"What about Dawn Talson and Melanie Shamera?"

"They're in protective custody."

"Hasn't anyone interrogated *them* yet? I need to find a lawyer. I should have done that first."

"Good question," he said, again taking out his cell phone. When he hung up, he said the women had refused to talk until they have a lawyer."

"We need to find one as soon as possible."

"I can help you with that," their bodyguard said. "Daniel Shipton is the best criminal attorney in these parts. I think I've got his card in my wallet."

"Where's his office?" Dana asked, impatient to wrap things up.

"In Casper. I'll take you there as soon as we can get an appointment."

"You're right. Lawyers aren't like walk-in beauty shops."

"A few of them are, but I don't recommend them. . . If we're lucky, we can get in to see him sometime this week."

"This week?"

"Yes, ma'am, he's a busy man." Jeff pulled a card from his wallet and punched in the numbers while Dana checked her watch. Her stomach said it was lunchtime.

"We're lucky he had a cancellation," Jeff said when he pocketed his phone. He's booked until the end of the month, but he'll see us at two this afternoon."

Dana smiled. "Let's try that new restaurant they're touting on TV," she said. "My treat."

After a lavish meal, Jeff drove them to Shipton's office.

"I didn't think there were many drug offenders here on the high plains," Kerrie said.

Their bodyguard shook his head. "More than you'd suspect."

Chapter Forty-Four

Jeff turned off the main street and pulled into a parking space. "It might be better if I talk to him first, "he said. "I know him pretty well from cases I've worked for the PD."

Undecided, Dana bit her lip. She considered him trustworthy, but why did he feel it necessary to pave the way for her. "All right," she said. "We'll wait for you."

Sarah shifted her weight in the backseat. "I'm so relieved that everything's coming together."

"We have made a dent in the firewall," Kerrie agreed.

"I'm worried the district attorney won't accept two plea bargains," Dana said. "He may think Melanie's testimony is all that's needed, but I promised Dawn that I'd get her immunity. Without her, none of this would have come together."

Their bodyguard returned twenty minutes later. Smiling, he said, "Dan will take the case, but he's got another client coming in ten minutes."

"I need to talk to him," Dana said, opening the passenger door.

"Make it quick. All he really needs from you is a substantial down payment to cover his expenses."

"No problem, but when does he plan to interview Talson and Shamera?"

"Late this afternoon."

A receptionist showed her into the attorney's office. Dan Shipton was a large man with transparent eyes and a white receding hairline. She wouldn't have called him handsome, but impressive seemed to fit. He was seated in an oversized leather chair in a rather plush office. How strange, she thought that a criminal attorney is doing so well. Weren't his clients drug dealers, thieves, and burglars? She didn't want to consider the implications. He stood when he noticed her and extended his hand.

"Ms. Logan?" he said. "I understand you're financing the immunity cases of two druggies. Why, may I ask?"

"It's the only way to bring the drug ring to justice." Dana took a seat before his massive desk. "My sister was murdered, along with at least five other people, including my friend, Matt Brown."

"So I've heard, but why don't you leave this case to the police?"

"The drug ring hired a high profile Denver attorney to defend one of the drug dealers. I'm afraid he'll escape prosecution."

His brows lifted and he pursed his lips.

"Both women need immunity," she said, "or neither one will testify."

"You understand that what you're asking is highly unusual."

"I've heard that you're up to the job," she said returning his smile. "And I'm willing to pay for a successful resolution to the case." She withdrew her checkbook from her purse and was told to pay the receptionist. They then shook hands and she left his office.

Seated again in Jeff's car, she closed her eyes and silently repeated her mantra. When she began to relax, Matt's face floated through her mind. "You don't look your age," he said. "I've always been attracted to older women."

Oh, Matt, why did they have to kill you?

264

A hand on her shoulder shook her awake. "We're home, Dana. Why don't you take a nap?"

"I think I just did. We've still got work to do, Sarah."

"What kind of work? I was thinking of taking a nap, myself, after that lovely lunch."

"Please do. Kerrie and I can handle the paperwork."

The women trooped upstairs to the office, where Sarah reclined on the couch.

"What kind of paperwork, Mom? I thought we had already investigated everyone within a hundred miles."

"Not quite."

"Like who?"

"Those on the fringes of this case: Beardsley, Musgrove, Zumwell . . ."

"But I thought they were above suspicion."

"They probably are but I'm taking no chances." Dana booted up the computer and clicked on her favorite places file. The webpage was loading when someone knocked at the office door.

"I didn't think you'd mind me interrupting," Jeff said, poking his head inside. "I finally heard from the informant I told you about. He knows the whereabouts of the sheriff's South Dakota hideout, but I'm afraid the information is going to cost you a small fortune."

Dana was so ecstatic that she didn't bother to ask the price. "Have you notified the police?"

"Yes, ma'am."

"Then take us there."

Their bodyguard frowned. "To the hideout?"

"Of course, where else?"

"But, Ms. Logan, that's dangerous."

"As if we haven't been in danger all along, Mr. Mailey.I don't mean drive up to the door, just in the vicinity or as close as the police will allow. I want to see those murderers in handcuffs or body bags."

"Mom."

Sarah sat up on the couch, rubbing sleep from her eyes. "That's my Dana. Always wanting in on the action. You'd best do what she wants, Jeff, or she'll hound you forever."

"If that's want you want, ma'am, but be prepared for disappointment. They may not allow us within five miles of the place."

"I'll settle for that."

"All right. I suggest that you all get packed for the trip."

"Will there be room for a bag of dog food in the trunk?" Sarah asked.

"You're taking Bert, Mom?"

"Of course. He's been on this case from the beginning."

"Okay with me," Jeff said, "Let's get going."

They hurriedly packed and loaded suitcases into the trunk. Without telling Jeff, Dana hid the Glock in her purse.

"What about our outside guard?" Sarah said.

"I don't think we'll need him anymore." Jeff stopped the car in the driveway and she walked over to lay him off. Smiling, she returned to the car.

It was nearly three o'clock and they wouldn't arrive at the South Dakota cabin until hours after dark. They would discuss the case thoroughly before their arrival. She hoped the entire gang was in residence when the police showed up at their door.

"Do the Wyoming police have any jurisdiction in a neighboring state?" Sarah asked.

"Depends," Jeff replied "If the officers are in hot pursuit they can legally cross state lines. But in this case, the South Dakota police will have to make the arrest. It'll probably be made by the local county sheriff's department, although I understand that the FBI has been called in."

"I hope the local sheriff isn't a friend of Will Turnsby's."

"I doubt that Turnsby associated with other sheriffs. They might have come across his criminal record."

"I hope they've all been notified," she said.

"Of course. They've not only received phone calls and faxes, they have photographs of the suspects and descriptions of them and their vehicles. Unless they're hiding on a mountain top with a 360 view, they'll be taken by surprise."

"Where exactly are we going, Jeff?"

"The cabin's in the Black Hills on the South Dakota side of the border. It's more like mountains than hills."

"So they could be sitting on a mountain top?"

"Theoretically, but that's not what my informant told me. He said it was this side of Rapid City. He drew a map."

"Looks like it's going to be quite an adventure, Mom. Now I know where I inherited my wanderlust."

"You have to promise that you won't sneak through police lines to get a better look," Jeff said.

All three women laughed. "We packed our binoculars." Sarah displayed hers from the back seat. "That's close enough."

Apparently unconvinced, he gave Dana a questioning look.

She shook her head, smiling. "We promise."

When he finally relaxed against the seat, she felt sorry for him. He didn't know what he was getting into.

Chapter Forty-Five

Their first pit stop was in Wright, a company coal town planted in the high desert. Jeff told them that a tornado had struck the small town several years earlier, killing a number of residents.

"How long before we're out of this desert?" Sarah wanted to know.

"Not for a while. The next town is Gillette, which is inhabited by quite a few methane gas drilling crews. There's a lot of exploration and recovery going on in these parts."

"And recreational drugs?" Dana asked.

"They're everywhere, ma'am, with more coming across the border every day."

"I just wondered why the sheriff chose this region for his new headquarters."

Jeff shrugged and shook his head. "Supply and demand, I guess."

They stopped in Gillette long enough for a quick dinner before continuing on their way. It was twilight when they left town. Jeff asked if they wanted to spend the night in Sundance, a small town located on the western edge of Wyoming's Black Hills. He told them it was beautiful there although they wouldn't see the landscape until morning.

"I doubt the law will be converging on the cabin until morning, anyway," he said, "although they've probably got spotters in place by now, watching the gang's movements.

I'm sure they'll arrest anybody who leaves the cabin during the night."

"Then we need to leave early," Dana said, "before anything happens." Tired but exhilarated, she decided to take a nap. When she woke they were pulling into a small motel that stayed open during skiing season. They stayed in two rooms, Bert bunking with Jeff.

Dana woke at 5:43 that morning and promptly woke her companions.

"It's too early," Sarah groaned.

"It'll be daylight soon. Let's get going." She called Jeff's cell phone and started packing her things into the trunk of his car, her gun hidden in her coat pocket.

"You're a real whip cracker," Kerrie said, handing her mother a cup of lukewarm coffee from yesterday's thermos. "I never knew that about you."

"You'd understand if you knew how badly I want this nightmare to end."

Jeff appeared with Bert in tow. "Head 'em up," he said, sliding his small suitcase into the trunk. "We should be there in about an hour."

When the sun came up, the countryside was beautiful with a fresh coating of snow as they climbed into the mountains and crossed over the border into South Dakota. Jeff kept them entertained with stories of the Black Hills' colorful history before they stopped at a country inn for breakfast. While there he checked his hand drawn map, assuring them the *outlaw* cabin wasn't far away.

"There'll probably be a roadblock already set up before we get there," he said, hooking sunglasses across his nose as he drove. "I'll talk to whoever's in charge and see how close we can get to the cabin."

Dana glanced into the backseat, noticing that her companions seemed equally excited. Even Bert was unable to sit still.

Jeff pulled onto a narrow dirt road and stopped. "That's strange. This short private road is supposed to lead to the cabin." He leaned forward to look through the windshield. "I don't see any signs of a stakeout."

"They probably arrested them all last night," Dana said, disappointed. "Maybe you should call your friend and find out."

"No cell service here," he said when he glanced at his phone. He then tried his CB radio. All they heard was static. "Too many trees. I think I'll take a hike up the road a ways."

"Are you armed, Jeff?"

"You bet." He patted the left side of his jacket. "Stay put. I'll be back soon." He quietly closed the driver's door and crept off into the trees along the road.

They had waited for nearly an hour for his return when Dana decided, "I'm going to look for him."

"No." Kerrie gripped her arm. "If anyone's going, it's me. At least I have some self defense training."

"We'll all go," Sarah said. "Bert will find Jeff."

"I don't think you're in any shape–"

"I'm in great shape."

Dana hesitated. "Okay, let's go. Quiet as you can." Bert led the way as they trudged single file through the trees and dense undergrowth where Jeff had disappeared. When the dog stopped with his ears pricked forward, she noticed a clearing ahead. Pulling the binoculars to her eyes, she saw a two-story cabin setting on the edge of the clearing. Smoke curled from the chimney. Parked in front of the cabin was a dusty red pickup truck.

"Rob's there. He must be out on bail."

"Where's our bodyguard?" Kerrie whispered back.

"Probably watching from somewhere nearby."

"But, Dana, where are the arresting officers?"

"Could this be the wrong cabin, Mom?"

"Jeff would have returned to the car if it were."

271

"Yes, you're right. You two stay here while I'll sneak around back to listen."

Before Dana could object, her daughter disappeared into a thick stand of evergreens. Kerrie's vanishing act was becoming a habit. Sighing, she indicated a smooth-surfaced rock for Sarah. Dana kept her field glasses trained on the cabin and surrounding area. The only movement she saw was the smoke, which was growing blacker and thicker by the minute. What were they burning in there?" She thought of the crematorium and shuddered.

A twig snapped behind her. Swiveling on her heels, she could see nothing moving, not even a squirrel. She caught her breath and looked at Sarah, whose eyes were as round as pizzas. Somehow that description seemed apt, she thought, despite the situation. Swinging her binoculars back to the clearing, she thought she saw movement in the trees on the far side of the cabin. It must be Kerrie, but how did she get there so quickly? And where was Jeff?

Bert chuffed and seemed to be pointing his long nose. Dana stepped behind him to look down his body like a rifle site. There in the trees behind the cabin was someone crouched behind a grove of evergreens. She adjusted the focus and zeroed in on Kerrie. Her head was tilted at an angle and she appeared to be listening. Be careful, she thought. Those monsters would kill their own mothers. She shoved her hand into her coat pocket to grip the gun.

"What's happening, Dana?"

She raised her index finger, signaling Sarah to wait. Nothing seemed to be moving and the only sound was her own ragged breath. Then, the cabin's front door opened and two men walked onto the porch. She refocused the binoculars and was shocked to see that one of them was pointing a gun.

"Jeff." she said quietly. "They've got him, Sarah. I'm afraid that Kerrie's going to try to rescue him. I have to get over there," she said, gripping her own gun. "You stay here with Bert." She handed her the binoculars and took off through the trees, circling around behind the cabin.

A limb scraped her face as she hurried through the trees. Where was Kerrie? Had she miscalculated her path to the cabin? She then saw a flash of blue in the trees ahead of her.

Chapter Forty-Six

It had to be Kerrie. She's wearing a blue sheepherder's jacket. Dana hoped her daughter wasn't planning an attack on an armed man. Logs were visible through breaks in the trees and she altered her course toward the cabin. When she reached the grove of evergreens, Kerrie was no longer there. She must have gone around the other side of the cabin. Dana crept low in that direction. Hearing voices, she stopped to listen. She thought she heard a woman's voice but it didn't sound like Kerrie.

"Get rid of him," the woman said. The voice was familiar.

"We'll tie him up and leave him here." It was Rob.

"Don't be stupid," she said. "If somebody finds him, he'll tell them where we've gone."

"Your secret's safe with me," another man said. It had to be Jeff.

The woman laughed. "If you're that big a coward, give me the gun."

"Oh, no, you don't." The voice was Kerrie's. Dana rushed around the cabin, her gun at the ready.

"Shoot her," the woman yelled as Dana rounded the cabin and the porch came into view.

"You'll have to shoot me too." She pointed the gun upward at Rob. Poised on the porch like a batter, Kerrie held a large limb, ready to strike.

"I know how to use this gun." She motioned Kerrie and Jeff off the porch.

"Kill her, you coward."

"Drop the gun, Rob, or I will shoot." Dana moved in closer, her heart threatening to pound from her chest.

"She won't shoot," Amanda said, reaching for the gun. Rob jerked it from her reach and swung it back in Dana's direction

She instinctively fired, hitting Rob in the lower groin. He screamed in pain and the gun clattered to the porch floor. Kerrie rushed to kick it from the porch before Amanda could get her hands on it.

"Give me one good reason why I shouldn't kill you both?" Dana said, moving in close.

Doubled over, he wailed, "I didn't kill Georgi. My brother—"

"I don't believe anything you say."

Rob crumbled to the porch floor, holding himself.

"Coward." Amanda yelled. She then tried to jump from the porch, but Kerrie stopped her. Twisting her arm behind her back, she wrestled her to the deck.

"Ma'am," the bodyguard said, taking the gun from Dana. "I'm grateful you saved my life but guns and tempers don't mix. Let's get these two into custody."

"Where in the world are the police?"

"They must have arrested the others last night," he said, pocketing Dana's Glock.

"These two arrived just before we did. I was careless and they got the drop on me."

The bodyguard asked Kerrie to find rope in the cabin, along with something to bandage Rob's wound. He then handed Dana his car keys.

Dana collected Sarah and Bert before driving back to the cabin. There wasn't enough room for seven passengers so Rob and Amanda were ushered into the back seat with their hands tied behind them. Before they left, Jeff returned her gun. Kerrie then slid into the passenger seat to keep an eye on the prisoners. As soon as they had cell service, she would contact the police and meet them en route to Rapid City. Jeff assured Dana they would be safe in the cabin until he and Kerrie returned.

Sighing with relief, the two women made themselves at home. Jeff had left the bag of dog food and they found a well-stocked pantry. Wandering about the large, well-furnished cabin, Dana remarked, "So this is what drug money can buy. The sheriff must have spent a million dollars to build and furnish this place."

"With drug profits," Sarah reminded her.

Dana noticed Bert sniffing everything in the living room. When she mentioned it, Sarah said, "He's as jittery as a hummingbird. You don't suppose that he was trained to sniff for drugs." She took a deep breath and said, "Aha."

"What?"

"Marijuana."

"How do you know what it smells like?"

"I spent some time in Los Angeles as a teenager and you never forget the smell.

"They smoked marijuana that long ago?"

Sarah gave her a withering look. "I wrote a paper about it in school," she said. "People have been using pot for nearly 5,000 years. They thought it helped their rheumatism and women's labor pains."

Dana groaned.

Sarah walked to the window and sniffed the drapes. She did the same with the furniture. "Smells like a pot party."

Bert barked from the kitchen and they found him with his paws against a full length cabinet door in an alcove near the outer wall. When they looked inside, they discovered another door that led down a flight of stairs to the basement.

Motioning Sarah to follow, Dana pulled the gun from her pocket and started down the stairs, Bert taking the lead.

The large, well-lighted room resembled a commercial greenhouse. Built-in rectangular grow lights marched in rows across the entire ceiling. At the end of the room gardening tools were lined up neatly on an elaborate plant stand. A computer sat among the trowels.

"It's marijuana, all right." Sarah stroked a long, narrow leaf with serrated edges.

"I don't even want to know how you know that."

"Somebody forgot to turn off the computer," Sarah said, moving the cursor. "Oh, my, look at this." A marijuana website appeared on the screen. "It says: 'Why smoke when you can vaporize?' And look at that contraption."

When she scrolled down the page, Dana noticed an article describing how to pass a drug test. "By the looks of this place, they were arrested before they could get rid of the evidence."

"I wonder why the arresting officers didn't destroy this crop, unless . . ."

"You're getting paranoid again, Dana."

"What do you expect after what we've been through." She searched the room, looking for outside exits or small rooms off the main basement greenhouse.

"What if all the gang members weren't arrested?" Sarah said. "They'll come back here to harvest this crop. We need to get out of here."

"Now who's paranoid?"

"You both are," a man said from the bottom stair.

Chapter Forty-Seven

Dana turned and aimed the gun at him. "Sheriff Turnsby, himself."

"Go ahead. Shoot. Two of my boys are upstairs. I guarantee you won't get past 'em."

"But I can take out their leader."

The big man shrugged. When he came closer, she noticed his blank expression. He had to be high on something stronger than marijuana.

"Don't you recognize me, Will," she said, lowering the gun. She held her breath, hoping she could pull it off.

"Georgi?" he said, squinting.

"You only thought you had killed me, you naughty boy."

The sheriff took a step backward. "It wasn't me, Georgi. It was Kim. She gave you the pills."

"But you told her to do it. Why, Will?"

The big man appeared confused. "But they cremated you . . ."

"That wasn't me. It was one of Rob's girlfriends."

"Which one?"

"Linda Johnsbury. Why did you want *me* dead?"

A voice called from upstairs. "Sheriff? You all right down there?"

"Yeah, yeah," he said, waving his hand dismissively.

Dana's heart pounded in her throat. "Tell them to check the cabin's perimeter," she said. "You never know who's going to snoop around."

"Go check outside," he yelled. "See if you can find Rob. His pickup's still parked out front."

"His truck's got a flat tire," the voice said.

"Then go fix it, you idiot."

Dana glanced back at Sarah, who looked as though she were going to faint.

Turning back to the sheriff, she said, "Tell me, Will. Why did you want me dead?"

"It was Rob's idea. I just went along with it."

"Why would my loving husband want to kill me?"

Turnsby wrung his hands. "He needed the money."

"Why? Didn't you pay him his share of the drug profits?"

"Sure, sure, but he and his women were skimming off the top. You know I couldn't let 'em get away with that."

"But you've been doing the same thing. What are you on now?"

When he hesitated she raised the gun. "Ecstasy, washed down with a little Jim Beam." Grinning, he reached into his pocket and withdrew several colored pills. "Put the gun down and have some," he said, carelessly dropping two of them to the floor.

"Sure, Will, but first I need to know who killed Matt Brown, Tonya Beardsly, and Linda Johnsbury?"

"Ecstasy first," he said, extending his hand.

Dana didn't want to excite him so she accepted three pills. She palmed them, pretending to swallow. "Better pick those up," she said. "You know how valuable they are."

When he bent to retrieve the pills, she slid hers into her pocket. Off balance, he grabbed one of the plant stands, nearly overturning it. When he had righted himself, he said, "Rob lied to me. He said you wouldn't take the good stuff."

Smiling, she said, "He lies about everything. You know you can't trust him."

The big man closed his eyes, swaying on his feet.

"Tell me, Will. Who killed Matt, Tonya, and Linda? She was afraid to ask about the others.

"Amanda. The two of us are a regular Bonnie and Clyde. But she didn't kill Linda. Rob did."

"Why would he kill the mother of his child?'

"She was gonna turn him in. What else could he do?"

"I thought Rob was too much of a wimp to kill anyone."

The sheriff laughed. "My little brother surprised me. But who cares. Let's party." He turned and staggered toward the stairs.

"Who was Laura, Will?"

"I think it was Kim."

Signaling Bert to attack, she watched as the German Shepherd leaped against the sheriff's back, knocking him to the concrete floor. He would have a doozy of a headache when he came to, if he ever did. Turning, she told Sarah to grab the potting twine and wrap it securely around his wrists. They then each grabbed a leg and, breathing heavily, dragged him to a corner of the basement where they covered him with bags of potting soil.

"Let's get out of here," Dana said, tiptoeing up the stairs. When they reached the living room, they found it unoccupied. The gang members must still be changing a tire on Rob's pickup. The sheriff's truck was parked nearby. She peered out a front window and saw that they were tightening the lug nuts, so now was the time to move. She motioned Sarah to restrain Bert and quietly opened the entry door. Standing on the porch, she leveled her gun at them. They couldn't have been more than eighteen, young enough to be frightened of an angry woman holding a gun, she thought. Slim and dark-haired, they looked enough alike to be brothers.

"Take your boots off," she said, "and start walking. If you turn around, I'll blow those new Stetsons into the next county. I just killed the sheriff so I won't hesitate to shoot the two of you."

Both boys dropped to the ground and hurriedly removed their boots.

"Throw them in the back of the truck," she said. "Start walking and don't stop until you reach Rapid City."

They started off at a run.

"Are the keys in the truck, Dana?"

She hurried to the driver's side and opened the door. Reaching around the steering wheel, she realized the keys were missing. She shook her head when Sarah asked again.

"Then we're in duck pucky up to our eyelids."

"One of those boys must have the keys," Dana said. Taking a step toward them, she fired a shot into the air. "Whoa," she said, "Come back here with the keys." She fired another shot for good measure, aiming at the road ahead of them.

As if on cue, they separated, each diving into the trees on either side of the road.

"Now what are we going to do?"

Dana reached into the truck for the boots and set them on the porch.

"What about the sheriff's truck?'

Dana found it locked. "We'll have to dig him out of the potting soil to get his keys," she said. "I'm not feeling lucky enough to chance it. Are you?"

Sarah shook her head.

"Then let's go inside and wait for Jeff and Kerrie." They grabbed the boots on the way.

Once inside, they locked the outside doors. They then wedged a chair under the doorknob to prevent the sheriff from escaping from the basement. They would have to stand guard until the others returned.

"I don't understand why the gang is still on the loose. What happened to the FBI?"

"They could have arrested the wrong people at another cabin," Dana said.

"The government has been known to make mistakes." Sarah grimaced. "I hope no one was shot in the process."

"There's been enough shooting to last me a lifetime." Sarah was staring at her.

"Are you in there, Dana?"

"What do you mean?"

"You're not the same person I started the trip with."

"I've never had reason to kill anyone before. Now, I've not only killed a man, I've wounded another, assaulted an officer of the law, threatened two young men and shot at them. All in the name of avenging my sister's death."

Without a word, Sarah embraced her.

"I'm also responsible for the death of a good man, Sarah. Make that two good men, who were only trying to protect me."

"You did what you had to, Dana."

They heard an engine start and rushed to the window.

"Those boys are taking Rob's truck. Are you going to shoot them?"

"No," she said, lowering the gun. "They're barefoot and escaping in a truck that every lawman this side of the Rockies is looking for. Let them go."

"Would you shoot the sheriff if he breaks out of the basement?"

"I'd only wound him. He has a lot of answer for."

"With all that potting soil, he'll have marijuana plants growing out his ears."

Dana laughed, her first real laugh since before her sister's death.

Sarah shared in the laughter but her expression soon changed. "We may never really know who killed Georgi."

"I don't think it was Rob, although the sheriff said he killed Linda Johnsbury. For that he'll spend years in jail, if they don't execute him."

"You think the sheriff told the truth about Amanda? She's the most bloodthirsty female I've ever met."

"We still don't know for sure whether it was Amanda or Kim who called herself *Laura*."

"It'll all come out at trial, Dana. I think it was Amanda who ran down the housekeeper with a step-side pickup. She may have also murdered Matt and the others. We're lucky she didn't kill us too."

"I know, but you almost have to feel sorry for poor, weak Rob."

"Almost, Dana? I thought you hated him?"

"Hate's a destructive passion I no longer need. I can't wait to get back to the house and start making it my own–our own. I'm beginning to like this part of the country. We've got a lot more exploring to do, starting with the rest of Wyoming."

Sarah held her hand for silence. "What's that noise? Those boys coming back for their boots?" She rushed to a front window facing the yard.

Dana grabbed her gun and followed. "Who's out there?"

"You'll never believe this, Dana, but the cavalry has arrived."

"The police?"

"Three carloads of them."

Dana sighed as she hid her gun beneath a chair cushion. "Prepare to be handcuffed, Sarah. Our presence here is going to be hard to explain."

Sarah smiled. "I don't think so. Dana. Our bodyguard is leading the charge."

Murder on the Interstate

Chapter 1

Lulled by a lack of traffic and the steady beat of rain, Dana was in danger of nodding off when a convertible roared past, followed by a late model pickup. The heavy downpour obscured her view, but they appeared to be coupled like boxcars. She wondered why they were driving that dangerously close, and why so fast in the rain?

An I-40 highway sign signaled an approaching curve so she clicked off the cruise control and slowed to forty-five. Their taillights had vanished and she glanced in both side mirrors. The earlier truck traffic had also disappeared and no headlights were visible in either direction. Darkness was closing in on her.

Sarah groaned from the passenger seat, apparently still asleep. It m*ust be the anchovies.* Her friend had insisted on stopping for pizza at a Kingman roadside cafe. Dana groped for the Tums. As she rounded the curve, she noticed two sets of brake lights not far ahead.

The motorhome swayed as she stepped into her own brakes and skidded on the pavement. Road signs had warned of animal crossings. The convertible appeared to have swerved to avoid hitting a deer and had gone off the mountain road. Dana pulled onto the shoulder as the pickup following the convertible screeched back on the pavement. Why didn't the driver stop to help?

Bolting upright in the passenger seat, Sarah said, "What happened?" Her words were thick with sleep.

"We're about to find out."

Headlights angled upward from somewhere off the road, illuminating a huge digger pine. Was it the convertible? Dana opened her door and climbed down. The steps were slick with rain and she nearly lost her balance. She heard the passenger door slam as she started off down the embankment. Chilled and miserably wet, she slipped and landed in a bed of pine needles. Why hadn't she grabbed the flashlight?

Dana glanced up at her friend, who stood shivering on the shoulder. "Sarah," she yelled, "Call 911 and hurry."

The smell of gasoline was strong, despite the heavy rain. The convertible had missed several pine trees but a boulder had stopped its forward motion. Both doors were locked. Peering through the driver's window, she could see nothing more than shattered glass, a dime-sized hole centering the web design. She then heard several backfires and a ping of metal as though the convertible had been struck with a rock. Realizing it was a gunshot, she dropped to her knees in the mud.

Sarah.

Slipping and clawing her way up the slope, she crawled onto the shoulder. A pickup was parked behind the RV. The driver had a nervous foot. A moment later another set of headlights emerged from the curve down the road. Tires squealed as the pickup roared off. As it passed, the RV's headlights caught a dark red truck, which appeared to be a newer model.

When Dana glanced in the passenger window, Sarah was crouched between the seats, the cell phone clutched in her hand. She took her time unlocking the passenger door.

"Are you all right?"

"I'm not sure." Sarah patted her chest, breathing heavily.

"What happened?"

"He shot up the motorhome."

"Did he shoot at you?"

2

"I don't think he saw me. He only seemed interested in wounding Matilda."

Dana hated the name Sarah had christened the RV, but that was the least of her worries. Grabbing a flashlight, she climbed back down the steps. A quick inspection revealed inside tires still inflated but the outer ones in the back were flat. She heard an engine shift down and was caught in the glare of headlights. Signaling with her flashlight, she was relieved when the big truck slowed and pulled in behind the motorhome. The driver seemed to be endlessly checking gauges before leaving the cab. Once on the ground, a warm, plump hand gripped hers in greeting.

"The name's McCurdy," a husky voice said. "Everybody calls me Big Ruby."

At nearly six feet, she was Dana's height although nearly twice her girth.

"I'm Dana Logan. There's a Mercedes convertible down the embankment. Gasoline is leaking and both the doors are locked."

"Lead the way."

Rain had slackened and the area still reeked of gasoline. She signaled Sarah to stay in the coach.

"Ruptured gas tank," Ruby said. "That low slung buggy must of hit a rock." She tried both doors before resorting to her knife that she pulled from a sheath on her belt. Slicing the canvas top, she reached inside the car to unlock the door. Her flashlight illuminated the interior where a young woman was slumped across the steering wheel. Her long blond hair was stained with blood and she didn't appear to be breathing. The vintage car had no airbags.

Ruby felt for a pulse. Lifting the woman as though she were a child, she pulled her from the car and carried her some distance before settling her gently on the ground. The flashlight spotted a wound on the left side of the woman's head. Her wide blue eyes then disappeared under Ruby's windbreaker.

"I'm afraid we're too late."

"She's so young," Dana's pizza threatened to return from her stomach. "And so small."

"We'd better find some I.D."

Dana hurried back to the car to retrieve the woman's purse. Shivering in wet clothing and the cool mountain air, she returned to Ruby and the body.

"The pickup driver had to have killed her," Dana said. "He then came back to disable the motorhome. My friend and I are lucky to be alive."

"Tell me about the pickup." Ruby started back up the slope.

"Dark red or burgundy. A Dodge Ram, fairly new."

"You get the license number?"

"I'm afraid not."

"We'll catch the bastard. I'll call the sheriff on the way."

"There's no cell service here."

"No trucker's without a CB."

***

Dana took the passenger seat after Sarah crawled into the sleeper. As rain drummed the windshield, she wondered aloud whether animals would find the body before the police arrived.

"Not likely," Ruby said, "The smell of gasoline should keep the critters away." She picked up her microphone to determine whether anyone was in the area. It was several minutes before someone answered her call.

"What's your twenty, lady?"

"West of Flag. How 'bout you?"

"East of Albuquerque. You've got one helluva power booster," a male voice said, "or we're talkin' some damn good skip." The volume rose and fell as though the other driver were out to sea.

Ruby swore beneath her breath. "Friggin' weather acts like a damn snow blower. Sucks up radio signals and spews 'em across the country." She glanced at her passengers and apologized for her language.

"No problem," Dana said. "I've heard worse on TV."

"You meet a lotta nice drivers out here on the road, but some of 'em are always talkin' trash. It gets lonely on long hauls. If you're out here long enough, you start to sound the same."

Just a matter of fitting in, Dana thought as she squinted through the windshield. There was no sign of the pickup.

Ruby tried her cell phone and reported only static. She returned to the CB. Keying the mike, she said, "Breaker, one nine. This is Big Ruby askin' for some help. Anybody out there got your ears on?" She adjusted the squelch when no one answered.

Dana sighed. "Maybe we should have stayed with the body."

"And let that so-and-so get clean away?"

"Yes, you're right." *I couldn't leave Sarah there alone.*

"Tell me again about the pickup. Did you get a good look at the driver?"

"No, but Sarah might have." She turned to determine whether Sarah was listening from the sleeper.

"A dark red Dodge Ram." Sarah said. "I remember the name on the tailgate. It looked like a young man's truck."

"Was it jacked up?" Ruby asked.

"Don't think so."

"Notice any dings or rust spots?"

"It looked shiny new."

"Rain shines up most trucks." Ruby patted the dash. "Even Old Bertha."

Bertha was barreling down the highway much too fast for prevailing road conditions. Dana hoped Ruby was a competent driver.

"What about bumper stickers?"

Dana closed her eyes and tried to remember what she'd seen.

"One said something about a Las Vegas casino," Sarah said, "but I don't remember which one."

"Nevada license plate?"

"I didn't notice."

Dana cringed. Some sleuths they were. She consoled herself with the fact that they'd been taken by surprise. If the murder hadn't happened, she might have fallen asleep at the wheel. The motorhome would have run off the road like the Mercedes.

She knew that convertibles have a low center of gravity, but the high profile RV probably would have overturned and killed them both. She shuddered, remembering the young woman with a bullet in her head. No one deserved to die that way.

Ruby said, "It'll come back to you. It's surprising how much we remember the next day."

Truckers seemed like bartenders, roadside psychologists who seemed to know more about human nature than their high-priced counterparts.

"I wonder if the killer went back."

"I doubt it." Ruby picked up her phone. They had reached the top of the grade where cell service might be available. "A lotta people coulda stopped there by now."

While the trucker punched in some numbers, Dana held her breath, hoping the call had gone through. She listened intently as Ruby reported the murder to a 911 dispatcher.

"No, I can't return to the crime scene. I gotta load of produce that'll spoil. In case you didn't know, drivers foot the bill if the lettuce wilts before it gets to market."

Replacing the receiver she said, "I'll drop you off in Flag. Somebody there can take tires back to your rig."

"What about the killer?"

"Soon as the rain lets, up, I'll warn the other drivers to keep a lookout."

"But how will they know it's him? Or if it's a man, for that matter?"

"You're right. Plenty of women drive pickup trucks in Northern Arizona. Quite a few of 'em Hopis and Navajos. There's more than a few dark red pickup trucks."

Sarah startled her by gripping her seat back. "I forgot to tell you, Dana, I got a look at the driver when he grabbed his gun from his glove compartment."

"Why didn't you say something sooner?"

"I was too busy thanking my lucky stars he didn't shoot me too."

"What's he look like?"

"Dark hair with a thin beard that runs along his jaw line. Connects with his hair."

"Long or short hair?"

"It was slicked back but I didn't see a pony tail."

Dashboard lights illuminated Ruby's grin. In profile she resembled a queen-sized Sarah, although her hair was darker. "Most people wouldn't remember anything but the gun."

"We're amateur sleuths," Sarah said.

Dana groaned inwardly. She'd hoped Sarah wouldn't tell anyone about the murders they'd solved, but nodded confirmation when Ruby glanced at her. The driver shook her head in disbelief.

"Dana captured a killer single-handed."

Ruby laughed. "What are you? Two traveling Jane Marples?"

"I'm only sixty," Sarah said. "Dana does facial exercises so she looks much younger. But we're the same age."

Sarah's main spring had snapped. If she didn't calm down, she'd be hyperventilating.

"Tell me about the cases you solved." Ruby reached to adjust the wipers.

By the time Dana filled her in on all the murders, the rain had stopped and they were taking a Flagstaff exit. The road curved down to a large truck stop and they pulled into the nearest fuel lane.

"All out for Flag." Ruby grinned as she descended from her truck. Her bright red hair was dazzling in the overhead lights.

"She's no spring chicken either," Sarah muttered as they prepared to leave Old Bertha.

Dana reached for the handle, reversed directions and swung down to the step, comparing the dismount to that of the motorhome. She could drive this rig as well, with a few instructions from Ruby.

Sarah's short legs flailed in mid-air when she groped for the lower step. Dana reached to help her down. Groaning and stretching on solid ground, they offered to buy their benefactor a cup of coffee. Ruby agreed, but before she could hook Bertha up to a diesel pump, Sarah stopped mid-stride and gasped.

"It's him."

"Who?"

"The pickup driver."

Chapter 2

"Where?" Dana craned her neck to scan the service area.

"Getting in his truck." Sarah nodded toward a lighted area beyond the café.

Dana glanced at the dark red Dodge. It appeared to be the same truck, but she couldn't be certain. "Don't stare, Sarah. Keep walking."

The truck door slammed and a dark-haired man glanced into his rearview mirror. The pickup backed slowly and pulled into an exit lane. He was too far away to read his license number.

"No lights on the license plate holder," Ruby observed.

Obviously excited, Sarah said, "What'll we do?"

Ruby rolled her big brown eyes. "Follow him, of course. Good thing Bertha's not hooked up yet. We've still got half a tank of fuel."

Dana told them to wait. Someone had to go back for the motorhome.

"I'm the only one who can identify him," Sarah said. "I'll ride with Ruby. We'll meet you down the road after we report his license number."

Ruby pulled a small notepad from her shirt pocket and wrote down her cell number. "Call as soon as you're on the road. I'll drop Sarah at a motel after we nail the creep."

"Get in touch with the police as soon as you write down the number." Dana was well aware of Sarah's excitement.

Like a bloodhound with the scent, she wouldn't give up until the suspect was caught.

She hurried into the truck stop store as Ruby pulled from the lot. Retrieving her cell phone from her purse, she called emergency road service before inquiring about new tires. While she waited for the service truck, she punched in 911. She was told a deputy was on his way to the murder scene. Ruby had reported the nearest mile marker, and he couldn't miss a thirty-six foot motorhome parked along the road.

Dana glanced down at her clothing caked with mud. No wonder people were staring. She headed for the restroom to make herself presentable. After cleaning her clothes as best she could, she combed her shoulder length auburn hair. People said she resembled the actress Geena Davis but tonight she looked like the Wicked Witch of the West.

Half an hour later they left the truck stop, headed west toward Ashfork. The new tires had cost a small fortune but Dana didn't complain. *They* could have been killed instead of the tires. No more driving after dark, if they had to spend their nights in Walmart parking lots.

The crime scene resembled a carnival, complete with flashing lights. The woman's body had been removed to an ambulance, which appeared ready to leave. As soon as the wrecker came to a stop, a sheriff's deputy walked over to question her. He accompanied her to the motorhome where she retrieved the victim's purse. Dana watched as the young officer rifled through the soft leather handbag.

While she waited, she asked the dead woman's name.

"I can't tell you that."

"I could have searched the purse on my own."

He hesitated. "All right, but this is confidential." The deputy withdrew a wallet and pulled the driver's license. "Her name was Lori Murphy, age twenty-seven. That's all I can tell you."

"Was she married?" Dana asked.

"Why?"

"The killer could have been her husband."

"That's a possibility, but he probably would have killed her at home."

"Not if she had a head start."

He appraised her for a moment before dropping the wallet back in the purse.

"Where's she from?"

"If you looked at the car, ma'am, you'd have seen the Arizona plates."

"I'm aware of that."

"Interstate 40 is a heavily traveled truck route. It was probably a random shooting."

"Random killers don't return to finish off the job. Not with people standing around who can identify them."

"And how would you know that?"

"I read a lot of mystery novels."

He flashed his light in her face. "Can you identify the pickup driver?"

She shook her head, telling him that her friend Sarah could.

Too much time had elapsed and she needed to call Ruby's cell number. "My friends may have already spotted the killer and are in need of police assistance." She told him about Ruby McCurdy and that Sarah was riding with her.

"Two women chasing a killer in a produce truck?"

"I'm afraid so, officer."

"You expect me to believe—"

"Call my friend, Sheriff Walter Grayson. He's an old friend who helped us solve a serial murder case." Dana didn't tell him that Walter was in love with her.

"Murder case?"

"That's right."

"You need to come down to the sheriff's office to file a report."

"But I can't leave Sarah stranded."

"I'm afraid she'll have to wait. As soon as the RVs ready to roll, you can follow me back to the station. By the way, you could have driven into Flagstaff on the inner tires."

I wonder why Ruby didn't tell me that.

***

Several miles east of Flag, construction barriers necked the highway down to two lanes. Light rain resumed and traffic slowed to the speed of a centipede. Every trucker in Arizona must have been waiting at the truck stop to pull out ahead of them. Ruby's CB chatter was getting on Sarah's nerves.

"Listen up," Ruby said every few moments. "There's a bad dude driving a dark red Dodge. Late model four-wheel drive. He's not far ahead. Keep your eyes peeled 'cause he killed a young lady west of Flag. This guy's armed and definitely dangerous."

"What are you?" a baritone voice drawled. "One of them bounty hunters?"

"Makes you wonder, don't it?" Ruby put the mike aside and reached for a pack of gum.

A new voice filled Bertha's cab. "Breaker one-nine for Big Ruby."

"Go ahead, Breaker."

"This is Johnny Reb. There's a red Dodge four-wheeler ahead a me. Describe the driver, will ya?"

"Hold on, Johnny Reb. There's somebody here who saw him." She handed the mike to Sarah.

"Ever used one of these?"

When she admitted she hadn't, Ruby said, "Press the button and talk in the slotted side."

For once in her life, Sarah was speechless. With Ruby's urging, she said, "Dark hair and a thin beard all the way to his sideburns. He might have a pony tail."

"Can't hear ya, lady. Speak up."

Sarah yelled into the mike.

"We can hear ya now." An unfamiliar voice laughed as he turned up his radio. Rock music briefly filled Bertha's cab.

Ruby retrieved the mike. "You morons give us truckers a bad name."

"Aren't they going to help?" Sarah peered through the windshield to scan the endless lane of traffic.

"Come back, Johnny Reb. What's your twenty?"

"I'll let you know when I see a mile marker."

"How far are you from Flag, and can you still see the Dodge?"

"'Bout fifteen miles out and right on his tail."

"You s'pose he's got a CB?"

"No antenna that I can see."

"Good. What're you driving? I'll call it into the highway patrol."

"New Peterbilt," he said with obvious pride. "It's bright royal blue with white striping along the cab."

"Who're you with?"

"Independent bull hauler. John Reb Trucking."

"Are you loaded or deadheading it home?"

"Made my last drop in Flag. I can keep up with him, if necessary."

"Great. By the way, how far does this construction mess go?"

"From here, looks like all the way to the White House."

Ruby sighed. "Guess I'll be eating this produce myself. I'll never make it to St. Louis in time."

"Wish I could help, but it's bumper to bumper far as I can see. I don't know how the cops are gonna nab this guy."

"How about writing down his license number, Johnny?"

"Will do. Hold on."

When he came back on the air, he said, "Must be the creep, all right. There's mud caked on the license plate. I can't even tell which state he's from."

"Stay with him, will ya? If you coulda seen the girl he killed, you'd know why we can't let him get away."

"I ain't got nothin' better to do. I'll keep you posted, Ruby."

"Don't forget me," another driver chimed in, followed by several others.

Ruby sighed. "Listen up, gentlemen. Soon as we get the hammer lane back, we'll put him in the cradle and keep him there, you hear?"

"What's in it for us?"

"A cuppa coffee in Winslow."

"Ah, Ruby, you can do better than that."

Wipers thumped hypnotically as rain smeared taillights across Bertha's windshield.

"What's the cradle?" Sarah asked.

"You ever watch that movie, 'Smokey and the Bandit?'"

"As a matter of fact, I have."

"You'll be watching a reenactment soon." Ruby picked up her cell phone and punched in 911.

* * *

Dana repeatedly tried to call Ruby's cell while following the deputy into Flagstaff. When she finally had service, Ruby's line was busy. The patrol car's blinkers reminded her where she was going and she followed him down the ramp. Heavy rain still splattered the windshield and lights emitting from a service station streaked across her vision. Her eyelids were heavy and she knew she couldn't drive much longer. Hopefully, a hot cup of coffee was waiting at the station.

After she had filled out the paperwork and produced her I.D., Dana was free to leave. Punching in Ruby's number, she was relieved when the trucker answered her phone.

14

"Where the hell are you?"

"I'm just leaving Flagstaff. Please put Sarah on the phone."

A moment later she heard Sarah's voice. "For heaven sakes, how long does it take to buy a new set of tires?"

"I'll tell you when I get there. What's your location?"

"Our twenty is south of Holbrook." She was beginning to sound like Ruby.

"Why are you still with her? I thought Ruby had a load of produce to deliver."

"We can't let him get away."

Dana sighed, frustrated. "Has Ruby notified the highway patrol?"

"That she has, and we've got a caravan of trucks for escorts."

"All of them after the killer?"

"I guess so, Dana. Must be a dozen of them."

"Good grief."

"They're placing bets about how far the killer will get before he's captured."

Dana blinked her eyes, blinded by oncoming traffic. "He must know everyone's after him."

"He probably thinks they're all tired of the highway construction."

"He'll have to stop for gas unless he filled up at the truck stop."

"That's when we'll nab him," Sarah said.

"It's too dangerous. Leave it up to the police."

"Ten-four."

"Has Ruby had any sleep?"

Sarah lowered her voice. "I don't know, but I saw her taking some pills."

"She must be on Vivarin. I could use some myself."

There was excitement in Sarah's voice when she said, "Here comes the cavalry."

"The police are there?"

"I can see their flashing lights in the side mirror. They're coming up behind us."

"How many of them?"

"It looks like three highway patrol cars that are traveling awfully fast."

"Good, I hope they catch him soon."

"The road's so narrow and the trucks are so wide, I don't know how they can pass."

Dana sighed. "I'm so relieved the chase's coming to an end."

Sarah's scream nearly shattered her soul.

"What's wrong?"

"There's been a terrible wreck."

"What happened, Sarah?"

"An eighteen wheeler swerved out in front of the patrol cars."

About the Author

Jean Henry Mead is the author of 15 books, seven of them novels, including the Logan & Cafferty mystery/suspense series: *A Village Shattered, Diary of Murder and Murder on the Interstate.* She's also an award-winning photojournalist and children's author. A southern California native, she lives in Wyoming with her husband and Australian Shepherd.

www.ingramcontent.com/pod-product-compliance
Lightning Source LLC
Chambersburg PA
CBHW071110250626
47159CB00002B/678